ANA LEE KENNEDY

PERSEPHONE'S BEASTLY LOVER

WEREWOLVES OF REBELLION
BOOK THREE

For more information contact:
Riverdale Avenue Books
5676 Riverdale Avenue
Riverdale, NY 10471
www.riverdaleavebooks.com

Design by www.formatting4U.com
Cover by Scott Carpenter
Digital ISBN: 978-1-62601-361-2
Print ISBN: 978-1-62601-362-9

First edition, March 2017

Chapter One

He should never have answered his cell phone.

"Please, Jack," Tina whined. "Just give me one more chance."

"We've been split now for four months, Tina. I don't want to get back together."

"I'll join the Werewolves of Rebellion," she rushed on as though he'd said nothing.

He sighed and wrestled with himself not to yell into the phone. "Being a member of Frank's MC was never an issue, Tina. You know that."

"I miss you," she whispered.

He remained silent. Holding the phone away from his ear for a second, he contemplated just ending the call, then Tina spoke again.

"Don't you miss me, Jack?"

"No," he said a little too forcefully. "I'm sorry, Tina. What we had was nice while it lasted, but it's over."

"Why won't you take me back?" Her voice began to rise and Jack grimaced. "I love you!"

"If you had truly loved me, I wouldn't have found you fucking two guys at the same time." He reined in his anger. "It's over, Tina. Stop calling me and go on with your life. Leave me alone."

"I can't go on without you, Jack!"

"I'm sorry. You have no other choice."

He slid his thumb over the End Call symbol on the screen.

Jack sat out on the front porch of his home. Evening had descended an hour ago. He should never have answered the call, but he hadn't even looked at the screen, figuring it was someone from the MC checking in on him as many of them, such as Luella or Frank, were prone to do. Sadly, Tina had suddenly crushed his decent mood.

Their time together had been great while it had lasted. He'd been serious when he told her that, but finding her in the backseat of her car with two bikers, both members of the Wraithkillers, had knocked him for a loop. Tina had been really drunk that night, something she'd never done in the time they'd been going out, but it was no excuse. Two dudes at the same time? He was all for an occasional threesome, but in the back of her car parked in a local bar's parking lot where anyone could have walked up on them? With the way the municipal cops patrolled the area around the bar on a regular basis, it was a miracle one of them hadn't chanced upon her and the two bikers.

Jack had jerked open the back door of the Sebring, wished her a good life while she'd had one guy's dick in her mouth and the other had his cock in her pussy, then he'd walked away as though it hadn't mattered—and it hadn't. At first what she'd done had hurt like hell, but within a couple days, the pain wasn't as sharp and he'd realized he really hadn't loved Tina. Really, she had done him a favor.

But she thought otherwise. Every couple weeks

or so, she'd contact him, but for the last month he hadn't received any calls from her, so he'd thought she'd finally accepted their breakup.

It looked like she'd only given him a brief reprieve.

With resolve, he pushed thoughts of Tina into the back of his mind and fervently hoped *this* time would be the last phone call from her. Maybe he should go ahead and have his phone number changed.

A cold breeze stirred gooseflesh over his arms. The wind reminded him of the other problem at hand. If he changed into werewolf form, he could stay warm when the temperature dropped after midnight, but he was tired of having to go outside at night to get away from *it* in the house, and living at the Werewolves of Rebellion Motorcycle Club instead of his house when he hadn't been a full member even six months yet, bothered him. His mama had always said one should never wear out his or her welcome. So he suffered through cold nights, thankful for a fold-out cushion to lie on and his fur to keep him warm.

Although it was mid-April, tonight the air smelled like one more snowfall might be possible. A few weeks ago, Jack had finally finished the restoration of the old Indian motorcycle he'd found abandoned and buried beneath a mountain of junk in one of the property's decrepit outbuildings. Over last summer and during the recent winter, he'd painstakingly restored the Indian. Frank had offered to restore it for him in the Nightshade's Wolves shop, but Jack wanted the satisfaction of doing it himself.

Last week, he'd taken the bike out when the weather had been unseasonably warm, but the summer-like temperature had only lasted a day and the cool bite of spring had returned in full force. Still, that brief afternoon ride on his Indian had been what he'd needed to get him out of his funk and calmed his shredded nerves.

He rose to move out onto the steps where he would have a nice view of the stars. A crash from the front room sent a frisson of fear through him and he stiffened. Breaking glass and the tinkling of pieces, as if they had been scattered across the coffee table, followed the first noise, then a thump against the window directly behind him shot adrenaline into his bloodstream.

If he turned around, he knew what he'd see. It was the same every time.

No, he wasn't going to look.

Couldn't look.

Would *not* look.

Thump!

No. No way. He'd had enough adrenaline highs the past few days to last his entire life.

Thump! Thump!

Jack sighed in resignation. *Fuck it. She'll just keep banging on the window until I look at her.*

Summoning courage and finding very little, he turned around to face the inevitable. The young woman stared back at him, sorrow and despair in her big, vaporous eyes. She mouthed the words *help me*.

He possessed such sympathy for the woman that whenever he saw her, Jack could never keep himself from reaching out to her. He moved to place his hand on the glass and, as it often happened, a frightening, demonic face appeared next to the woman's and bared its fangs at him, roaring its disapproval.

He stumbled backward, frightened to the very

core of his heart and simultaneously pissed off that he'd again fallen for the pretty woman's silent plea. The thing flashed red eyes and pointed—at him.

Was that a threat?

"Fuck off you red-eyed bastard!" he yelled. Anger sluiced through him. "This is my house, so get the fuck out!"

The window exploded. Jack found himself airborne, the sensation curious yet disconcerting. The impact with the ground, abrupt and final, knocked the air from his lungs. Lying flat on his back, he finally managed to gather his wits. He struggled to his feet, his senses spinning slightly, and looked up at the window. Nothing was there, only the gaping hole where the glass had once resided and the soft amber glow of the kitchen lights filtering through.

"You son of a bitch," he screamed. "You're going to leave. You just don't know it yet!"

He staggered over to the bottom step and plopped down on it, the wood's coldness penetrating his thin pajama bottoms. He gazed up at the sky, the clarity of the heavens soothing him. At a young age, he'd known there were other things on earth besides human beings, such as himself—a lycanthrope—and that there was black and white witchcraft. Hell, he'd even witnessed some of the shit that had gone down when an incubus and its harem of succubae had infiltrated Frank's MC, but ghosts and spirits—or whatever the hell these things were in his home—those wielded power he hadn't known existed, or hadn't really believed. Until recently, he'd never had a reason to consider that the afterlife could reach into the mortal world and shake it up like the flakes of a snow globe.

5

Jack sighed. But now he did.

Maybe once the research team arrived, he could get some answers, but more importantly, some peace.

He hated to give up, but for tonight, he decided to go over to the MC. He'd sleep on one of the sofas. At least he'd get relatively decent rest. It wasn't sweetbutt night, so there shouldn't be too many people wandering through the main house.

Turning to look up on the porch, he half expected to see red eyes glaring back at him. Instead, the amber glow from within highlighted the window. The feeble light bled through the hole at just the right angle that it lit up all the glass shards littering the porch. He shifted for a better view and glass crunched under his ass. Damn. Now that he was paying attention, he saw there were even slivers and pieces of the window all the way out in the yard where he'd landed.

The idea of jumping on his bike to ride over to the MC appealed to him, but it was too cold. He could transform, but any late-night travelers seeing a werewolf on a vintage Indian would probably drive right off the road and straight into a ravine. He smirked. Sort of funny, but then again, he'd hate to terrify someone or cause them any harm.

Rising, he thanked God that he kept his truck keys under the driver's floor mat. If he'd have left them in the house, he'd have to chance going inside and meeting a worse fate than exploding windows.

Looking forward to some genuine rest, he headed toward his truck parked in the pole barn.

* * *

Feeble morning light spread across the compound. A gentle breeze wafted over the parking lot, forcing Persephone to zip her windbreaker the rest of the way. One of the researchers slammed the SUV's back doors, the sound finalizing the preparation for the trip to Southeastern Ohio. Seph glanced at the display on her smartphone. At barely seven in the morning and having just finished a case a little after one a.m. that night, no one on the team had had more than three hours of sleep, but Queen, their team supervisor, had already booked an investigation with a guy who was adamant he couldn't wait a couple more days for their arrival. Usually the team's cases were in cities, sometimes large towns, but this was Seph's first trip to a tiny, Podunk, in-the-middle-of-nowhere location. She wasn't even sure if Rebellion could be classified as a town. From what she'd read online about it, Rebellion's total population hovered around 2,500.

Inwardly, she groaned. Flyspeck towns meant no entertainment, and the only shopping available often consisted of general stores. From the GPS on her phone, she'd discovered that the big cities—Pittsburgh and Cleveland—were 90 minutes to two hours from Rebellion. Even Wheeling, West Virginia, was a 40-minute drive. If Rebellion had a restaurant, it would probably be some sort of café or hole-in-the-wall bar. Seph would go mad on this trip. Then again, if the situation at the man's home was as dire as he was saying, she probably wouldn't have much time to do anything outside the investigation.

She was only three months into this new job. Funded by a wealthy businessman in Detroit, who had a huge fascination with the paranormal and the supernatural, this position paid Seph well. After losing her apartment and her car to a fire, she had to recoup her losses, especially since her auto insurance wouldn't cover an act-of-God fire and the only insurance she'd had on her apartment was for the worth of her computer and television. Answering an ad for a field team assistant who was willing to learn about unique technology and methods of researching the paranormal for an organization called Weird, Hidden and the Occult, otherwise known as WHO, had seemed a lark to Seph. To her surprise, the team was legitimate.

In the three months she'd been with the crew, she'd done well at hiding her abilities from everyone. Tapping into spirits was difficult and draining. If Queen knew she could do such things, Seph knew she'd never get any rest…or peace. She'd been orphaned at a very young age and had never been adopted, so Seph knew nothing about her parents or why she had her strange ability. One thing she did know—she hated it. Whenever she communed with the dead, they drained her like pulling the plug on a bathtub to watch all the water drain out.

"Seph?"

Most importantly, the job paid her bills. And, for now, she had a roof over her head, whether at the base in the bunk room, out in the field sleeping wherever clients gave them a bed, or in motels and hotels when the need called for it. If she could save enough, she wanted to put a down payment on a condo…

"Persephone Jones!"

Seph jumped and nearly dropped her phone on the pavement. She shot her gaze up to meet Queen's. "Oh, sorry. I sort of blanked out there for a few minutes."

The stocky, curvy Samoan woman smiled sympathetically, her dark eyes kind. "We're all exhausted, but once we arrive at our next case, having us there will give our client some peace of mind. We'll be able to crash for a few hours, then start work." She indicated the trunk with a curt nod of her closely shaven head.

Seph's heart sank. The drive across Ohio was a long one.

"Got all your personal stuff packed that you'll need?" Queen asked.

"Yeah, just loaded it."

"Did you do a count on batteries, battery packs and power cords?"

She dipped her head firmly. "I did that last night after we got back to base while my brain was still functioning."

Queen chuckled, the sound soft and melodious. "Good. We'll leave in 15." She started walking away, but called over her shoulder, "Make sure everyone's thermoses are full of coffee. We're going to need plenty of go-juice for the long drive."

Her supervisor's short, fast strides moved her quickly across the pavement to the tech van. Seph liked Queen, who was fair and a great teacher, but the woman was as demanding as her name. She blinked sleepiness from her eyes and sighed. It would be so nice to crawl into bed for a few hours.

"Hustle, hustle," Dean, the other head paranormal researcher, said jovially. He opened the SUV's double doors and loaded a silver case marked *EVP Devices*, then shut the doors again. He removed a clipboard from where he had it stashed under his arm and held it out to her. "Here's the file and notes for this particular case."

9

Dismayed, all she wanted to do was get a nap during the drive. "Can I type it in once we get to the location?"

"Sorry." He offered her a placating expression. "Queen will need all the details neat and ready to go so she can review those once we're lodged somewhere."

"Damn." She took the clipboard with the pinned folder. Papers and sticky notes poked out around the manila cardboard edges.

"Once you're in the truck," Dean added, "don't be surprised if Queen gives you notes to transcribe from her phone. She uses her Samsung S Notes when she can't find any paper. Saw her jotting stuff on it last night. The longer you're with us"—he started walking away—"the more you'll adapt to these long hours without any sleep. Hang in there."

Seph strode around to one of the back passenger doors still standing open, set the clipboard on the seat, then headed inside to fill half a dozen thermoses with black coffee. The coming hours were going to be torture. With a sigh, she hurried toward the break room.

Chapter Two

"Where are you off to so early in the morning?" Luella asked.

Jack poured himself a cup of coffee. He glanced at the tall, blonde woman as she washed cups and spoons discarded by the earlier members who had already left for work. He hadn't known Luella long, but he liked her a lot and respected the hell out of her. She took care of the main house as well as the MC's community, managing everything and making sure all ran smoothly. He set the pot back on the burner and faced her.

"I'm headed home. Got some people showing up there anytime now."

"'People'?"

When he didn't say anything, she let the water out of the sink and stood watching the bubbles drain. "Look, Jack," she began, "I know that you're having some... Well, for the lack of a better term—some odd things happening at your place."

"Oh?" How the hell did she know that? He eyed her suspiciously.

Luella rinsed the sink, a cocky smile on her face. "I overhead you talking to Frank one evening, asking if Bernadette knew anything about how to get rid of ghosts."

She turned slightly, reaching for the tea towel where it lay crumpled on the counter, then wiping her hands dry on it. Glancing over at him, she rushed on. "Don't worry. Frank hasn't said a word to anyone." She shrugged. "Except maybe Bernadette, since you were inquiring about her help, but Frank's not the type to run around to others and blab your problem. I just happened to be standing at the china cabinet in the dining room putting dishes away when I overheard the two of you talking."

Relaxing, Jack inhaled the rich aroma of the Columbian coffee. The scent soothed his frayed nerves. "I had thought about approaching Scary Mary, but the woman freaks me out and I didn't want to invite anything else into my house, even if Scary Mary has good intentions."

"She's not bad, Jack. Bernadette works with her and is her apprentice. You know that."

"Yeah, but…" He shrugged. "You'd just have to spend a couple nights at my place to understand my caution, Luella." He chugged back a couple big swallows of his cooling coffee. "I took Frank's advice and did some research into paranormal investigation teams. Found one that has an excellent reputation up in Detroit, and they were willing to drive down here to check into my problem."

"Where are they staying?" she asked. "With you?"

"Probably the motel in Rebellion."

She wrinkled her nose in distaste. "Well, if the motel doesn't suit them, there's a free bungalow in the community with two or three bedrooms, I believe. And I'm sure Tractor will allow someone to stay in his big camper."

Beastman wandered in, his expression disgruntled,

eyes sleepy and unfocused. He patted Luella on the ass as he passed her, then stopped at one of the cupboards, opened it, withdrew a travel mug and held it out to her. She quickly filled it for him.

"I'll see you tonight," Beastman mumbled.

"You okay, baby?" she asked.

"Yeah, just didn't sleep worth a shit."

"Back still hurting?"

"Yep."

"Well, I'll give you a good massage tonight. Maybe that'll help." She grinned and batted her eyes.

"For *that* sort of massage, I'm already feeling better." He leaned over and nuzzled her neck, earning him a deep, throaty giggle from his mate.

Jack nodded to Beastman as he shuffled by, placing the lid on his travel mug.

"Morning, Jack," Beastman said. "Love ya, babe," he called over his shoulder. He halted before he stepped down into the sun porch and looked pointedly at Jack, his thick, bushy, gold beard giving him the air of a bristling bear. "Babe is Luella, not you."

Jack burst out chuckling. "I understood what you meant."

With a curt nod, Beastman grabbed a jacket, then pushed out into the chilly morning air. Luella's gentle laughter trailed him out to the carport.

"Don't mind him," she said. "Beastman's grumpy because he pulled something in his lower back yesterday when he was helping cut and stack wood. He's a big baby."

The loud exhaust system of her mate's pickup vibrated through the house. Gradually, the sound dissipated.

13

Jack finished the last gulp of his coffee and passed the cup to Luella. "I better get moving."

"Morning!" a voice called an instant before Bernadette entered the kitchen. "Luella, I need a strong cup of joe this morning. I haven't been able to get warm."

"You ain't coming down with something, are you, honey?" Luella asked as she reached for one of the clean mugs in the dish drainer.

"I don't think so. Probably just this yo-yoing from warm afternoons to damn cold nights and mornings."

The redhead glanced at Jack as she maneuvered around the table to accept the mug Luella held out to her. Jack had to admit one thing—she was incredible. He wasn't a man for redheads, preferring women with darker hair to pure black locks, but if Frank's mate had been free, he would've made an exception. Although short, Bernadette was also compact, but not in a chunky way, more built to perfection in a small package. Big breasts matched round, flaring hips, giving her the perfect hourglass shape. Her flaming-red hair matched her fair complexion, and the green of her eyes immediately drew a person's attention. Jack didn't think he'd ever seen eyes so vivid a green before. He let his gaze wander over her in a nonchalant manner as she poured half-and-half she'd gotten from the fridge into her mug. Although Bernadette was a looker, her bubbly personality and bright smile for everyone only added to her beautiful wrappings. Frank was a hell of a lucky man.

She caught his gaze and smiled. "Frank told me you're having a spirit problem in your home."

Nodding, he replied, "Yeah, but it's more than a spirit."

Her eyes widened as she studied him more intently. "Oh? How so?"

"There's two—as far as I can tell—and one seems more…"

"Demonic?"

He startled. "Yes. How'd you know that?"

"As my powers mature, I can tell more and more things about a person or situation. I see a dark aura around you. It's not heavy, more like a slate-gray smoke cloud above you, which means it has touched you in some way."

Quickly, he explained what had happened last night.

"Holy hell," Luella exclaimed.

A worried expression settled over Bernadette's porcelain features. "Want me to get with Scary Mary on this and see if she has any suggestions?"

"No, I've called in a paranormal research team, so let me get back to you on that. I'd handle this myself, literally, but if this were a human pissing around my place it could be easily stopped. Humans smell like sport or food to us, so it's simple to scare the hell out of them, and if they tell others, no one would believe them anyway. But this…" He shook his head slowly. "I can't fight this, Bernadette."

"You know where to find me, Jack." She pulled out a chair, sat, then reached for a basket covered with a hand towel that she removed. She selected a muffin, the aroma of spices and bananas wafting up to Jack.

"Hand me one of those, please," he said.

She passed him a fat muffin.

"Thank you. Luella, I'm out of here." He snagged his jacket from where he'd slung it over one of the other chairs and headed toward the porch.

"Bye, Jack," they both chimed behind him.

He headed outside juggling the banana muffin from one hand to the other as he shrugged into his jacket. After clambering into his Dodge and taking the keys from under the floor mat, he started the truck and drove down the slope toward the MC's community. He passed the homes, waving to those wandering around outdoors in the cool, damp morning air. Young leaves blushed the orchard with green. Out at the end of the drive at the gate, Puppy sat planting early spring flowers around the short brick pillars the gate was fastened to. She hollered a greeting he barely heard through the rolled-up window. Waving to her too, he pulled out on the road and headed west to his place.

He dreaded going home, but maybe WHO would be able to figure out what was going on there, why his house was being haunted and what could be done—he prayed *something* could be done—to make the woman and her tormenter go away.

* * *

Bernadette looked up at Luella. "I'm worried about Jack alone out there at his place."

"I overhead him and Frank talking a few nights ago," Luella replied as she slipped two slices of bread into a toaster. "I didn't hear everything, but it sounds like Jack has a hell of a nasty problem in his house."

"Yeah, Frank told me that things explode, furniture is thrown and that the woman ghost is desperate to get Jack's attention." She shivered, almost sloshing her coffee onto the tabletop. "I grew up on stories about ghosts. My grandma swore the next life walks side by side with this one so that's why we see spirits and other beings from time to time. And the more I learn through Scary Mary, the more I realize Grandma was right." A flood of sympathy for Jack moved over her. "Jack must be so scared."

"What's odd is that he has lived in that house for a couple years now," Luella told her. "He started building it when he moved here from Cadiz, but I don't think he had any trouble like this until recently."

"That *is* strange," Bernadette replied.

"Well, if this research team he has hired can't help, maybe you and Scary Mary can." With a jar of jelly in one hand and the toast in the other, Luella sat across from Bernadette. "I bet she has a few aces up her sleeves."

"Let's hope it doesn't come to that. Dealing with the dead can be dangerous."

"If the dead is even what Jack is dealing with."

"Yeah, that's a concern too," Bernadette agreed.

Somehow, some way, Bernadette knew she'd get pulled into Jack's problem. She didn't mind helping him, but after dealing with the incubus Ezra and his succubae a few months ago, Bernadette worried that Jack's "haunting" could turn into something even more dangerous.

Chapter Three

Seph hopped out of the SUV and gazed around at the house and surrounding property. Sunshine streamed through the tree limbs, creating a lacy pattern on the ground. She would bet when the trees were in full foliage they provided a heavy, cool canopy over the house and lawns. Despite the chilly spring, porch chairs and an old rocker sat on the porch. A cold breeze whispered through the trees to the right, then wafted over the driveway. Gooseflesh rose on Seph's neck and she shivered.

Queen, Theo, Sandra and Dean exited the vehicles and stood glancing around curiously.

"Do we have the right address?" Queen asked.

"This is where the GPS led us," Dean answered loudly as he rummaged for something in the van.

Foreboding emanated from the house. Seph approached the structure. This case was going to be a difficult one, perhaps even dangerous. Something powerful resided in the home. It tickled her senses, kissed her consciousness with warnings, and whispered to her with venomous promises she couldn't quite hear. Unnerved, she couldn't fight her attraction to the place, but she halted when something glimmered in the grass. She knelt, peering closer. Shards of glass lay everywhere. Following the path of slivers with her eyes, she mapped out the range of the pieces and caught the shining of more glass up the porch steps. There, just to the right of the steps, a front window was missing the glass, one curtain dangling through the big hole.

She rose, pointing at the house. "Queen, something has happened here. It looks like the window has exploded, and there's glass all the way out here by my feet."

Her boss sauntered over to her, an element of surprise in her dark eyes. She assessed Seph quickly, appeared to be on the verge of asking her a question, then suddenly changed her mind and walked off to the side of the debris to pause at the left of the steps. After a moment, she looked back at Seph. "Good observation skills, Seph. Whatever happened here…" She shook her head. "If this is paranormal, we've never dealt with anything so powerful before."

"So where's the owner?" Theo asked.

"My guess is that whatever happened here scared him badly enough that he left," Queen stated.

"Why don't you call him?" Dean suggested. He looked at Seph. "His number is in his file."

About to return to the SUV for her laptop, Seph stopped at the sound of an approaching vehicle.

"That might be the owner now," Queen said.

A pickup appeared through the trees, then rounded the bend leading to the area where the team had parked. The driver stopped by a pole barn, shut off the engine, then hopped out to approach them. Seph tried to keep her face neutral as her gaze landed on the man. Tall, probably more than six foot four, the guy appeared as if he could take on a gorilla barehanded. He wasn't overly muscled, but something about his stance coupled with his size spoke volumes about the hidden power beneath his clothes—or rather pajamas. He must've been in a big rush when he'd left.

The sun revealed him in stunning clarity right down to gilding his reddish hair with gold and copper. At this distance, Seph couldn't tell what hue his eyes were, but she guessed brown to go with his coloring. Even from several yards away, she could tell he was attractive, his closely cropped beard adding a rakish look to his features. Something within her stirred and rushed to her core. Flustered, she turned and focused on the gaping window again, and the sensations she picked up from the opening quickly intensified.

"Jack Henessy," he said, holding his hand out to Dean, who gripped it. Jack pumped Dean's hand several times before releasing him. "I'm relieved to see you guys."

"I'm Queen Galu, the head of this team," Queen said, drawing Jack's attention. "What happened here?"

"The ghost woman came back asking for help," Jack began, tension filling his face, "then this…this *thing* appeared next to her, and when I yelled at it, the glass exploded. The explosion knocked me halfway out in the yard, where I landed flat on my back."

"Are you okay?" Seph asked.

For the first time, he noticed her where she stood closest to the house and behind everyone. His gaze lingered for a second longer than it should have, then he nodded.

"Yes, I'm fine. I haven't found even a scratch, but

the blast and sudden impact with the ground stunned me for a couple minutes." He motioned toward the house. "We can go inside. It's *usually* safe during the daytime. It's at night when the shit hits the fan."

He passed through the small crowd on his way to the house. As he reached Seph, his gaze met hers and a strange thrill wound through her. Light brown eyes, almost sandy. A tattoo peeked from the short sleeve of his shirt, but she couldn't tell what it was. He nodded slightly, the corners of his mouth quirking, his eyes alight with…interest?

"Watch for the glass," he said. "It's everywhere on the porch and steps." At the threshold, he paused, looked behind him to make sure everyone was coming, then pushed the door open. "Anyone want coffee?"

"Oh heavens, yes!" Queen answered.

A chorus of "me too" drifted across the lawn.

Jack nodded and stepped inside. To Seph, it was as if he'd walked into the maw of a monster.

* * *

Shaking, Jack opened the door. The eye contact with the pretty, black-haired woman had sent a frisson of excitement through him. It left him unsettled and his cock hardening. What the hell? He dismissed it as the effect of a night of chaos, unsettled sleep and not enough coffee this morning. When he looked back at the research team, he sneaked a glance at the woman, who stood staring at the house as though she expected it to fall on her. Yeah, he knew that feeling well.

"Come on in," he invited. "I'll put on a pot of coffee, and if anyone is hungry, I have a couple boxes

21

of mini donuts in the kitchen. I live here alone, so I don't usually keep much on hand. Half my time is spent at the MC."

"MC?" Seph asked as she stepped into the small foyer.

"Motorcycle club," he said, averting his gaze. "The Werewolves of Rebellion—but don't worry. We're not an outlaw gang. We all have jobs and families, and there's even a small community of our members who live in the shallow valley below the club's main house. We take care of our own and help others when we can." He began making coffee, dumping the old grounds, finding a filter and the can of coffee, the mundane actions soothing his nerves. "Have a seat."

The scrape of chair legs on the tile overwhelmed the small kitchen. Jack pushed the Power button on the Bunn, then turned to find everyone sitting except the black-haired woman, who stood against the wall by the doorway leading to the hall. For an instant, he imagined her sprawled naked across his bed, her limbs pale in the dim light, legs spread for him... He blinked hard a couple times.

Wondering what the hell was wrong with him, he focused on finding the donuts, then set the boxes on the tabletop. "Help yourselves." The coffeemaker beeped. "And do the same with the coffee. There's creamer and sugar there on the lazy Susan. Cups are in that cabinet." He pointed.

Shaking again, he occupied himself with rummaging through the refrigerator for odds and ends he could add to the meager breakfast. Why did just looking at that woman rattle him so badly? He straightened with a bag of raisin bagels in one hand and a tub of cream cheese in the other. He placed the items on the tabletop, his attention going back to the woman.

She was gone.

And that really bothered him.

"I'll be right back," he told everyone.

The woman wasn't in the main hall. He strode past the laundry room, the bathroom, the spare bedroom and paused at the back door leading out on to a small porch big enough for a tiny table and two chairs and that overlooked rolling fields beyond a couple huge hickory trees. A noise to his right forced him to turn. Down the short L-shaped hall, the woman stood at the threshold of the master bedroom—his bedroom. The instant he saw her there, looking at his rumpled bed, his cock hardened even more. Jack shook off the erotic thoughts.

She seemed oblivious to his presence. Standing with one hand on the doorframe, her ebony ponytail tickling the spot between her shoulder blades, she kept staring into the room as though there was something intensely fascinating inside. Jack let himself have a moment to check her out. He traced the curve of her neck with his gaze, allowing his eyes to feast on her, and enjoyed every smooth plane and curve of her body right down to a little round ass that had enough padding to stick out slightly and beg to be bitten. Gulping, he drew his gaze down her jean-clad legs all the way to her Aviva sneakers and back up her body again. His cock, still straining against his sweats, throbbed painfully. Hell, he couldn't recall ever being this attracted to a woman before. The sweetbutts at the

MC were super sexy, but none of them compared to this woman. He shook his head as he willed his dick to abate. Something about the brunette spoke to him, urged him to talk to her, to learn about her, to look into her eyes and see the real person who dwelled on the inside of that lovely package in which she resided.

He cleared his throat. She jumped.

"Oh!" Turning sideways in the threshold, she gaped at him, surprise all over her face. "You scared the hell out of me."

At the color infusing her cheeks, he smirked. "What are you doing back here?"

"I'm sorry." The red blooming over her skin spread down her neck. "I was drawn back here for some reason."

Now her disappearance made sense. He nodded. "Ah, I didn't know that the team employed a medium."

"They don't."

"Excuse me?"

"Well," she said, "they don't know that they do, and I don't call myself a"—she moved over to the end of the short hall and glanced down the main one toward the kitchen—"medium, or a psychic or even a sensitive. I just…know things." She lowered her voice. "I see things other people can't, things no one else can even sense."

"So why doesn't the team know that you're a…?" He waved one hand in her direction. "Whatever."

"It's a long story," she replied quietly. "I just don't want them to know." She frowned and gazed up at him. "I'm not even sure why I told you this. I've never said anything to anyone about what I'm capable of, so please don't say anything to them."

At her direct eye contact, Jack froze. Her eyes weren't brown, nor were they gold or even a sandy hue. Amber, hers were amber. Deep, rich, startling orange-gold eyes. He let his gaze wander up to her hair swept back into a tie. Raven-wing hair, hair that set off her striking eyes.

The air grew cool around them, the temperature dropping sharply. She gasped and something odd settled over her face, something he couldn't quite label, but it seemed part shock and part fear. He opened his mouth to say something to her, but the temperature had fallen so rapidly that only fog puffed from his lips.

"What the hell? What's going—"

The cold speared him straight through the center of his chest. He stiffened, uttered a low "oomph," then, without any way to stop himself, he pushed the medium backward until he had her wedged in the tiny corner between the doorframe and the wall. She blinked several times, her gaze locking with his, then a huge smile brightened her face, and Jack found himself kissing the hell out of her.

* * *

Persephone struggled with someone inside her body. Only once before had she been possessed, and it had been so briefly that she'd managed to quickly force the spirit out of her body, then said a prayer aloud to keep the spirit at bay. This time was different. This ghost was female and almost…familiar. But that didn't make any sense. As the coldness of the spirit's energy sluiced through her veins and into her muscles, sadness also washed through Seph until she looked up and met Jack's eyes. It was Jack, but not Jack. The energy inside Seph recognized something in him and happiness rushed through her body.

He pressed her to the wall and kissed her—hard. Shocked, she tried to fight him, but the presence welcomed the kiss, pushing closer to Jack, running her hands over his body, untying the string of his sweats…

"Stop this!" she told the entity. *"Leave me. I did not give you permission to possess me!"*

No one replied, but the energy to maintain control over Seph's corporeal form grew stronger.

Jack groaned low in his throat and rubbed his hard-on against her belly. Despite her lack of control and fear, Seph couldn't help being aroused. Or was it the spirit's arousal? She couldn't tell.

"Jack?" someone called from the kitchen. "Do you have any half-and-half?"

Queen's voice provided the interruption needed. The entity within Seph fled from her. Seph sagged, but found Jack holding her up. He blinked down at her.

"What the hell just happened?" he asked, his expression bewildered.

"Whatever is here just possessed us," she said.

"Fuck!" He stepped back, but still held her by the shoulders until she got her feet soundly beneath her. "Does that mean that…that thing had control of me? Did I hurt you?"

"What's going on back here?"

Seph glanced over to find Queen standing at the hall's junction.

"Fucking ghosts or whatever is here just took over both of us," Jack snapped. The edge in his voice transformed into a low growl. "Until now, the weird shit always happens after dark, seldom during daylight."

Queen blinked and the color drained from her cheeks.

"Sorry," Jack rushed on, "I didn't mean to bite your head off. This just…well, it scared the hell out of me."

He raked one hand through his hair. Seph wanted to smooth the places that stood up at odd angles.

"And I feel like I haven't slept for a couple days," Jack added.

"Spirits will access your energy so they can materialize," Queen explained as the rest of the team filed into the hall behind her. "And possessions are a hundred times more draining. It will take a few hours before you feel like yourself again, so count your blessings that the possession was brief."

"What happened?" Dean asked.

"I'll explain in a few minutes," Queen answered. She looked pointedly at Seph. "And so will Seph and Jack."

Seph met her gaze boldly, hoping to convey innocence.

"I don't think it's safe for anyone to be here." Jack jerked his head toward Seph. "And I don't think it's safe for her—"

"My name's Persephone," she offered. "Persephone Jones."

He held her gaze for just an instant and smiled, then he focused on Queen again. "It's not safe for Persephone and me to be here together. I don't want to be used, possessed, taken over or whatever the fuck it's called nowadays."

27

He pushed past Queen, Theo and the others, who moved against the wall out of his way.

For some reason Seph couldn't pinpoint, Jack's anger hurt her. Did he think she'd somehow staged this ordeal? Was he repulsed by her? The erection he'd been rubbing against her belly stated otherwise, but that very well could have been caused by the entity that had possessed him.

Feeling used, and shame prickling her skin, she suddenly needed a cup of very stout coffee and a few minutes to regain her bearings. She passed Queen, who placed a hand on her forearm.

"Don't," she said to Queen. "Not now. After what just happened, I don't know whether I want to cry, throw up or just pass out."

"Right." Queen let go. "Go take a few minutes to compose yourself."

"Damn straight I will." Head spinning, Seph headed down the hall and straight to the coffeemaker.

Chapter Four

Later, after three cups of strong coffee heavily laced with sugar, Jack began to feel like himself again. He'd explained his side of the occurrence to the team, answering as many questions as he possibly could, but finally he had no more to offer. Queen, a tenacious and bubbly Samoan woman whom he'd quickly decided he liked, had taken detailed notes on an iPad mini as he'd talked. A tiny, mousy woman named Sandra, who looked to be in her early thirties and probably aerobicized every morning and every night, wandered the house with what he was told was a K2 meter. Walking around the home with her, a tall man who looked to be in his mid-40s with a body that seemed composed of all sharp angles, held another gadget and muttered quietly to Sandra as they worked. Jack thought he'd heard one of the team call the guy Theo.

"Are you going to talk to Persephone?" he asked Queen as he rinsed out his mug.

"She prefers Seph," the big woman said, "and I want to give her a little more time to chill." She stared up at Jack, her onyx eyes showing him that she knew more had transpired between them than they were letting on. "I've noticed she can become very temperamental on cases. I have suspicions as to why, but no solid proof. Seph does her job well, but she keeps her thoughts and emotions under lock and key."

He nodded and turned his thoughts to other matters. "Does the team have a place to stay?"

"I saw a sign for a motel when we drove through Rebellion." Queen jotted a couple notes into her iPad. "I thought I'd inquire whether or not it has enough rooms for us."

"I'm sure you can stay at the MC. I'll drive over and double-check. I need to get out of here for a couple hours anyway."

"Are you okay with us poking through your house and over the property while you're gone?" Queen asked.

"Make yourselves at home." He looked around the kitchen and through the doorway into the living room. "That is if you're able to after what happened earlier to me and Seph."

"Thank you," Queen said, her expression sympathetic. "Would you mind taking Seph with you? If your motorcycle club is fine with putting my team up for a while, Seph can make the arrangements, then get with me on them later. And if you have time, you can give her the history of this house."

To Jack's surprise, he quite liked the idea of having some alone time with Seph. "Sure, but what's the history of the house got to do with spirits here? There wasn't anything on this land except a few old, falling-apart outbuildings."

Queen frowned at him quizzically. "There was no house?"

"No. I built this place, but I've only been living here since last fall. Why?"

"Usually a haunting is tied to a house or a structure, but it could be the property itself." She shrugged. "For example Gettysburg is haunted due to the battle and deaths there. Lots of emotional energy was released there, so it's glued to the area."

He walked around the table and stood at the hall. "Nothing has ever happened here as far as I know."

"All right. See you later," Queen said, returning her attention to the notes she kept adding to her iPad.

Jack passed Theo in the hall, then paused at the junction that led to his bedroom. Sunshine streamed through the backdoor's glass, and more spilled into the room through the big panes on either side of the master bed. If he stepped into his bedroom, would he be attacked again? Claimed and left to a spirit's control?

He shook off the thoughts and steeled himself to enter and find a change of clothes. He'd invested many thousands of dollars into this house, the pole barn and a tool shed, so he'd be damned if he was going to let something on another plane of existence pull his strings as though he were a puppet.

After taking one step into the room, he paused. Of course, if he was possessed, couldn't he remain that way never to be himself again?

The very thought sobered him.

Still, he couldn't allow himself to be ruled by fear. Hell, he was a lycanthrope and they were one of the most dreaded creatures in myth and legend, let alone reality. But even a werewolf was at the mercy of magic and hidden powers.

With a deep breath, he focused on the idea of taking Seph with him to the MC. Quickly, he rushed into the room, then rummaged through the chest of drawers for clean underwear, socks, jeans, a beater and a flannel shirt. Next, he grabbed his cowboy boots. After he snagged his cut from where it hung over the back of a chair, he headed down the hall to the bathroom. At least there he had a semblance of security. Hell, he didn't know if he'd ever be able to sleep in his bed again after today.

Once he'd dressed, Jack stopped in the kitchen. "Why don't you and your team follow me to the MC instead? If there's a problem lodging there, I'll escort you into town and help you get rooms at the motel. I know the woman who manages the place, so I'm sure I can get you a good rate if the MC doesn't pan out."

"Oh?" Looking away from the notebook's screen, Queen tipped her head to one side and sized him up. "Does our being here alone worry you?"

"Maybe. Right now I don't know what to expect. Besides, we have paperwork to sign for this case, right? And the Werewolves of Rebellion are my family, so it's time I let the entire MC know what's going on. That way, the members can aid in protecting you and your team if the need should arise."

Laughter resided in Queen's voice. "Your MC is going to protect us from ghosts and demons?"

Jack shook his head, his frustration with her mounting, but he knew she didn't know any better. Although WHO might have experience with spirits and demons, Jack doubted any of the team members were equipped to deal with werewolves. An image of Bernadette and Scary Mary popped into his head. Or for that matter, witches.

"There are two other MCs in this area," he

continued. "You're all new faces in town, so you might draw unwanted attention. The one MC has a tentative truce with the Werewolves of Rebellion, but the other club is devout one-percenters who have caused *a lot* of trouble the past few months."

"Do we really need to worry?" Queen asked.

"It's just a precaution." Grinning wryly, he added, "And trust me, you'll be more comfortable at the MC than at the motel. The motel is almost like camping. No TV, basic phones, no room service except for towels, and tiny bathrooms with only a toilet and shower stall in each."

"Hell, you have my vote," Dean said as he entered the kitchen.

"Mine too," Sandra called from the living room.

"We'll pack up," Queen said, "and meet you outside."

He took his keys from the hook by the door, but on stepping outside, he changed his mind about the pickup and returned them to their place. The sun had warmed the air enough that a short ride on his Indian would be the ticket to banishing his unsettled feelings. He found Seph at the SUV, its double doors open. She sat in the back of it, a thermos next to her as she sipped from its screw-on topper.

Emboldened by the unexpectedly warm day, Jack asked, "Would you like to ride over to the motorcycle club with me? I'm going to double-check on accommodations for you and your team."

She looked at him warily, but the idea seemed to intrigue her. Slowly, the wariness faded and interest lit her eyes. "Sure. I think it would do me good to get away from here for a bit."

Her acceptance relieved Jack, which surprised him. Why should he care? Hell, why had he asked her to go with him? Inwardly, he chuckled. That was easy. Every time he looked at her, his cock saluted.

"Great," he said, suddenly changing his mind about riding the Indian. "Give me a minute and I'll pick you up here. Better put your jacket back on."

* * *

As he walked away, Seph retrieved her jacket from where she'd tossed it on the floor of the SUV, then shrugged into it. The sound of something loud and rumbly cut across the drive. A motorcycle? Now she understood the need for a coat.

The engine revved a few times. In moments, the sound drew closer and Jack rode up the lane to her on an old motorcycle with wide tires, wide fenders and a rounded gas tank. She knew very little about motorcycles of any sort, but this one looked like it was old, possibly restored. Black, gold and red paints complemented one another and shimmered in the blazing sunshine. On the sides of the gas tank, someone had airbrushed a realistic image of an Indian chief in a war bonnet with a wolf's head alongside it, as if the Indian were also the wolf.

"Hop on." Jack held one hand out to her.

She gaped at him. The sound of the motor vibrated her body, the sensation both disconcerting and thrilling.

"Never ridden on a bike before?" he asked with a sexy-as-hell smile.

She swallowed and shook her head.

"All you need to do is relax and let me do everything."

His words struck her as insinuative, seductive... sexual. Before Seph could stop herself, she took his hand and followed his instructions on where to place each foot as she swung herself onto the passenger cushion behind him. Once seated against his back, she found herself pressed so tightly to him that her entire body flared with sudden, intense heat.

And holy hell did he smell good! The aroma of freshly laundered clothes and crisp, spicy cologne overwhelmed her senses, but another smell tantalized her further, something wild, heady and intoxicating— his own personal scent. She closed her eyes and drew in the wonderful combination of odors that were all Jack, allowing herself a private moment to enjoy the hard planes of his body, the delightful heat emanating from him. She'd experienced attraction before, had had a couple of great sexual partners, but this guy... Jack had already become that delicious candy she just had to keep nibbling.

Vaguely, she noticed her team hopping into the vehicles. Queen shot her an amused look before climbing in behind Dean, who usually drove.

Seph slid her hands around Jack's waist, expecting him to stiffen at the contact, but he didn't. Sitting still, she waited. The bike thrummed beneath her, the vibration in the seat stimulating her pussy. The sensation aroused her, but the man pressed to her breasts did so even more. This ride was going to be sweet torture.

"Ready?" he asked over the bike's motor.

"Yes," she replied loudly.

"Remember to relax with the bike's motions."

With that, he pushed off and slowly maneuvered the drive to the two-lane road.

Once they were out on the pavement, it didn't take Seph long to feel the movements of the bike and blend with them. She wanted to place the side of her face against Jack's back and just enjoy his body, but the thought of the team following them kept her from doing so. Instead, she admired the countryside. Although she'd always been pure city girl, she had to admit the f the Appalachians were dazzling.

Jack suddenly downshifted, decelerating. Looking ahead, Seph discovered the reason. A flock of huge birds crossed the highway. Some flapped their enormous wings and half lifted off to land on a high bank while others ran in a comical manner across the road to disappear in the briars and brambles that were just beginning to glow with tiny spring-green leaves.

"Are those…turkeys?" she asked over Jack's shoulder.

"Yes."

"I'd forgotten they're not white." Feeling a bit embarrassed by the admission, she laughed softly.

He laughed too. "Beautiful, aren't they? A lot prettier than the plain white ones raised for American dinners."

"And big," she added.

He chuckled again and gunned the Indian.

They rode past farms, sprawling hayfields turning deep, vibrant green, and ponds and lakes reflecting the spring sun. As Jack turned off the main road, Seph caught sight of a creek meandering through some trees, and soon the ribbon of water followed alongside the gravel road. In a bend of the creek, a tall gray-blue bird stood on one long leg, the other drawn up against its body as though it were a feathery statue placed in the water. Jack slowed the Indian again and crossed the water via a covered bridge, then started up a steep hill. At the top, he turned left and traveled a narrow paved road until he made another left. Soon, a gate appeared ahead, and they made a right onto a lane with the WHO team pulling in behind them. The lane led through open fields, then orchards on either side. Finally, a small community sprawled in a shallow valley. Little single-level clapboard homes, some white, some tan or light gray, all crouched on either side of the track. A house trailer here and there sat behind some of the homes. Above the community, the lane wound up a knoll to the crowning jewel, a beautiful Victorian home.

"What a gorgeous house," Seph commented.

"It's the actual MC," Jack replied over his shoulder, "but it's an actual home too. Our president and his woman live there, as well as other couples and some of the single members and prospects."

They reached the summit and Jack slowed, then duck-walked the bike over to one side of a big garage with the sign *Nightshade's Wolves*.

"Although I know virtually nothing about motor-cycles," she said to Jack, "I've heard of Nightshade's Wolves. This place custom-makes bikes."

He shut the Indian down. "How have you heard about this place?"

She allowed him to help her off the bike. "One of the guys in WHO's office—whom Queen has good-naturedly reprimanded a few times for always being on this workshop's website—dreams of someday owning a

Nightshade's Wolf. He's always boasting that he puts ten percent of every paycheck in his motorcycle savings account."

Jack laughed, the sound low and rumbling, reminding Seph of the motorcycle's motor. "Is he a young guy just starting out in the world?"

She nodded.

"Well, I hope he achieves his dream. These bikes"—he hooked a thumb over his shoulder toward the big shop sign—"aren't cheap. That kid will be saving for a long time. Most of Frank's clients are those with plenty of money lying around or have access to loans."

"Frank?" she asked as the WHO vehicles pulled in and parked.

"President of the Werewolves of Rebellion," a deep voice said from the shop's office doorway. "Jack, I'm still drooling over how fucking amazing that Indian turned out."

"Thanks, Frank." Jack chuckled.

Seph glanced over at a very tall, very broad-shouldered man dressed in jeans, a blue-and-white, long-sleeved flannel, and a cut identical to Jack's save for different patches and more wear. She had to admit the man was striking with his dark hair, eyes, and neatly trimmed beard. He moved out onto the carport, letting the door shut behind him, and held out a massive, long-fingered hand to Seph.

"Frank Nightshade. And you are?"

"Persephone Jones. Call me Seph. I'm part of the WHO team."

Frank turned questioning, deep brown eyes toward Jack.

"This is the team I told you that I'd contacted to help me with the problems at my place," Jack explained.

"Ah...well, let's go inside and talk." Frank dipped his head toward the big house. Laughter and bluegrass music spilled from open windows. "It's getting close to lunchtime, so I'll have the girls put out some extras and we'll have a meal together."

"Sounds awesome," Dean said as he approached.

The others tumbled out of the SUV and van, murmuring their agreement. Seph worked with a great crew. She had to smile, though. Food and coffee ran neck and neck with their investigations.

Chapter Five

Bernadette helped Luella gather dishes and stack them by the kitchen sink. She turned to find Seph, the young woman Jack had brought with him, standing next to her.

"Can I help?" she asked.

"You're our guest," Luella answered.

"But I feel useless." She blinked large amber eyes at Bernadette.

An odd feeling washed over Bernadette. Not a bad sensation, but one that tickled her senses and whispered something was different about this woman.

"Well," Bernadette said, "you could load the dishwasher."

"Deal."

Shirley waved to them as she stepped around the other side of the little kitchen table. "I wiped down the tables. I'm heading back to my place. I still have forms to send to work and the wireless was down all morning."

Everyone within earshot called out their good-byes.

"I'm heading out too," Callie May announced as she entered from the dining room with dirty paper napkins and a couple stray glasses. "I really need to do some laundry, or Devin might divorce me." She laughed and dropped the napkins in a trashcan before passing the glasses to Seph. "See you all at suppertime."

"See ya," Bernadette, Luella and others called after her.

"Well, it's settled," Jack said from where he appeared in the dining room doorway.

Bernadette turned toward his voice.

He locked eyes with Seph and grinned broadly. Returning his smile, Seph lit up, her cheeks pinking and her eyes bright.

Bernadette caught Luella's attention and they smirked at each other.

"Your team is staying on the MC's property until the investigation of my place is over," Jack continued. "There's a vacant house, two empty trailers, and Tractor has a big RV that can be used too, so there's plenty of room for everyone."

"Why don't you go unpack your stuff?" Bernadette suggested. When Seph met her gaze, the sense the woman belonged with the MC grew even stronger in Bernadette. "That drive from Detroit isn't a short one. I bet you're tired."

"I'm beat." Seph yawned behind her hand. "We came straight here from another case we wrapped up last night, so none of us has had any sleep."

"Go on, then." Luella waved a soapy hand at her, then wiped it on a towel. "Go unpack and get some sleep. Jack's house will still be there tonight."

"I have the keys to each place except the RV," Frank stated. He took keys off the pegboard by the sun porch door. "I'll have to stop at Tractor's house and get the RV key. Everyone can follow me down."

"Thank you for lunch. It was wonderful!" Queen entered the kitchen, slipping her notebook into its case. "I think we'll all crash for a while."

Bernadette made mental notes of which team member was which as they filed through the kitchen thanking her and Luella for the food. They all followed Jack and Frank out onto the carport.

When the screen slapped shut on the sun porch, Luella turned to her and said, "Well? What do you think?"

"I think that those two are going to be doing the nasty very soon," Bernadette joked.

Luella giggled and returned to washing the odds and ends in the sink.

"But I do get the sense that Seph will be a new addition to the family," Bernadette said. "She's…different. Not bad different, but just..." She shrugged.

"We'll figure it out," Luella said. "We always do."

* * *

Seph waited as Jack unlocked the door to the RV. He swung it, along with the little screen door, open and stepped up inside the big Winnebago.

"Come on in. It has power, so you can cook, watch TV and even use the heater. Tractor keeps the RV self-sustaining in case we have guests who need a place to crash." He showed her how to turn on the heat. "It'll get cold tonight, so boost this up and stay warm. There is plenty of water to shower and flush the toilet, but"—he opened the cupboards to find them empty—"you'll need to buy a few groceries if your team decides you'll be here more than a couple days." He shrugged. "And you're always welcome to have your meals up at the main house."

"Tractor?" She couldn't help grinning. "That's an odd name."

Jack took her bag from her and set it on the sofa. "He takes care of most of the MC's field work such as mowing the hay and plowing. It seems like the only place anyone sees him besides the supper table is on a tractor, so that's how he got the nickname."

"Does this Tractor take the RV on trips often?"

"Twice a year," he answered. "He just got back a couple weeks ago from Florida. He takes his family there where they have extended family. Tractor says he likes to warm his fur on their private beach…"

She met his gaze. Why did he look so…annoyed?

"Warm his fur?" she asked, trying to lighten the mood.

"Uh…just an expression."

She continued looking at him. He had such expressive eyes. Right now confusion filled them.

"You know"—he shrugged abruptly—"like an old dog on a sunny porch warming its fur after it's been out in the cold all night."

"You mean a cat?"

He frowned. "Pardon?"

"It's usually an old cat, not a dog."

He scrubbed one hand over his face and nodded.

She peeked into the bathroom, looked back the hall toward the bedroom, then back to Jack. Although not one of the high-tech recreational vehicles, this one was still very nice, even decorated with little things that seemed island-ish. She pointed to a decoration on a wall and quirked an eyebrow.

"Oh, Tractor and his family are Filipino."

She nodded. "Thank you for everything, Jack. The RV is perfect, and for once it'll be nice not to have to share a room with one of the team members."

"I should be thanking you and your people," he replied seriously. "And I'm sorry about what happened this morning."

"That wasn't your fault, or mine. Spirits can be very unpredictable. Some of them tell me—show themselves in unexpected ways." She averted her gaze, then made like she was checking out the little TV set.

"Still, it was embarrassing, and I'm sorry."

He was embarrassed he'd kissed her? She gulped. "We'll see what, if anything, we can find out tonight."

"Uhm, sure. I'll just let you unpack and get some rest."

She moved toward the sofa and caught her toe on a rubber mat by the door. Stumbling, she threw her hands out to catch herself, but Jack swept her into his arms and steadied her.

"You okay?"

"Yeah." She nodded vigorously. "Caught my toe on that doormat, that's all."

She straightened and looked up into his eyes. Big mistake. Riveted, she couldn't avert her gaze, couldn't break the strange pull to the man holding her. He blinked slowly, as if hypnotized. He tightened his grip on her upper arms, tugging her slightly toward him. Unable to resist, she hoped he'd kiss her hard and thoroughly but this time as Jack, not the spirit that had possessed him that morning. This time she'd be free of

44

the entity that had claimed her too. Seph wanted to taste Jack and discover the sexual fire she sensed simmering just under his skin.

Again, his fingers tightened on her arms. The pupils of his eyes grew darker, wider. His spicy, wild aroma seemed to intensify and wrap around her in a warm, comforting blanket.

She found herself rising on tiptoe to reach him. He was so tall, his shoulders wide, powerful... What would it be like to smooth her hands over them? To feel the hardness of his muscles beneath her palms? If only he'd stop torturing her and just kiss her...

* * *

If his fucking cock got any harder, it would burst right through the zipper of his jeans. Seph was part of the team he'd hired to investigate the paranormal activity in his home and here he was about to kiss her. Hell, he wanted her so damn badly that he could bend her over the drop-down table and bang her until it collapsed under them.

Jack tugged her maybe half an inch toward him and stopped himself from crushing her body to his. He wanted to possess her mouth, taste her, feel her breasts squashed against his cut. But the foot or less between them might as well have been the Grand Canyon. She was here to help him. If he followed through with his desires, it would put them in an awkward position and possibly create problems for Seph if Queen found out she'd fucked their client.

He gripped her arms a second time. His cock throbbed with impatience. Hell, if she even brushed against his crotch he might come. What the fuck had caused such a sexual attraction to her? Sure, she was gorgeous, but he knew nothing about her. This raw, carnal need was enough to drop him to his knees.

He shook himself and stepped back. "I'll let you get settled, Seph. Queen has my number should anyone need to reach me."

She blinked several times and suddenly sat on the couch as though her legs had collapsed under her. "Uh, yeah. Thanks for everything, Jack. See you later."

He practically fell out the door, then caught himself, spun, and shut the RV with enough force that it rocked a bit. Standing for a moment gathering his senses, Jack mentally cursed himself and drew in a big lungful of air. What the hell was wrong with him? On shaking legs, he stalked across the lawn and around Tractor's garage to the little slab of concrete poured in front of it where Jack had parked his Indian. He straddled the bike, started it up, then pushed off and accelerated out onto the gravel lane.

Hormones finally abating, Jack began to think more clearly.

"Warm his fur?" He shook his head as he rode through the orchards, his pulse subsiding. "What the fuck was I thinking? I might as well have said that Tractor liked to shift into werewolf form and lie on the hot beach." He sighed. "Dumbass!"

Jack rode home enjoying every second of the ride. The spring sunshine beat down on him, heating his head and shoulders. He couldn't wait until summer weather settled into the Appalachians for a few months so he could ride his Indian every day. There was nothing like hugging the curvy mountain roads on his bike to sooth his inner animal and calm his human side.

He turned onto his lane and rumbled slowly down it to the house. His beast detected something off, something malevolent. Coming to a full stop, his feet planted on either side of the motorcycle, he sat quietly as the machine thrummed under him and let his lycanthrope senses analyze the sensations wafting through the trees and up the last few feet of the lane.

Had someone been here? He closed his eyes and scented the breeze. Maybe. Whoever had trespassed had left very little odor behind, but the vibes hitting him from an unknown source prompted his inner animal to surge to the forefront of his brain and simmer beneath his skin. He willed the change to obey him and succeeded. With his senses tuned for trouble, he kicked off, gunning the Indian a bit, and rode the last few feet up the lane, then down the path that led from the drive to the pole barn where he kept his bike. The entire time, Jack remained poised for an attack that could happen from any direction. Part of him felt foolish, for there was obviously no one here. Regardless, his lycanthrope self whispered not to let his guard down.

Inside the building, Jack duck-walked the Indian over to its parking spot, shut off the engine, then yanked a heavy-duty tarp over it. He was halfway across the dirt floor when a thought struck him—what if whoever had been here came back to steal his Indian? A low grumble built in his chest that he eventually let out in frustration. Jack left the building and strode to the toolshed, where he found a length of medium chain and an old padlock. If someone really wanted to steal his bike, the chain could be cut, but at least chaining it would give him a bit of security.

Jack returned to the pole barn, secured the bike, then

pocketed the keys and headed to the house. One thing he must do today was patch the broken window. He sighed. A pane of glass that size would cost a pretty penny. He'd nearly choked to death on his own spit when he'd chosen the windows and found out the price, but he wanted a good view and lots of light in his home when he'd built it.

He climbed the steps, glass crunching under his boots, and reached for the door. He paused. Curtains were hanging outside the window. Frowning, he moved over to investigate. Only one of the two curtains panels hung over the sill. The other remained inside along the window frame. He searched the porch for anything unusual but found nothing.

With his unease growing, Jack returned to the door and stepped inside the little foyer. He entered the living room and approached the broken window. If someone had been in the house, he or she could have easily dragged the curtain out upon leaving and not realized it. But maybe a draft had blown it outside. If that where the case, why weren't both panels hanging through the window?

Someone had been here, though. He couldn't detect any unfamiliar odors in the house, but he sensed the essence of someone who had fouled his den.

Worried, he strode to the kitchen and halted in his tracks. On the table lay four large zip bags of pot.

"Fuck," he whispered.

* * *

"Where's Frank?"

Bernadette stood in the shallow corner by the living room doorway and blinked rapidly at Jack's barking tone on the other end of the landline.

48

"He's not answering his fucking phone!" Jack yelled.

"It went dead, so it's on the charger," Bernadette replied, trying to use a soothing voice. "What's wrong?

A sigh followed. The worry within that long, gusty sound tugged at Bernadette's heart, which in turn tickled her witch senses. A wave of foreboding fell over her.

"Jack, answer me. I know something terrible is happening. Is it the house again?"

"No, it's something else entirely." Quiet followed for a few seconds, then, "Is Frank there? I really need to talk to him, because if the situation I have here isn't handled properly, it could not only affect me, but the MC too."

At that, Bernadette began to tremble. "Hang on. I'll find out where he is."

She let the receiver dangle down the wall and turned to come face-to-face with Luella.

"What has happened?" Luella demanded, her blue eyes bright with worry.

"I don't know yet. Where's Frank?"

"He went down to the community to make sure everyone in the team were all settled in," Luella replied in a rush. "I'll call the empty bungalow number and see if—"

"Shit, what now?" Frank said from the sun porch. "I barely get back to the house and you two are freaking out." He stepped into the kitchen and looked at first Bernadette, then Luella.

"It's Jack. Something is wrong." Bernadette reached for the receiver. It rose into the air and settled in her hand. She held it out to him.

"Jack, what's going on?" Frank said the instant he held the receiver up to his ear.

The look on her mate's face pushed a needled of fear through Bernadette. She hoped no one was hurt— or worse. Anxiously, she stood nearby with Luella and tried to piece together what was so important through Frank's side of the conversation.

"Call Deputy Williamscot," Frank said. "I'll wait ten minutes, then I'll call his private cell phone to back up what you've said, okay?" He listened for a moment, his expression grim. "Don't worry, Jack. Craig is well aware of what most of us are. I'll vouch for you, and so will Bernadette, Luella and Beastman if needed. Craig knows the Werewolves of Rebellion are on the up and up. We've helped the county sheriff's department put away several of the River Rebels and even interrupted their human-trafficking ring, so Craig won't judge you. Just be honest with him." He nodded, the furrow deepening between his eyebrows. "All right. Like I said, I'll give you ten minutes, then I'll make my call."

He hooked the receiver into the old sixties-style wall phone, hanging it up. "Fuck, fuck, fuck!"

"Three fucks in a row," Luella said. "That's not good."

Frank shook his head, raking the fingers of both hands through his wavy locks, a habit Bernadette had learned meant that he was either frustrated or about to lose his temper. Her worry increased. The MC had been through so much the past year, and so had she and Frank. Could they handle more upset so soon after what had transpired last October?

"Get your riding gear on, babe," he told her.

"After I call Craig, we're heading over to Jack's place."

"Is it the spirits in his house?" she asked.

"No, something that has the potential to be much worse," he answered as he headed toward the stairs.

"It pisses me off when men demand that you spill your guts on cue, but when we want to know something, they have to be all Mr. Mysterious," Luella groused.

"I just hope this isn't the start of more chaos for the MC," Bernadette said. "We've all been through hell the last few months."

"But we're strong," Luella said and hugged her. "Don't forget that."

"I haven't. It's just that we need a breather now and then."

"Honey, it's been quiet since Halloween. We've had six months to breathe. That means you better grab your fireproof thong and hang on 'cause we're about to enter hell again."

On that note, Bernadette stuck her tongue out at Luella, earning herself a throaty chuckle from her friend, and headed upstairs to eavesdrop on Frank's call to Deputy Williamscot as she put on her riding gear.

Chapter Six

First thing Jack planned to do once the deputy, Frank and Bernadette left was board up the window. When he had a chance, he'd buy a replacement and install it. He felt really stupid for not having done it earlier. Although he'd known he was taking the chance of a bird or a wild animal getting into the house, he honestly hadn't thought much about a trespasser doing so since no one except the MC members knew he lived here.

The fact someone had penetrated his home uninvited awakened his wolf. He wanted to kill the person, transform and rip out the perpetrator's throat, watch the blood spray as the trespasser gurgled his last breath… Jack shook himself. He might not be a member of Frank's blood clan, but he observed the same practices the Nightshades and their extended relatives did and that was to control the beast. Letting the animal have its way would be devastating to anyone near enough for Jack to reach and he didn't want that. He had to exercise human reason and make his lycanthrope counterpart obey.

"I'll take care of this, Jack," Deputy Williamscot was saying. "You've turned this in to me, so as long as you swear none of your prints are on any of the bags, I'm going to take your word as the gospel."

"Craig, really?" Frank said.

"Hey, you know I have to attempt to do my job the best I can, Frank." The deputy scribbled something on a little notepad, then slipped it into a breast pocket of his black-and-gold uniform. "I trust you, you know that. But I still have a wife and kids to support and can't afford to lose my bread and butter."

Deputy Craig Williamscot was a good man. He'd helped Frank's MC and clan through many tight spots. Jack was going to say that he understood the deputy perfectly, but Frank beat him to it.

"Yeah, yeah. I'm sorry, Craig. You've never done me or any of my clan or the MC wrong." He raked his right hand through his hair, dislodging a black-and-white do-rag.

Bernadette picked it up and handed it to him. "Who knows about your place back here, Jack?"

"That's just it." Jack pegged the deputy with a direct look to get his point across. "No one but MC members knows about my home here in these woods. If you haven't noticed, I don't even have a mailbox to show someone lives back this lane. My mail goes to a PO box in Rebellion."

"It appears someone is trying to set you up," the deputy insisted. "Why?"

Jack leaned against the sink, crossing his arms, and sighed heavily. "Beats the hell out of me. I'm not one for barhopping; my trips into town are usually for groceries or other household basics. Hell, I haven't even gone to see a movie for months, since I rent them through satellite, and I've spent the winter restoring an

Indian motorcycle." He held both hands out, palms up. "I get along with everyone at the MC too."

"What about your workplace?" the deputy asked. "Any problems there?"

Jack shook his head. "Nope. I work for an aggregates company on the river hauling stone. I've been so busy running gravel to the new fracking pads that 99 percent of my communication with anyone at work is through my cell phone or the radio in the truck."

"Any run-ins with another MC?" Deputy Williamscot questioned. "Maybe a row at one of the local bars?"

"No," Jack said with force. "Nothing like that. Like I just said, I'm not a bar hopper—or a barfly. I'm telling you I've had a quiet winter, a quiet spring, and all my interactions, until recently, have been work-related or with Frank and the MC. I've hired a paranormal research team to investigate some crazy shit happening in my house, but they were all accounted for when"—he gestured at the bags of weed—"this happened."

"You hired a what?"

"It's a team called WHO—the Weird, Haunted and Occult. Whether you believe me or not, I don't give a flying fuck, but there are two spirits in my home, one that's really nasty, and that's how the window got busted."

The deputy picked his hat up off his head, revealing a round imprint in his blond hair, then resettled it. "After I encountered Frank and his clan"—he jerked a thumb in Frank's direction—"and I now know there are werewolves, I'm not at liberty to dismiss anything out of the ordinary." He shrugged.

"Well, if anything else happens, Jack, anything suspicious at all, call me. Not the office, me. Or have Frank call me, okay?"

"Yes, sir." Jack breathed a sigh of relief. "What happens to the pot?"

"Dig a hole, burn it to ash, then cover it and set the sod back over the hole—and do it far away from the house." The deputy walked into the living room. "And Frank, you better keep your eyes peeled out at the MC. If someone is targeting Jack, they might do the same to more of your people. Your clan has been through a lot the past few months." He tipped his hat to Bernadette and grinned. "Keep Frank on the straight and narrow, Bernadette."

"You know I will," she said, laughing softly.

Once the deputy was gone, Frank looked at Jack. "What do you make of this?"

"I honestly don't know," Jack replied. "I'm at a loss."

"Do you think it was just someone's way of saying they know you're here and they have access to you?" Bernadette suggested.

That gave Jack pause. "You mean the person who did this didn't want to set me up but show me that they could if they wanted to?"

She nodded. A thick lock of flaming-red hair fell across her eyes.

"Fuck." He shifted his gaze to the bags on the tabletop. "That idea never occurred to me."

"Who could be responsible?" Frank rummaged in the pantry closet and produced a black garbage bag. He then picked up the broom from the corner, gave Jack the bag, and waited while he opened it. "You better think long and hard on it," Frank stated. "You've missed someone on your list of people you associate with."

"Shit, Frank." Jack held the bag open while Frank used the bristle end of the broom to shove the bags of pot into it. "With the way some people in this world are so fucked up, it could be anyone with a nose out of joint. Some people take offense if you look their way funny."

Frank put the broom back in the corner, then drew Bernadette to his side. "Regardless, you watch your back. Maybe you should live at the MC for a while."

"I appreciate the offer, Frank, but you know I'm not comfortable with that. I was raised to live on my own, support myself—"

"Don't be a fucktard," Frank growled, startling Bernadette. He tightened his grip around her, then kissed the top of her head. "One of the purposes of my MC is to protect my people, whether clan or members."

Jack bobbed his head once, slowly, then a couple more times. "You're right. I'll think about it."

"And if you decide to stay there," Frank continued, "you don't have to ask for permission. Just come over, got it?"

"Yeah, got it."

"Do you need anything?" Bernadette asked. "Like maybe our help to board up the window?"

"I saw some plywood in the lean-to by the pickup," Frank stated. "We'll also help you dig a hole, burn and bury the weed."

Jack smiled. He thanked his lucky stars he was

one of Frank's wolves and that he had such an amazing extended family to rely on.

"I'd appreciate your help," he said. "I might be a lycanthrope with special abilities, but holding up a sheet of plywood while swinging a hammer at a nail isn't one of my strong suits."

Frank laughed. "Let's get busy."

* * *

Damn, she'd slept soundly—and hard. Seph sat up on the bed and tried to focus on her surroundings. At first she didn't remember where she was, but within seconds the memories flooded her mind, especially the one of nearly kissing Jack a second time. The memory shot a bolt of desire through her, followed quickly by disappointment that it hadn't happened.

She swung her legs off the bed and sat there staring at the gold, brown, and black flecked carpeting. Why was she so attracted to Jack? Yes, he was a hunk, but there were lots of hunks in the world. So what made him so different?

Better yet, why did she care?

She'd always used guys to scratch an itch, but none of them wanted to spend any more time than that with her. A quick roll in the sheets, a 'come here and let's fuck against the wall,' or even an occasional two-or-three-night relationship, but nothing serious. No guy had ever wanted her after they picked up on her strange ways, and even if the guy didn't notice her oddness, she was forced to send each one packing. The men who had spirits hanging around them were the worst. Usually relatives or extremely close friends who had died stayed close to the living in the event they could somehow convey a message. When the deceased homed in on her as a medium—a very powerful medium at that—they would not leave her alone.

Within a few hours to a couple of days, the cute guys, the handsome guys, the sweet, funny ones and even the arrogant jerks who were simply great in bed ended up with an "It was great, but it's time for you to go" from Seph.

And there had been one or two that it had really torn her up to send on their happy trails too.

Getting involved with Jack was not an option. Besides, it would cause a conflict of interest with her job. She didn't think Queen would really object to a romance brought on through an investigation, but for Seph, she didn't need a handsome, tall, broad-shouldered, sandy-eyed, sexy-as-seven-kinds-of hell, smiling He-Man distracting her from her task. Besides, it was becoming more difficult with each case to hide her abilities from Queen and the rest of the crew. She didn't want to be a medium, hadn't asked for the ability, but she knew she'd resent it if someone tried to force her to use it commercially, and she respected Queen too much to watch her friendship with the woman fall apart.

Seph's belly rumbled. She wandered through the darkening RV to the kitchenette where she'd left her belongings, including her cell. After she fished her phone out of her bag, she pressed the Screen button to see the time. After 6:00. No wonder she was hungry.

She quickly took her hair out of the ponytail, brushed it vigorously and let it hang around her shoulders. A fast teeth cleaning at the sink, then a baby wipe over her face and neck helped to wake her fully. She took her wallet-purse and slipped the cell into its designated compartment, then left the RV. Maybe the rest of the gang was hungry too. She figured the main house had already served supper, but a trip into Rebellion for a meal sounded like a good idea.

It didn't take her long to discover that Dean, Susan and Theo were nowhere to be found. At the bungalow, there was a Do Not Disturb sign scrawled in Queen's handwriting and taped to the glass on the front door. Seph smirked at the announcement. Queen was such a bubbly, happy woman, but when tired and finally resting, a person didn't dare disturb her without facing an enraged bear. It was ironic, if Seph really thought about it.

With no idea where the others were, Seph glanced up at the beautiful Victorian on the hilltop, then decided against going up there. Until she got to know the residents better and was more comfortable with them, she didn't want to encroach on their space. Maybe if she drove into town—she glanced over at one of the trailers where the rest of the team was staying—she'd bump into them somewhere. Her belly gurgled and a hunger pain forced her to grimace. Screw it. She was famished. If the van or SUV wasn't available, maybe someone would lend her a car or she could call for pizza delivery.

That last thought stopped her in her tracks. The sun had set. Gold and orange bled into the sky, but a black cloud bank was beginning to move across the brilliant hues, snuffing them out. The temperature had grown chillier and the landscape had darkened drastically. Hell, she had no idea if anyone would even deliver out here in Bum-Fucked Egypt.

Groaning, she headed toward the trailer. On the other side, she found both vehicles gone.

"Damn."

She had two bars on her phone, but a search revealed there were no cab companies, which was what she'd expected anyway. Well, she might as well push her discomfort aside and walk up to the main house. Maybe Bernadette or Luella were around. Seph was so hungry that even a peanut butter sandwich sounded lavish. She returned to the RV and retrieved her jacket, wondering if the garment would even be warm enough for the trek up the hill, then she exited the camper and began the walk.

Until she got out on the lane and started on her way, Seph hadn't realized just how far it was up to the MC—or how cold. She had been strolling along for several minutes when a motor and the crunch of tires on gravel drew her attention to a spot halfway up the incline. Headlights swept over her, but she kept her back to the vehicle and focused on placing one foot in front of the other. The cold had already numbed her nose and fingers. If she stopped now, the soles of her sneakers might freeze to the ground.

A pickup stopped alongside her, and the power window on the passenger side hummed down.

"Seph?" Jack called. "Whatcha doin' walking out in the cold, baby?"

Something in Seph leaped at the sound of Jack's deep, raspy voice, especially the way he said "baby." It wasn't that he'd said the word in an inappropriate manner, nor was it self-assured or arrogantly male. No, the way he'd drawled "baby" simultaneously delighted her and warmed her right down to her pussy. In fact, it stopped her in her tracks.

"You all right?" he pressed.

She couldn't ignore him, couldn't even if she'd wanted to. Instead, she kept a tight rein on how happy she was that Jack had stopped to talk to her. She walked over to the truck.

"I slept longer than I wanted to," she explained, trying not to sound excited to see him. "I woke up starved, and none of the team seems to be around this evening, so I have no wheels. Thought I'd hike up here and beg for a sandwich or something." As she spoke, her breath bloomed around her face. She laughed nervously and heat rushed to her cheeks. "It's a lot colder out than I expected too."

"Get in. We'll go to my place."

It wasn't a suggestion. The command in his voice left her no choice. Before she actually realized what she was doing, she'd opened the passenger door and had climbed into the warmth of the cab. After she slammed the door and Jack had put the window up again, Seph marveled at how easily she'd given in to him, and it scared her somewhat.

"The team heading to my place later?" he asked as he put the truck in gear. "I haven't heard from anyone yet."

"Probably. We do most of our investigations from about midnight until three a.m."

He glanced over at her, the lights from the dashboard backwashing his face in a blue-white glow. "Why midnight to three?"

"It seems to be the time that the spirit world—and anything strange for that matter—is the most active."

"Yeah, I guess you're right, but the spirits in my house usually start their shit about dark." He reached the top of the hill and turned around on the carport, then headed back down to the community. "But with these ghosts, or whatever they are, they made it clear today they can do a lot during the day too."

"Ghosts can make themselves known during the daytime," she agreed, "but something about the darkness and the way the two…" She searched for a word that wouldn't sound ludicrous to him.

"Two planes of existence?" he suggested.

Seph looked at him sharply. "Yeah. How did you know?"

He applied the brake a little more firmly as they reached the bottom of the slope. "Let's just say the MC is more open-minded. And we…"

She waited expectantly, suddenly very curious about what he was going to say.

"Well, you'll probably find out soon enough." He waved to someone sweeping their porch as they jostled past. "Bernadette is a white witch, and she works as the apprentice for another so-called white witch who lives deep in the woods, so I've seen some crazy shit happen." At the gate, he stopped the truck and looked both ways before pulling out onto the road. "Plus I've known from a young age that there is more to the universe than meets the eye. The difference is that not everyone is able—or open, I guess is a better word—to experiencing it."

Seph couldn't help but gape at him.

He finally noticed her staring and asked, "What? Did I say something wrong?"

"No, you just surprise me."

"Baby, if you're around me long, you'll find I'm packed with surprises."

His use of "baby" again rendered her speechless as she basked in the glow of it. It took her a long moment, but she finally shook it off and set her mind straight again. She was about to ask him what he meant about being packed with surprises but suddenly realized they'd left the community and were headed somewhere. She'd been so wrapped up in looking at him and the sound of his voice she only vaguely recalled that he'd said he was taking her to his place.

"After I patched the broken window at my place, I decided I better stock up on groceries." He tossed her a sidelong grin that nearly ignited her panties. "If I'm gonna have company, there needs to be food in the house." He chuckled, the sound sending more heat to her pussy. "You're hungry, I'm starved too, and the team should be along later tonight, so we might as well see what we can throw together for a meal."

Her belly let out an embarrassing gurgle at the mention of food.

He laughed. "Maybe we should make something quick and easy so you don't start chewing on my furniture."

At that, she giggled, unable to help herself. The more she talked with Jack, the more she liked him and the sexier she found the man.

That sobered her. She was doomed if she didn't keep her distance. She had to maintain a level head and brace herself against the chemistry they seemed to share.

It seemed like only seconds before he turned onto the lane to his home. The pickup bounced down the narrow road, the headlights sweeping over trees and bushes boasting tiny green leaves.

"You might want to text Queen so she knows you're already out here," Jack suggested.

She dug her phone out of her purse. "Good idea." With a couple swipes and rapid-fire thumb strokes on the sensors, she sent a brief text to her boss. "All done."

"Good." He slowed the truck, then turned it around and backed up close to the steps. "Let's enjoy a meal before the shit hits the fan later."

"You're that convinced there will be activity?" she asked.

"You saw that window and how far the glass was blown, right?"

"If that's the case, I hope no one gets hurt during this investigation." She looked up at the porch. One window glowed brightly, as well as the little glass panes in the front door, but at the next window only blackness greeted them. At this angle, she couldn't tell what he'd put over the window, but she guessed it was a large sheet of some of wood since no light even leaked around the edges of the frame. "Besides, I imagine those windows are expensive."

"Hell, yeah." He exited the truck and hurried around to her side. "I hope I can come up with something the insurance company will believe."

His gallantry surprised Seph, but she let him take her hand and help her down. When he placed his palm on the small of her back and maneuvered her out of the way so he could close the passenger door, her insides seemed to turn into piping-hot jelly and her knees threatened to give out. Holy hell, if he had this effect on her, what would he be like in bed?

At that thought, she gasped and shut down the mental image. Jack glanced at her.

"You okay?"

"Th-that breeze is so cold," she lied.

"Forecast is calling for a dusting of snow tonight."

He frowned and stared up at a sky of heavy clouds. "Good thing we had our ride in the nice weather today," he mused, "but hopefully this will be the last of the cold weather until next fall." He turned to go up to the house. "I locked the door for the first time since I…"

He tensed and shook his head.

"Since you what?" she prompted.

"Nothing. Never mind." He headed up to the house. "I'll unlock the door. You might as well make yourself at home while I bring in the groceries," he called over his shoulder.

"No, I will help—and no arguing with me," she said firmly.

He held his hands up and laughed. "Okay, okay."

Seph made several trips from the truck to the house, passing Jack as he headed the opposite direction each time. They finally met up at the truck, where he had climbed into the bed. She couldn't see what he was doing, but judging by the sound of it, he was picking something up.

"Did a bag bust?" she asked.

"Nah, the tie came off it. There were taters all over the place, but I've got them all now." He placed the bag on the edge of the bed, then hopped over the side. When he landed, he jostled Seph, knocking her backward against the cab and catching himself by bracing his hands on either side of her. "I'm so sorry. I didn't realize you were standing that close…"

She met his gaze and something kindled in the pit of her stomach. It flamed all the way down to her pussy where throbbing began in earnest. A big knot formed in her throat and no matter how much she tried, she couldn't seem to swallow it. He moved his right hand to smooth hair out of her face, but the wintry breeze blew it back over her eyes. Cold had nipped each of his fingertips, but it didn't prevent them from shooting more fire over her nerve endings.

"In the darkness, I hadn't realized you'd taken the ponytail out," he said softly. "Your hair is beautiful."

She basked in his compliment, even as shyness peppered her skin with heat. Warmth radiated from the man, and the scent of his crisp, spicy cologne, slight sweat and that wild, unnamable but intoxicating essence all blended together to relax and arouse her again. Standing so close to him, the security light bathing the driveway, Seph looked directly into Jack's eyes, eyes that held a strange expression she couldn't identify. It was almost as if it were part curiosity and part desire, but there was another element in them, something…feral? She shivered, whether from the cold or her reaction to the man standing toe-to-toe with her, she wasn't sure.

Transfixed, she couldn't break eye contact as he lowered his head and claimed her lips.

Chapter Seven

The moment Jack's lips touched Seph's, he wanted to devour her, claim her as his. For a second, a section of his brain worried about his reaction. Sure, some lycanthropes took human women as their mates, but it wasn't an everyday occurrence. There were a few human mates at the MC, but most were turned, eventually. However, this overpowering need welling up within him nearly forced him to transform. He jerked his hand away from her face, fearful she'd feel his claws just beginning to emerge, but instead of pulling away, he pushed up against Seph, crushing her between his body and the truck's cab. He wanted to feel her soft, pliant form beneath him, wanted to shred her clothing and penetrate her with one hard shove, experience the silken heat of her core.

The growl that bubbled up from deep in his chest brought him back to reality, but Seph hadn't seemed to notice the sound as she opened her mouth to him, then wound her arms around his neck.

Fuck! If he wasn't careful, he'd have her on the stony, cold ground in an instant, fucking her into the dirt. Why did he have this phenomenal need for her? What made her different than the sweetbutts and even the women outside the MC who he'd dated or fucked?

She moaned softly, the noise spurring him onward. He kissed her harder, more demanding, and she took every bit he offered. A subtle aroma of powder wafted up into his nostrils. The wind gusted over them yet again, this time tossing a sheaf of her long, silky hair over the side of his face as he plundered her mouth, the powdery scent she wore becoming even headier. The tickling sensation of her hair excited him further and he wondered what she would look like naked, all her hair hanging to one side of her face as he fucked her from behind, one hand on the back of her neck, the other gripping the side of her round, perky ass. Unable to restrain himself, he opened her jacket and pushed even closer to her, rubbing his hard-on into her belly. Her approving murmur almost unleashed his inner beast. The rational human side of his brain hollered for him to stop, and he did—barely.

Jack broke the kiss but couldn't force himself to step away from her. Not yet. The sensation of her body, the heat emanating from her, proved too delicious. Heart thrashing crazily, he tried with major effort to will his hard cock to abate, but it continued to throb painfully. Blood pounded through his body, roared in his ears, and the urge to shape-shift kept trying to overtake him. He gulped hard and tried to slow his breathing. Seph moved slightly, just enough that her hips thrust against his, which exited his cock all over again. A little groan escaped him. He'd move away from her…in a moment.

* * *

Seph couldn't seem to make her brain respond. She stood with her head back, lips bruised and swollen, the cold air drying them until she knew they'd be chapped. Jack placed his forehead to hers, breathing as though he'd just finished a marathon. All she wanted to do was spread her legs for him. She was willing to even go at it right here in the driveway. Who did that? Surely not she, but here she stood, pressed to the side of his pickup, desire raging in her leaving her irrational, needy. Hell, all she could think about was having Jack's cock inside her as she locked her legs around his driving hips. Worse, there was this burning itch that plagued her skin from the roots of her hair all the way to her toes. The more Jack kissed and rubbed up against her, the worse the sensation became. It wasn't unpleasant, but it was irritating when it flared white-hot. She'd never experienced this skin sensation before during an erotic moment. Could it be the cold? The air now blasting over them proved harsher than it had been for a few days.

She fluttered her eyes open to look at Jack. He stared back at her with... She blinked. His eyes weren't light brown anymore. They glowed bright gold. She gasped, but he shook his head and clenched his eyes shut for a moment, then looked at her again. The glow was gone.

Had she really seen the weird effect or was it just the way the security light was hitting his eyes?

"Let's get inside," he managed to say. "That wind is freezing, and if I don't get you indoors now, I might fuck you right here against the truck."

The way he said the words in total sincerity excited her even further. It shamed her a bit that she was thinking so wantonly. Regardless, she realized she truly wanted him to make love to her right there, right now.

With a hesitant nod and willpower she hadn't known she possessed, she placed her hands on his chest. She resisted the urge to slide them up under his shirt instead. He took the hint and stepped back. He then grasped the bag of potatoes where it still lay on the truck bed's edge and hooked his other arm around her waist as they climbed the path to the house.

She leaned into him for the continued contact, but also to have some way to steady herself so she didn't faceplant. Her pussy throbbed so insistently, so hot and hard that it annoyed her. If he touched her there right now, she'd orgasm. And no man had affected her this way—ever. That thought troubled her so deeply that she shoved it lightning-quick into the dark recesses of her mind. She couldn't get involved with Jack, no matter how much she wanted it. The thought of him turning her away because of what she was…well…that stabbed something cold and steely through her heart.

She glanced sharply up at Jack. At the steps, he stared down at her, his pupils still big with arousal, his lopsided, sexy grin stabbing her heart a second time.

Without a doubt she was already hooked on the guy.

What was she going to do?

* * *

Inside, Jack started a fire in the free-standing wood burner. He liked this section of the living room where he'd laid heavy, flat creek rocks and cemented them carefully together before setting the ornate wood burner on them. A pipe arched over backward and went through the wall to vent the smoke. He'd thought about building an actual fireplace but had decided against it when he considered how much work it would be should he decide, years later, to rip out an entire wall made of brick or stone to convert to solar heat or even fuel oil or electric. For now, he'd enjoy the pretty woodstove with its open front.

As he lit the paper stuffed into the kindling, Jack realized he was so disturbed by his reaction to Seph that he was trying to distract himself. He leaned back so he could see her through the kitchen doorway. He'd shown her where to store the canned and boxed goods, and she was quietly humming to herself as she placed items in the upper cabinets.

He couldn't get involved with this woman. Oh, he wanted to, wanted to see what it would be like to fuck her until she begged him to stop, then fuck her again after she'd had a brief rest. Gulping, he willed his pecker to go back to sleep, the damn traitor. But holy hell how he desired this woman!

No. He couldn't even entertain the thought of being with her. She was a city girl. Even a long-distance relationship wouldn't work. Detroit was every bit six hours from here. Between his work and the driving time to go see her, they'd get very little time together.

Jack frowned and shut the stove doors a little too forcefully. He opened the vents so the fire could draw air, then stood, his back popping loudly. Why was he even entertaining such thoughts? Seph was out of reach, and if he allowed himself to get any more invested in her, it would tear him up to see her go. He had to be strong, had to block all sensations, thoughts and reactions to her.

"What should we make for a meal?" Seph asked from the doorway.

"How about kielbasa?" he suggested.

"Sounds great. I'll get it started." She turned and strode to the refrigerator, her ass swaying from side to side, her jeans showing her every curve and the plumpness of her butt cheeks.

"Fuck," he whispered. "This isn't going to be easy."

* * *

Later, after a dinner of skillet-browned kielbasa and sauerkraut with sides of mashed potatoes and canned biscuits, Seph stood at the dishwasher filling it with scraped plates. The team had arrived about five minutes after Jack had finished setting the table. Queen hadn't eaten anything, and since they'd left Detroit early that morning in a rush, the rest of the crew had gone into Rebellion for a few supplies and toiletries. When they'd finished shopping, all the little restaurants were closed, and no one wanted fast food that late in the evening.

"Thank you so much for supper," Queen told Jack with a huge smile. "I've never had kielbasa and sauerkraut, but I must admit it was really good."

The others rising from the table murmured similar comments.

"No problem," Jack said easily.

"Since Seph has the dishes under control," Susan said, "I'm going to start setting up some of the equipment."

"We'll help," Dean stated.

Theo nodded as he passed Seph his plate, glass and utensils.

"Time to cut the chitchat," Queen said. "Let the house grow quiet except for the sounds of normality. We'll set up everything. Lights out in an hour, okay?"

Seph bobbed her head as she placed the last dish in the dishwasher, then shut it.

"What do you want me to do?" Jack asked.

"Just find a place to chill and let us investigate," Queen replied with another one of her startling white, toothy grins.

The woman shot a pointed glance at Seph, who frowned.

"What?" She looked directly into Queen's eyes.

"If you encounter anything, let me know ASAP."

Seph frowned even harder at her boss. "Don't I always?"

"Mmm." Queen sauntered into the living room and immediately began firing orders at the rest of the team.

Rinsing out the skillet he'd cooked the meat in, Jack asked, "What was that about?"

"I'm not entirely sure," Seph replied, somewhat rankled. Although she did have a suspicion as to Queen's implication, Seph wasn't about to elaborate. And the last thing she was going to do was let Queen know her own suspicions were true.

"I think we're done here," he said. "Thank you for all the help."

"Thank you for the meal."

She avoided meeting his gaze and wiped her hands on a tea towel before hanging it on the oven door handle. There was work to be done, and Seph truly wanted to rid

Jack's home of any dark entities. He needed protection. Sure, he was a big, powerful man, but he wasn't prepared to fight something on a different plane of existence. The way he'd been tossed out into the yard from an exploding window was proof.

She caught him panning his gaze up and down her body several times. Each time she caught him, heat flamed across her skin. Frustrated with her response, she motioned for him to sit at the table.

"Have some coffee. Read a magazine, something." She picked up Queen's iPad she'd left on the table for Seph. "I'm going to get busy. If you notice anything strange, tell one of us."

"Trust me, you'll hear all about it," he rumbled.

At that, she couldn't help but grin. She liked his unique brand of sarcasm and the fact he could make her laugh so easily. Suddenly realizing she was once again letting her thoughts stray into dangerous territory, she nodded and hurried into the living room with the others.

A fire crackled brightly in the now-open woodstove. It cast golden light across half the room and warmed it thoroughly. Humming softly, an air system sucked the heat in through a vent and pushed it throughout the home. Much of the team's equipment had been tested and was ready to go.

"I just need to set up cameras in the back of the house," Theo told Queen, "then we're ready to start."

As Seph opened a file for notes on the iPad, she tensed when Queen approached her. She knew that expression.

"Can we talk?" Queen asked.

Inwardly, Seph groaned. "About?"

"Are you into Jack?"

"He's handsome and I'm attracted to him, but he's a client and I'm part of the team. Plus I live several hours away."

Queen stepped back slightly. "Good to know, but I was actually going to suggest that you get to know him. You're alone too much, honey. I never see you with a guy and—" Her eyes widened abruptly. "Wait. You are into men, right?"

At that, Seph had to laugh. "Yes, I'm heterosexual."

"So why don't you have a nice, handsome man waiting for you back home?"

Seph shrugged. "I have my reasons."

"Is it because you're a—?"

"Queen, we're ready to go," Theo announced upon returning to the living room. "Jack's going to hang out at the kitchen table."

Throwing Seph a pointed look that shouted "this discussion isn't over," Queen started turning off lamps and flipping the switches to overhead lights. "Let's get started, gang."

Relieved she'd escaped the dreaded talk, Seph kept within hearing distance of Queen and Tina as they asked questions to thin air and held out sensitive recorders to capture any spirit voices. Seph hurriedly wrote notes into the file with a screen pen when necessary, but mostly kept the notebook wedged into her waistband and focused primarily on the screen of a meter that detected unusually cold spots or areas.

She followed the women through the house, passing Frank at the kitchen table and refusing to look at him. They headed down the corridor, stopping in the guestroom, the bath, then finally Frank's room.

Nothing.

No flutters of light on the K2 meters. No cold areas were revealed on the Seph's screen. Neither Dean nor Theo called out about anything odd occurring, nor did they have any EVPs on their recorders that they could discern as actual words.

The house was vacant of spirits.

"We'll keep investigating," Queen said as she led them back to the kitchen, "but it might be that whatever is here is observing us from hiding places. Anything happening on the cameras?" she called into the next room.

"Not a thing so far," Dean said, "but we might've missed something while we've been asking questions."

"This is comforting," Frank stated grumpily.

Seph let her attention wander over him. Why did he suddenly seem so down? The urge to hug him almost had her putting her equipment down. Again, she reminded herself to keep her distance, that she was returning to Detroit in a few days.

"Don't worry," Queen comforted him and sat at the table. "This isn't unusual. If spirits are accustomed to only one or two people in the home, newcomers might make them wary, so they'll spend a couple nights watching and listening before they begin to draw attention to themselves."

"I hope you're right," he said. "It will piss me off royally if nothing happens only to have all hell break loose after your team goes back to Detroit."

Queen patted this hand. "If we have to, we'll break out the more technical equipment and set up a base somewhere in your house. We'll figure out what's going on here."

He nodded. "I hope so."

He sounded so forlorn. Whatever he'd been experiencing in this house, he hid it well. The brief possession had frightened Seph, but it was clear that Jack had endured much, much more. She wished she could step into his arms, hold him for a long time.

God, how she wished that.

Chapter Eight

"Have you heard anything from Jack or any of the WHO team?" Bernadette asked Luella.

"No, not a peep." Setting another folded towel on a growing pile, Luella looked over at Bernadette. "Why don't you go down and talk to Seph?"

Bernadette dropped the lid to the washer, and the agitator began thrashing the load of laundry she'd just deposited into it. She stooped and gathered jeans into a heap to wash next.

"I was thinking about it," she answered. "Something about the young woman draws me. She's different."

"Yeah, I sense it too, but I can't put my finger on what it is."

"She has a gift," Bernadette said, "but that's not all I'm picking up on. There's something else." She met her friend's big, blue-eyed gaze. "I'm betting that's the thing you're sensing too."

Luella quirked an eyebrow at her. "What do you men she has a gift?"

"I sense magic and other supernatural abilities in people. The more I step into my abilities, the more I can see power auras—at least that's what I'm calling it for now—around people." She straightened and leaned back against the washer. "Everyone has a little bit of power in him or her, but humans have suppressed it so much the last few hundred years that most people only have residual power, whatever it may be."

"And Seph?"

Tipping her head to one side, Bernadette thought for a moment as she stared past Luella and out the window at the back lawn bright with a dusting of snow glittering in early morning sunshine. "Seph has this white light around her. It literally emanates from her like heat. It's so strong that I have to pull my own magic about me to block it because it's distracting."

"Holy shit." Luella gaped at her. "She's that...that..."

"Powerful? Yes."

"Do you think she's aware of it?"

"Yes, she's very aware of it, but I think she hides it from others."

"And you think she's...?" Luella prompted with a grin.

"Oh, she'd definitely his mate." After taking the bottle of Downy down from the shelf over the washing machine, Bernadette poured its cap full of softener, then raised the lid to dump it into the agitator's cup as the machine filled with rinse water. "When Carol came in this morning, she said she was out sweeping her porch last night and saw Jack and Seph in his pickup leaving the farm."

"Looks like we're going to have another sister joining the fold," Luella replied, smiling.

"Seems that way." Bernadette grinned back.

Luella picked up the stack of towels and left the

laundry room. Once she was gone, Bernadette returned to staring out the window. Last night's snowfall had left the MC in white, sparkling beauty, but something about Jack's dilemma tainted the beautiful image beyond the laundry room. It worried Bernadette, niggling at the back of her brain. It poked at her powers, asking for help. She only hoped Jack would ask for her aid before it was too late.

The aroma of the fabric softener filled the room so abruptly that it brought Bernadette back to reality. She stepped into the kitchen and checked the wall clock—it was a little after ten a.m. Carol, Callie May and Puppy were setting out late-breakfast items for those in the MC who were late risers. Muffins, toast, a bowl of scrambled eggs and another bowl of fresh fruits took up most of the space on the little dining table. Puppy retrieved a bottle of orange juice from the fridge, then set it with the cap twisted off on a vacant spot.

She caught Bernadette's gaze and smiled, lighting up her huge, dark brown eyes that she was nicknamed for. She started to say something, but a bright, cheery hello interrupted her.

"How's it going this morning?" a tall, leggy blonde asked as she appeared on the steps leading from the sun porch to the kitchen. She shrugged out of a heavy jacket and hung it on one of the pegs by the doorway. "We still on for supply shopping today?"

"Morning, Daffodil," the women chimed together.

"Hey, you." Bernadette offered her a little finger-wave, then snagged a couple strawberries from the fruit bowl.

Daffodil looked amazing in a pair of formfitting, wide-legged slacks, platform loafers and a pink, lightweight, long-sleeved turtleneck with a darker pink vest edged in black piping. It didn't matter what her friend wore, Daffodil always looked like she'd just stepped out of a Fifth Avenue clothing store. After the incident with the incubus and his minions and busting the River Rebels' human-trafficking operation, Daffodil had come out of her shell and was beginning to experiment more with her own powers. As the months had passed, Bernadette's tentative friendship with the woman had blossomed. And Phil, Frank's second-in-command, was so in love with his new mate it was a miracle Daffodil had managed to get away for a day of shopping.

"Where's Phil?" Bernadette teased.

"Yeah, Daffi," Puppy joined in, "your shadow is missing."

"He had to work all week. Since the weather has broken, he's been busy, but trust me"—she winked—"he makes up for it in bed each night." She patted the area over her crotch. "And if he keeps *it* up, I'll develop a callus."

Everyone burst out laughing.

"But are we still doing the shopping for the MC today?" she asked again.

"We sure are," Luella answered as she walked into the room. "As soon as the late risers clear out, we'll head out too."

"I'm going to finish gathering the dirty laundry, then change," Bernadette said.

Luella waved one hand at her as she poured coffee into a mug with the other.

Upstairs, Bernadette gathered the odds and ends of soiled clothing Frank had left around their room. She added them to their hamper, then shimmied out of her sweats and T-shirt, standing in nothing but her panties and sports bra while she rummaged in the dresser for jeans to wear that day.

The door opened. She looked over her shoulder to find Frank appraising her with intent in his eyes.

"Oh no you don't," she said, trying not to giggle. "I have to get dressed, then I'm helping with the big shopping day for the MC."

He offered her his sexy, I'm-gonna-fuck-you-anyway grin that never failed to turn her insides to molten lava. "Actually, I came up here to talk to you."

"Oh?"

"It's been quite a while since we last talked about whether or not you've decided to be turned. You've been busy writing your latest manuscript, and I've been wrapped up in finishing the custom bike orders we received over the winter." He took a few steps toward her, and her heart rate sped up. "Thought we could spend the day together since Phil's overseeing the finishing touches on the bikes, but I didn't realize supply day had come around again."

"I'm sorry, babe." And she was. Disappointment filled her. It would be awesome to spend the day with her mate, but the MC and the community relied heavily on the small group of women who worked with Luella to keep everything running smoothing. Many couples in the community both worked, which made it difficult to find time to spend time with their children when they had to run errands, buy groceries and more. By collecting everyone's supply lists and making the shopping an all-day affair one day a month, it freed families to focus on what was important—being a family—and helped out the elderly humans who couldn't maneuver much anymore.

"Well, that comes with being the president's woman," Frank stated. "At times it sucks."

She strode to the closet and selected a long-sleeved blouse in deep green to match her eyes.

"Damn, sweetheart." Frank walked up behind her as she was shutting the closet door. "You're one fine woman."

He placed a hand on either of her hips, the heat of his palms almost scorching her skin. She tried to restrain herself, but couldn't help leaning back against him. Frank slid his hand around her and palmed her breasts through her sports bra. More heat penetrated her skin, her nipples tautening painfully.

"Frank…" she whispered.

"I'm not pushing you, but have you thought any more about letting me turn you?"

"Yes." She pressed her ass against his thighs. He was too tall and she too short for her to plant her ass in his lap, but his hard-on poked her lower back, telling her that he was ready to take her at any moment.

"And?"

"I'm still tossing it around. The pain of it scares me."

"I wonder if Scary Mary would have a spell or potion that could take the pain away?"

Her breath caught as he flicked her nipples, sending a bolt of electricity straight to her cunt. "I…I hadn't even thought of that."

"I want to start a family with you, sweetheart."

He leaned over and nuzzled her ear, his excited breathing hot and gusty over the side of her face.

She whimpered, desire streaking through her to settle in her core. "I know. I want children too, but I have to think further about the implications of having lycanthrope children, what they will face…" He rubbed his cock against her back, the fabric of his jeans both stimulating and frustrating. "And," she barely managed, "I realize the fact I'm human and you're lykoi makes it more difficult for me to get pregnant."

"In that case," he murmured, lips pressed to the curve of her neck, "let's practice."

"Frank," she protested, "I have to dress and meet the women. Today is too important to others to—"

He whipped her around and bent her over a wingback chair by the bed so fast that she could only gasp. A long, low growl rolled out of Frank, then the crisp sharpness of claws sliced through the elastic of her panties and they fell to her feet.

"Good grief, Frank. If only you knew what I spend on new panties."

"Worth every fucking penny," he growled out.

He palmed her pussy, inserting his fingers without claws and pumping them in and out of her several times.

"Oh…baby…" She shoved her ass out, impaling herself even more on his digits.

Behind her, the sound of a zipper lowering and rustling clothes told her that he was determined to have his way with her. More heat settled in her pussy and the constant throbbing in her folds intensified.

"Bernadette!" Luella's voice traveled upstairs. "We're leaving in ten minutes!"

"Frank, I really need to get—"

"Shut up and let me fuck you," he snarled.

"But…" The moment he placed the head of his cock against her opening, all thought vacated her brain. He pushed his hard length into her, parting her folds, stretching her pussy and invading her core. All Bernadette could do was brace her knees on the edge of the seat cushion, thrust her ass out to him, and hang on to the winged sides of the chair.

"Fuck," he whispered as he settled balls-deep into her. "I love your body. You're firm, yet supple, round, yet"—he withdrew slightly, then thrust into her to seat himself even more tightly to her tingling pussy—"athletic and yielding."

"Shut up and fuck me!"

"Yes, ma'am."

He began a rhythm that quickly tightened the special spot within her that would throw her over the precipice into utter pleasure. His member filled her to the point of being uncomfortable, but as she adjusted to the intrusion, the tingling and rhythmic tightening inside her grew faster and faster. Behind her, pumping in and out of her, Frank moaned and growled. He slowed his movements, leaned over her, yanked the bra over her breasts and palmed them, kneading vigorously.

Fire swept over Bernadette's skin. The frustrating sensation of want leaped higher and higher as she chased her orgasm. She desired the freedom of shattering with him impaling her, but at the same time she also wanted this moment, these sensations to never end.

"Bernadette!" This time Daffodil yelled up the stairs. "Frank's up there, isn't he?"

"Shut the hell up and let me finish!" he bellowed back.

Giggles poured out of Bernadette. However, Frank picked up his pace again, pummeling her body, banging her so hard that her head kept butting the inner curve of the chair's back and in turn, the chair would hit the wall. They set up a pattern of *pat, thud, bang, pat, thud, bang*, with Bernadette half laughing and half moaning.

Frank paused, buried all the way into her body. Slowly, he moved so it felt like he was actually trying to screw himself into her, then he moved the same way but in the opposite direction. His cock jumped inside her. Bernadette let out a cry and the coil within her twisted so hard, sending her almost to the edge of jumping off, then refrained from allowing her completion. She shoved her ass back, nearly unseating him.

"Come on, Frank. Fuck. Me. Hard."

The growl he issued shot goose flesh over her. He pumped like a man possessed, and she held on for dear life, relishing his every thrust.

A rhythmic grunting began behind her. She knew he was close, and so was she. The *pat, thud, bang* began again, harder, more frantic. Frank tensed. Bernadette pushed back, keeping him buried to the hilt within her. Frank withdrew and thrust, once, twice, thrice. He paused, his cock swelling even more, the tight fit growing snugger, his hard-on impossibly harder, then he thrust several more times and so deeply that he pressed Bernadette's face to the back of the chair and held her in that position as his cock throbbed deep inside her and warmth flowed into her channel.

The sensation served as the leaping point and the slow, rhythmic flutters inside her grew faster, firmer, then claimed her so suddenly that she could only scream as he held his cock deep within her as he milked the last of his essence into her body.

They remained that way for a moment, both panting heavily, both shaking. Finally, he moved backward, but kept himself firmly inside her as he helped her straighten before he withdrew.

"I love you, sweetheart," he rumbled in her ear. "You're the flame of my heart."

"I love you with all of my soul," she replied, voice trembling. "God, I love you."

* * *

Jack sat staring into the red embers of the fire. Frustration filled him. Last night had been a bust. No paranormal activity had happened and he felt like a fool. Why were the spirits suddenly so quiet? Sure, he had the busted window as proof of one attack, but unless WHO could find some evidence, he knew they would only investigate so long.

Then there was Persephone. She'd told him good night when the team had packed up and left by 3:30 in the morning, but she'd made sure she hadn't made eye contact with him. Did she now regret their encounter against the truck last night? He hoped not. He'd enjoyed it. Even now whenever he thought about her, his cock jumped to attention.

Yet, he had to remind himself that she was returning to Detroit soon. Maybe that fact was why she'd pulled away from him? Whatever the reason, he was torn whenever he thought about her exiting his life, and his animal whined inwardly at the notion as well. This left him so unsettled that he thought he'd explode from the sensation. How could he possibly be attached to a woman he'd only known for roughly 24 hours?

Jack had to get his mind off Seph and the lack of activity in the house. He rose, loaded the wood burner, then shut it down so it would simmer all day and leave coals for him to stoke upon his return. He hadn't changed clothes from the night before, having fallen asleep on the sofa. The idea of going to his bedroom right now for clean garments wigged him out too much, so he walked into the laundry room and took a shirt out of the dryer. He tossed the dirty one on the floor by the washer and headed back through the house to the front door where he snagged his cut and leather jacket. Pausing long enough to stuff his feet into his riding boots, he then locked up the house and walked to the pole barn.

The landscape wore a thin dusting of snow. The spring sun blazed down on it, the sharp sparkles wreaking havoc on his sensitive lycanthrope vision. It wouldn't take long for the sun's heat to melt away the white coating and send the aroma of warming earth into the air, a scent his wolf relished. For now, he'd take the Indian out despite the cold. He needed the wind in his face and flowing through his nostrils to cleanse him of the confusion that seemed to plague him of late.

Buzzing in his packet halted him in his tracks. He'd forgotten to remove his phone last night. It was a wonder it hadn't gone dead. He fished it out of his pants and looked at the display: Tina.

"No fucking way," he mumbled and turned the cell off.

More frustration claimed him. Desperate for a long, high-speed ride, he picked up his pace to the barn. There he uncovered the Indian to find a note taped to the gas tank.

I have eyes everywhere.

Puzzled, he checked the bike over thoroughly to make sure someone hadn't sabotaged it. Satisfied everything was as it should be, Jack unfastened the padlock and removed the chain.

He was about to straddle the bike and start it up when the gravity of the note hit him. Had this stalker seen them burn and bury the weed, and was the stalker the same perpetrator who had planted the pot on his kitchen table? Maybe there was more than one person involved. This was getting too serious for his taste.

Jack started the bike, the sound of its thrumming engine reverberating in the pole barn, and gave it just enough gas to coast across the dirt floor and out the parted double doors. He'd started to push off when something whined past him. He jerked, ducking instinctively. Holy fuck! Someone had just taken a shot at him! Another bullet grazed the top of the gas tank, not ten inches from his crotch. Jack nudged the Indian into gear, gave it the gas, and shot up the lane, praying the shooter didn't find his mark this time. The back tire spun slightly on some snow before finding traction and propelling him up the lane. If anyone else was hiding in the woods, they could pick him off like a pig in a slaughter pen waiting for that final blow.

He reached the road without incident and headed straight for the MC. He looked down at the tank, pissed to the hilt at the deep scratches the bullets had left in the paint job.

Chapter Nine

Seph stepped out of the RV to get some fresh air. She paused upon spotting Bernadette at a neighboring house. An old woman handed her a slip of paper, waved, then shut the front door.

"Morning," Bernadette hollered to Seph.

"Morning," she called back.

"If you're not doing anything today," Bernadette said, "would you like to go shopping with us?"

Seph thought about it for a moment. It would be nice to make new friends, and she really did feel drawn to Bernadette and Luella. However, it wouldn't be prudent when Seph had to return to Detroit in a few days. Her heart ached at that thought. It would be wonderful to have friends beyond the WHO team, friends who could be her companions and confidants.

"I think I'll pass this time," Seph answered, surprised at the sadness in her voice. "We didn't get back until four a.m. and I'm still tired. I'll need a nap if I'm going to return to Jack's place with the team tonight."

"All right. Maybe you can all have supper with us at the main house before you leave for the night investigation." The redhead waved and continued on her way to an idling black Suburban where other women were waiting for her.

"Oh, there you are, Seph."

She turned to find Queen walking over to her. "Hi. What's up?"

"Since it appears the team might be involved in this investigation a bit longer than I thought, I've rented an economy car that's easier on gas over these god-awful steep, windy roads. Also, I felt really bad when I found out you had no transportation last night."

"It worked out fine."

"Still, we need an extra set of wheels, and I know how you're backward about approaching people you don't know for help."

Seph said nothing. She appreciated the thought, and as long as Queen was happy, maybe she wouldn't broach the subject of Jack or prod her about her suspicions of Seph being a medium.

"There's a small car rental company in Rebellion," Queen continued, "but they won't bring the car out here, so Theo has offered to drive you into town to pick it up."

"Okay," she answered. "I need some deodorant and a new toothbrush since I knocked mine in the trash by accident this morning."

Laughing, Queen shooed her toward the SUV as Theo pulled up. "Good God, go on with you and do something about those stanky teeth." She ambled back toward her lodging. "We're meeting at Jack's at 11:00 tonight."

Seph chuckled with her boss, then got into the SUV with Theo. She rode into town with him listening to a bluegrass station he'd found that actually had some catchy melodies. She tapped her foot to the beats. Theo grinned at her a couple times as he drummed the fingers of one hand on the steering wheel.

"Certainly gorgeous scenery round here," he said over the music.

"It is. Sometimes I find myself wondering if I could actually live in a region like this."

"You? Leave the city?" He snorted and braked for a turn. "No way."

She grinned over at him. "Like I said, I just wonder about it. I'm not a froufrou girl, but I do like having easy access to shopping, restaurants and fun things to do."

"My point exactly."

The rest of the ride they listened to tunes, but when Theo drove down the main street of Rebellion, Seph paid special attention to what businesses lined the sidewalks. In the square, she admired the towering courthouse with its domed copper-colored bell tower. They passed the county seat, then a large four-story stone building that seemed to house many little businesses and offices, an auto parts place, a post office, a red-stone church, a Rite Aid, Dairy Queen and McDonald's. Rebellion may not be a big town, but it appeared to have a lot more available to residents than she'd initially thought. However, there didn't appear to be any entertainment in town, and the marquis she'd seen across the square from the courthouse appeared to have been closed for at least 20 years, so there wasn't even a movie theater.

At the car rental office, Theo made certain all the papers were signed and the insurance coverage added to the bill before they parted ways. He escorted Seph out to a little red Chevy Spark.

"I'm heading back to the MC," he said. "You okay on your own?"

"Yeah, I'm going to stop somewhere for a couple things, then I'll be heading that way too."

He nodded, got into the SUV, then pulled out of the parking lot.

Seph found a Family Dollar where she purchased a new toothbrush and a stick of deodorant. Once she had her purchases, she headed out to the Spark. As she crossed the lot, the rumble of motorcycles drew her attention. She looked up expecting to see the emblem of a howling wolfman on the back of cuts, but the riders wore heavy leathers with an emblem on them she couldn't make out. They stared at her as if they knew her. What the hell was their problem? She stared back, unable to look away until the bikers passed the entrance to the lot and on through the traffic light.

Unsettled, Seph quickly threw her bag of purchases into the car and hopped in to start it up. She drove out of Rebellion, hoping she remembered all the turnoffs along the way.

It wasn't quite noon yet, but the sun had melted all the snow except what remained in shaded areas. The eye-searing blue of the sky, the herds of cattle and horses grazing on new field grass, and the winding creek that peeked through the trees in spots gave her the sense she was where she belonged. But that didn't make any sense. She'd lived in the city her entire life. She liked having easy access to stores and movie theaters, and knowing a hospital was nearby was much more comforting than one being an hour or more away.

She poked a sensor on the screen in the center of the dashboard and pop music filled the car. The heat of the sun worked its magic on the trees and bushes. Little leaves peeped out everywhere. Their color reminded Seph of a spring-green crayon, one of many shades of green in the big box of Crayola crayons Sister Miranda had given to her for her eighth birthday. She'd loved Sister Miranda very much, had looked to her as a mother figure and still did. To this day, she couldn't see a bright spring-like green without thinking of the sister and that precious box of crayons that had given her many hours of creative escape from her life in the orphanage.

Something in the rearview mirror caught her attention. She jerked her mind back to the present, her focus zeroing in on what was behind the car.

Four Harley-Davidson motorcycles.

Fear clenched in her gut. There was no doubt in her mind they were the same riders she'd seen while exiting Family Dollar. Were they targeting her, and if so, why?

The bikers tailgated her as she climbed a curvy strip of SR 26. Blobs of melting snow fell from some overhanging tree limbs, the watery mess obscuring her vision. She braked for a hairpin curve, trying desperately to see the road while finding the windshield wipers control with one hand. Somehow, she managed to navigate the turn without mishap, but the roar of the bikes behind her was so close they sounded almost as if they were in the backseat. Shaking, Seph tried to concentrate on the dangerous road. She must've hit something on a lever. The wipers suddenly started working, clearing her line of sight.

At the top of the hill, the riders still hadn't backed off. She passed an oncoming flatbed truck hauling two ATVs and cringed as she hugged the white line running the edge of a steep incline. Just as she rounded yet another curve, two of the four Harleys separated and drove up alongside her driver's door, keeping pace. They wore helmets with dark visors, which struck her as odd. She caught a glimpse of their MC emblem on the back of the closest rider's leather jacket, something that looked like a ghost or maybe a screaming witch.

Driving out of the curve, Seph found the sun glaring on the wet windshield. The riders behind her rode so closely that she could actually see the zippers on their leathers. Panicked, she glanced back at the road only to find open air instead of more winding pavement. Her heart thrashed painfully. Adrenaline bulleted through her veins. She tensed, and the scream that tore from her mouth sounded deafening within the confines of the car yet simultaneously distant.

A tree rushed up to meet the Spark. The sudden impact abruptly threw Seph forward the instant the airbag erupted. Breaking glass and shrieking metal sounded incredibly loud in the little car. She blinked, stunned, but as the airbag began to deflate, the noises of groaning metal and cracking wood filled the interior of the Spark as the tree bent and snapped over. The car suddenly jerked to the right and slid farther down the incline. Another scream burst from Persephone, her heart flailing wildly.

"Oh my God! Oh my God!"

The airbag released the last of its air and flattened over the steering wheel, revealing the horror before

Seph. Nothing but trees on an impossibly sheer cliff beckoned the vehicle to plunge farther, inviting her to a premature death. She screamed again, her throat stinging with pain at the intensity of her cry. Another tree stopped the car, the abrupt halt so jarring that the seat belt jerked painfully over Seph's breasts and shoulder. Regardless, the impact jerked her forward, whipping her head toward the steering wheel. Her forehead hit it—hard. Stars burst across Seph's vision before total blackness fell over her.

* * *

The motorcycles on the next ridge drew Jack's attention. There were four and they looked like Harleys, but from so far away he couldn't tell for certain. The little red car they'd fenced in on two sides careened off the side of the road, plummeted over the hill and crashed headlong into a tree. The motorcycles performed U-turns and headed back down the hill.

Stunned, Jack gave the Indian some gas and raced along the road, praying the driver wasn't dead. He knew that turn well. Many drunks had driven straight off it. The curve sorely needed a guardrail, but had only a dangerous curve sign.

It took him a good couple of minutes to navigate to the next ridge. He passed through the curve, made sure nothing was approaching in the opposite lane, then turned the Indian around and parked on the edge of the road. He shut the bike off and knocked the kickstand down, leaping off the bike almost before it was stationary.

He paused on the berm. Shit, the vehicle had broken over the first tree it had come to rest against, then rolled several yards farther to be caught by a huge oak. The engine wasn't running, but music came from the vehicle, something that sounded a lot like Hozier's "Take Me to Church." He managed to scramble down the steep incline, nearly losing his footing and tumbling head over heels, but he caught himself against the broken tree, then skidded down the muddy, snow-crusted earth to the corner of the car's trunk. He stood for a few seconds, calming his nerves, adrenaline careening through his body. As he found his footing again, sunshine bounced off the Spark's back glass and glimmered along the edge of the roof. A breeze smelling of awakening earth and melting snow blew across the hillside, ruffling Jack's hair and nipping his ears. Carefully, he placed his boot heels firmly in the mushy soil and inched himself along the side of the car to the driver's door. Hopefully it would open without any problems, but the way the front end was crunched in the center, forming a big V in the hood, had him concerned.

The driver appeared to be a woman, but on a second look, Jack froze. He knew only one woman who had hair that color and length.

Fear unlike any he'd ever experienced before clenched his heart and nearly suffocated him. He blanked out, staring through the driver's window at the cascade of dark, gleaming hair hiding the lovely face he'd come to relish every time he saw her. He swore softly. If she were dead—no! He couldn't allow himself to think such thoughts.

He grabbed the door handle and pulled. It wouldn't budge. He yanked on it again and it still wouldn't open.

He looked around and listened intently, trying to

detect if a car approached from either direction. Hearing only wind and the footsteps of a deer farther down the hillside, Jack quickly shrugged out of his clothes and boots, dumping them in the mashed snow behind him, then he called upon his beast. Tingling assailed his skin, pain seared his joints and flamed along his bones. He growled in protest, but he'd learned to deal with the agony over the years. His fingers morphed into paw-hands, and fangs dropped from his gums, forcing his human teeth aside as his face and nose shifted into a wolf-like muzzle. The transformation, done countless times since he'd come into his beast at the age of 16, took only three or four minutes.

With pain still blazing through his body and his lycanthrope ears attuned to detect an approaching vehicle, Jack punched through the metal of the driver's side, found a firm hold, jerked the door off its hinges, then tossed it over his shoulder. It landed with a *thunk*, followed by the scratch of branches over metal as it slid down the incline. He leaned inside the car and pushed the deflated airbag aside. He reached for the curtain of hair obscuring her face. The clothing was unfamiliar to him, and Jack had never before noticed a telltale ring, tattoo or even a wristwatch on Seph, but he knew without a doubt that when he brushed her hair back it would be she, his Persephone.

His furry hand trembled. *His* Persephone.

Oh God. She couldn't be dead, couldn't…

He flicked the dark hair back to see Seph's smooth, lovely face, her bright amber eyes closed. He slid the pads of his first two fingers along her throat, careful to make sure his claws didn't nick her milky skin, and checked for a pulse.

The relief that swept through him was as powerful as the earlier adrenaline had been. His legs wobbled under him, but he ignored the sensation and gently tipped her back in the seat to exam her face. The sight of blood on her chest, shoulders and a couple places on her head frightened the hell out of him, but from what he could tell, the wounds were superficial and caused by the glass that had burst inward from the windshield.

Moaning, she opened her eyes. Panic fluttered through Jack. She couldn't see him in werewolf form! But no sooner had she looked at him then her eyes rolled back in her head and she was out again. A knot the size of a baby's fist above her left eye had begun to turn black and purple. Soon the swelling would spread downward to her temple. Other than the lump and lacerations, she didn't seem to have any other injuries, although he figured she'd be bruised from the seat belt too. Jack retrieved his coat and balled it up. He placed it on the steering wheel to cushion her face. The car was obviously dead and he didn't smell any gasoline. Music kept playing, so he reached over and touched sensors until the tune stopped. He wasn't about to move Seph any further and risk potentially hurting her neck or spine since he had no idea if she had whiplash or worse that remained undetected. He coaxed his beast into submission and shifted back into his human form, soon shivering in the cold. Quickly, he donned his clothes and pulled his boots back on.

Jack took his cell out of his pants pocket, then sat on the edge of the undercarriage frame with his back to Seph's side to generate warmth for her. He called Frank and explained what had happened.

"Holy shit, Jack!" Frank's voice shot across the airwaves. "Do you think she'll be all right?"

"Yeah, I do. Seph might have a serious neck or back injury, but I don't think so. The worst looks like the knot on her head, so at the most she might have a concussion."

"Did you see anything that might tell you who ran her off the road?"

"No, I was on that ridge where you can look across to the other one."

"Before you get to Drunk's Curve?" Frank asked.

"That's the one. I'm hoping Seph saw something that can be used to identify the fuckers who did this to her. Who the hell would target her like this, Jack? She's been in town a little over a day, and most of that time Seph's been with me."

A long silence came from Frank. Finally, a heavy sigh gusted into Jack's ear, followed by "Let's pray she saw something, then. My thought is River Rebels starting their shit again for some reason, but until Seph can be questioned, we'll have to sit tight. I'll keep this quiet until I hear back from you, okay?"

"There's more, Frank."

"Fuck. Tell me."

Jack relayed what had happened out at his place.

"There's no way in hell both incidents are coincidence," Frank said so quietly it stood the hair up on Jack's nape.

"I don't think so either."

"Your ass is staying at the main house. Until further notice, Seph is too. Anyone coming into our compound is ludicrous, especially after the Claiming and Maiming last summer, but just in case it is the

River Rebels feeling brazen, I don't want her in the RV alone." Frank muttered something, and an answering reply sounded a lot like Luella. "Whenever you have to go to your place with that investigation team," he spoke into the phone again, "I'm sending guards out with you, understand?"

"Yes, sir," Jack replied, showing his respect for his MC president. "I accept and appreciate your help."

"The house is bursting at the seams right now," Frank said, "but Luella says the little room under the stairs is vacant. It's tiny, but Seph will be safe and have privacy. "Since Tom's girlfriend dumped him, you can bunk with him. Call me when you find out something."

"I will."

The line clicked.

"Fuck!" Jack clenched his eyes shut, then let out a frustrated groan. He'd rather sleep on one of the sofas for the next six weeks than bunk with Tom, who talked in his sleep and stunk the room up with farts that could peel the wallpaper off the walls.

Until the e-squad and the cops showed up, Jack kept checking on Seph. He couldn't stand that she'd been hurt, that he couldn't do anything tangible to really help her. What if she had a serious spinal injury? What if she didn't have a mild concussion but one that was life-threatening?

The possibilities left him quivering. His stomach lurched.

"Jack?"

He turned suddenly, nearly sliding down the soft incline before he grasped the edges of the car's frame and righted himself. "Hey, baby."

"I'm…still in the car?"

"Yes." He stroked hair out of her face again and looped it over the back of her neck. "I called 9-1-1, and someone will be here any minute now."

"Four motorcycles…"

"I know. I saw what they did, but I was on the opposite ridge and couldn't get here in time."

"Why did they attack me?"

"I don't know, baby." He rubbed the backs of his fingers over her cheek. She leaned into his hand slightly, so he took that as a sign that his touch comforted her and his heart swelled at the thought. "Did you see who the riders were?"

"No." She batted her eyes drunkenly. "Weird thing on their coats."

"Really? What was it?"

She was silent for a long moment. At first Jack thought she'd passed out again, then she sighed.

"I'm…not sure." Her voice sounded weak. "Something like a ghost, but it had a scary face on it, maybe a witch's face? It was…"

This time she did succumb to unconsciousness.

He braced his feet in a semisolid spot he'd stomped into the earth and settled his back against Seph's side once more, blocking the cool spring air wafting up out of the hollow. His beast lunged to the surface, sending tingles across his body, but he forced the animal to bend to his will and go back to sleep.

Only one motorcycle club used the ugly emblem Seph had just described.

The Wraithkillers.

Chapter Ten

By the evening of the following day, Jack had to race to the hospital to see Persephone. She'd been in and out of consciousness the day before. Today, however, he'd hoped he could get off work early so he could spend some time with her, but with the spring thaw, orders for gravel were pouring in from not only the fracking pads but also wherever there was ongoing construction, townships needing to gravel their roads, and from residents for their private drives. His ass was sore from sitting in the truck for 14 hours, his arms tired from gripping the steering wheel in the same two or three positions. By the time he got to the hospital, he'd be lucky to have any time with Seph before visiting hours ended.

He parked his pickup by the main entrance, having been lucky enough to snag a vacant spot there. After shrugging out of his uniform jacket, he slipped on his cut, then slammed the driver's door and jogged into the hospital, dodging a couple ushering four quarreling children down the walk.

Inside, he passed the information counter on one side and the gift shop on the other, then made a left and followed the corridor to the elevator, which he took to the second level. Outside Seph's room, he discovered two prospects: Sledgehammer, who had transferred from the Cadiz MC to Frank's MC just after Christmas, and Beer Cans, a member who lived in Malaga, halfway between the hospital and Rebellion.

"Jack," Sledgehammer said from a hard plastic waiting room chair. He raked a large, meaty hand over his face, then yawned. "Visiting hours are almost over."

"Had to work over," he said.

"Hey, Jack," Beer Cans greeted him. "She seems to be much better today."

"Someone will be taking our place anytime now," Sledgehammer told him. "So she'll have guards tonight too."

"Thanks, guys."

He entered Seph's room to find her watching a rerun of *Ghost Adventures*. Besides the flickers of light from the TV mounted to the ceiling, only a small nightlight illuminated her bed just over one of her shoulders. Someone had sent her flowers, probably the WHO team. A vase of bright spring blooms sat on the stand next to her, and another vase full of pink roses and baby's breath on the windowsill had a red heart-shaped helium balloon tied to it that had the words *Get Well Soon* on it in stark white.

"Hi," Seph said, her cheeks pinking.

"Someone sent you pretty flowers," he stated, wishing he'd had the foresight to do the same. How could he be so fucking stupid?

She pointed to the ones next to her. "The team sent those, and the others are from the women of the MC."

"I should've brought you something nice," he said glumly. Holy hell, shame prickled his skin so badly he thought about making an excuse and leaving, but he couldn't bear not spending what little time he could with Seph. "I'm sorry."

"Are you kidding me?" she retorted. "You saved my life, Jack! That's all that's important to me. Besides, I think the team's flowers have stirred my allergies." She sniffed, then rubbed one of her eyes, laughing.

He chuckled, too, as he took in the purple-and-blue bruise that had spread from the side of her forehead over her eye and down her temple. The look on his face must have spoken volumes.

"I know, I've seen what I look like," she said.

"I'm just thankful you didn't break your nose or worse. Had a friend years ago who was in a car wreck and the steering wheel busted his teeth out. He was a mess." He sat on the corner of her bed. "You're lucky you just got a bad bruise."

"And a concussion, but I'm told I'm out of the danger zone now."

"Are you going home—getting out of here tomorrow?"

"That's what I'm told."

"Good." He wanted to pull her into his arms, hold her tightly, stroke her hair and never let her go. "The team has been lost without you."

"How's the investigation going?"

"It's not."

She frowned. "What do you mean?"

"Not a damn thing has happened. It's been four days and they haven't gotten any readings at all."

"Seriously?" She gaped at him, mouth forming a cute little oval. "I've been in here two days now?"

He nodded. "It's easy to lose track of time when suffering a bad head injury, baby." "Your team thinks I was imagining things and overreacting."

"I'm sure they don't believe that." She met his gaze steadily.

Actually, Jack had overheard some comments between the two men that maybe Jack had been smoking some weed or worse and had actually fallen through the window, breaking it. He'd wanted to slug them. Falling through the window didn't explain how glass had landed all the way out in the yard some 30 to 40 yards away, or the other crazy incidences such as when he and Seph had been possessed by the spirits. Still, WHO had been there for four days now. They couldn't continue investigating if the ghosts, or whatever they were, had decided to play nice.

He shrugged. Right now he had more important issues to address. "I wanted to talk to you about what happened with the bikers."

"Two deputies were here this morning who interviewed me."

"But I want to know what you remember," he coaxed gently. "Motorcycle clubs have their own ways of handling problems. Describe that MC emblem you told me about."

"I told you about the...?" She wrinkled her forehead and thought back, her gaze growing distant. "Oh, yeah." Her lovely amber eyes widened suddenly. "I remember now. I came to long enough to talk to you for a few seconds."

"You said the emblem looked like a ghost or a witch," he prompted.

Slowly, she began telling him about the climb up

the twisting road, the melted snow falling out of tree limbs onto the windshield and how she couldn't figure out how to activate the wipers right away. Gripping the blanket to her as if to provide a shield of sorts, she clenched it tight to her chest, her knuckles whitening until Jack scooted forward and placed one of his hands over hers. She realized what she was doing and loosened her hold but didn't slide her hands out of his. Relaxed somewhat, Seph went on to tell him the riders had worn plain helmets with dark visors, how two of the bikers had ridden up alongside her, then the sun had blinded her in the turn. The rest he knew, but she described the MC emblem in as much detail as she could remember.

"Those bikers were Wraithkillers." Jack kept his voice even so Seph wouldn't know how upset he was and scare her. "Their insignia is a banshee. That's why it looks like a witch that's part ghost."

Fury burned in his gut. He wanted to release his wolf and let it shred the Wraithkillers who had done this to Seph. But why would they break their truce with the Werewolves of Rebellion? Hell, he wondered if their president, Crow, was even aware of what had happened. Although they were one-percenters who dealt in all things illegal, the Wraithkillers had lost so many men in skirmishes with Frank's MC that Crow had decided he'd better call some sort of truce before there weren't any Wraithkillers left. And, from what he'd heard from Phil, who was bonded with a sweetbutt who once belonged to Crow's MC, Crow wasn't that bad of a guy, but he did have some members who were sociopaths or worse. An image of Bloodbath came to mind and he fought off a shiver.

That guy had been criminally insane, and if it hadn't been for Frank and Bernadette taking him out at the Claiming and Maiming last summer, the nutjob would have murdered even more people by now.

However, Crow hadn't known—and still didn't— that his gang was fighting an MC primarily comprised of lycanthropes, which was why so many of his members had been maimed or killed, but Frank was open to peace between their MCs. He hadn't wanted any further battles at the cost of more lives, and Deputy Williamscot had been reaching his limit on how many werewolf kills he could pass off as drug or gun deals gone badly. Their last encounter with Crow's MC had been over a missing crate of weapons some of Frank's men had found busted in the middle of a road. Wraithkillers had kidnapped Beastman's old lady to force a trade for the guns. It had been a tense trade, but Luella had been returned to them safely.

But targeting Seph made no sense. She wasn't even a member of the Werewolves of Rebellion, or anyone's woman…yet.

He blinked. Where had *that* thought come from?

"Are you all right, Jack?" Seph asked.

He snapped back to himself. "Yeah, just thinking. Targeting you doesn't make any sense."

She sat quietly. The fear in her eyes only flamed his anger hotter, not at her, but at the assholes who had done this to her. He wanted to take her back to the MC and keep her safely at his side, but judging by the way Queen had been talking last night, he was betting they'd head back to Detroit anytime now.

"Hi there," a female voice said behind him.

The rustle of a uniform followed, and he turned to

greet a short, stacked nurse with big green eyes and a bow mouth.

"Visiting hours ended five minutes ago," she said with a smile. "You can come back tomorrow morning at 8:00 a.m."

"I'm going home tomorrow morning," Seph said.

"So you are," the nurse replied as she looked at Seph's chart. "Well, your man here can take you home with him, then." She replaced the chart and walked over to the blood pressure cuff and began strapping it around Seph's upper arm.

Jack couldn't stop himself from smiling at the red hue creeping up Seph's neck. He wanted to give her a kiss and pass it off as a farewell kiss, but he gripped her toes through the blanket instead and tugged on them gently.

"Night, Seph," he said.

"Good night," she said, "and be safe."

He paused, maintaining eye contact. She actually looked like she didn't want him to go. Was it because she was frightened to be left here, worried someone might try to hurt her again? Surely not in the hospital, especially with guards at her door. The light shining in her eyes called to him, and damn if he didn't almost tell the nurse to start Seph's release papers right now so he could take her with him tonight...but he couldn't. First he had to make sure the doctor gave Seph a clean bill of health.

"Will I see you tomorrow?" Seph asked as he started toward the door.

He spun on his heel. Fuck, leaving her behind was turning out to be one of the most difficult things he'd ever had to do. "I have to work—but I don't want to. I'd love to take you back to the MC, but circumstances…" He lifted one shoulder in apology. "Besides, I figure your team will pick you up and head back to Detroit."

"Yeah…"

Good God, did he just see her lower lip tremble? That punched him straight in the gut, almost robbing him of breath.

"If… if I don't see you before you leave"—he gulped down the raw emotion crawling up his throat—"you have my number."

She brightened somewhat at that.

He couldn't bear to look at her any longer. If he did, he'd knock the nurse to the floor, grab Seph up in his arms and leave with her wearing nothing more than a hospital gown.

"Take care," he said and walked out.

When he left, he passed Sledgehammer and Beer Cans talking to their replacements to guard Seph that night. By the time he reached his pickup, darkness had settled over the town. Jack clambered into his truck and sat with his head against the steering wheel. He had to let Seph go back to Detroit. That was her home. Her entire life was there, not here.

But fuck, the thought of her leaving caused pain in his chest, pain that rendered him motionless for several minutes.

* * *

"Holy fuck, Jack!" Luella bellowed. "I said that we'll take care of her, okay? Damn."

Bernadette grinned. Poor Jack was so distraught

about not being able to retrieve Seph from the hospital that he'd been hovering around them for most of the morning.

Luella finished tucking in the end of the single bed beneath the stairs. "Persephone has been in the hospital two days and you've been there with her whenever possible, even visiting her last night. You have to go to work. You can't pay bills on just air. The last thing you want to do is lose your job over another woman." She spun and faced the doorway where Bernadette stood handing her bedding. "Shit, I'm sorry, Jack. I didn't mean that to come out so harsh or to imply the wrong thing."

Jack peered at her from around the edge of the doorframe. "I know what you meant, Luella. After Tina's craziness cost me my last job, I'm being ultra-careful. And with the WHO team having left early this morning for a new case, I feel like Seph is my responsibility now. It's just that…"

"What?" Bernadette prodded. The indecision and confusion in Jack's eyes poked at her heart. She met his gaze and knew without a doubt he was in love with Persephone. It was obvious by the way he acted around the woman, but the expression in his eyes told all.

"Seph is different," he said. "I can't explain it. And I'm really worried those assholes will target her again."

"For the love of all that's lycanthrope," Luella began, "Frank has had men posted either in or outside Persephone's hospital room since she was admitted."

Bernadette hid her smile and handed her a fresh pillowcase.

"We don't know why she was targeted," Jack snapped back. "Seph isn't even from around here. She has been either here or with me…" Realization crossed his face.

Bernadette frowned. "What is it, Jack?"

He shook his head, his eyes darkening. "I'll have to think about it and make sure I'm not jumping to conclusions, then talk to Frank about it."

"Go to work, Jack," Luella said again. "We've already made arrangements with the hospital to pick Seph up at eleven."

"Who's going as your guards?" Jack asked and moved directly behind Bernadette to lean in over her head, his hands braced on either side of the doorframe.

"All the trucks are in the garage for spring maintenance, so Beastman doesn't have to work today," Luella said as she tugged the case over a fat pillow. She plopped herself on the edge of the bed. "Tom and Tractor are escorting us too, but Tom is peeling off to watch over Maeve and Mildred at the clinic while the rest of us go on to the hospital." She tossed the pillow at the head of the bed and fixed her bright blue gaze on Jack. "Go to work before I kick your ass, Jack. You're on my last nerve."

"Go on," Bernadette urged, looking up at the worried man. "Seph will be fine. We'll all be fine. You know no one is going to get within 20 yards of us with Beastman as one of our guards."

"What if the Wraith—"

"Jack!" Luella stood abruptly, ducking the ceiling just in time, and placed her hands on her hips, eyes flashing silver. "Get the hell out of here and go to work!"

He stared at her for a good minute. "Someone took potshots at me the same day Seph was run off the road."

Mouth ajar, Luella stared at Bernadette.

"We hadn't heard anything about that," Luella said."

"Frank didn't tell me anything, either," Bernadette added, suddenly uneasy.

"Now do you see why I'm so worried?" Finally Jack sighed, the gust of breath stirring the hair on top of Bernadette's head. "All right. I'm sure Frank will call me if there's a problem."

"He will without a doubt," Bernadette soothed him while wishing someone could calm her too. "You know that."

"Yeah." He stood behind her for a few more seconds, then, with another gusty sigh, he turned and left.

Luella smoothed the cover on the bed. "Fuck me sideways and bent over. If someone shot at Jack, do you think it was a warning or the shooter was just a bad shot?"

"My guess is a warning."

Silently Luella nodded.

"He's smitten with Persephone," Bernadette stated, changing the subject.

"That's an understatement."

"Wonder how long it will take before they're officially mates?"

Luella straightened and bumped her head against the drywall forming the slanted ceiling. She absently rubbed the offended spot. "I give them a month, tops."

"I bet they're bonded mates within another week." Bernadette backed out of the room when Luella shooed her out.

"That soon?" her friend questioned skeptically.

"I'm betting on it, if you will."

"A real wager?"

"Sure." Although still a little nervous, Bernadette was relieved she'd lightened the mood. "Why not? How about 50 bucks?"

"Okay, but make it more interesting," Luella said with a leer.

"Damn, I know that look. What do you want to add to the wager?"

"Fifty bucks and laundry duty for a month." Luella turned off the light and shut the door.

Making a face, Bernadette managed a disgusted "Ugh."

"Is it a bet?" Luella asked on her way to the kitchen.

"Yeah, okay." Oh how Bernadette hated doing laundry. She just *had* to win the wager.

"Good. If by one week from today they're not officially bonded mates, you better stay on top of the laundry. It gets out of hand so quickly."

"I'll be so glad *not* to do laundry," Bernadette quipped, following her into the kitchen.

Luella chortled. "You can talk the talk, but let's see if you can walk the walk."

"Seriously?" Bernadette shot back. "That's the best you can come back at me with?"

One of the women turned on the vacuum in the dining room, drowning out their laughter.

"Grab your jacket and purse," Luella shouted over the sweeper's whine. "If we head out now, we won't have to rush. And give your mom a quick call that we'll be down to pick her and Mildred up in five."

Chapter Eleven

Luella stopped the SUV in front of Bernadette's mom's cottage. Her mother, Maeve, walked out of the house with Mildred on her arm. It was nice her mom had become such good friends with the elderly lady. The sentient woman at Maeve's side looked like she could be anywhere between 60 and 80 in human years, one of those people who never looked their true age. From what Bernadette had been told, Mildred was well over 150. Natural-born lycanthropes lived exceptionally long lives, aging much slower than humans did, but Bernadette still had trouble comprehending their lengthy lifespans. Turned werewolves lived longer than average, too, but not nearly as long as true-born wolves. Although Bernadette had to wonder how long she'd live if she agreed to let Frank turn her, and if she did, would she eventually have to leave and live elsewhere to hide her age? Sometimes it was avoided, but the idea of waiting for a generation, or two, of humans to pass away who would recognize her so she could return to Rebellion struck her as morbid. Then again, that was how the Cadiz branch of the MC had come into existence.

"Hi, Maeve," Luella said to Bernadette's mom. "Morning, Mildred."

From the backseat, Puppy said hello to the women too.

"Mom, Mildred," Bernadette said. "You both look really nice this morning."

They both murmured greetings and thank-yous. Once they were settled in the back passenger seat, Tractor shut the door.

Beastman revved his Harley and started out the lane again, the howling wolf emblem on his cut glistening in the morning sunshine. Tractor and Tom brought up the rear on their bikes.

"Puppy is going to the clinic with you two," Bernadette said. She twisted around so she could see her mom and Mildred. "Tom will be your guard. While you're at the clinic getting your checkups, Luella and I are going to Barnesville to pick up a young woman who is part of the paranormal investigation team working for Jack. She was hurt the other day and has been in the hospital."

"Oh dear," her mom said. "Is the girl alright?"

"Yes, she's fine now, but if it looks like it will take longer than necessary to discharge her, we'll call the main house and Carol will come get you."

"That's fine," Mildred said. "Me and Maeve always have fun when we're out together. Maybe we'll pick up a couple fine-looking men hanging out at the doctor's office. Isn't that right, Maeve?"

Her mother blushed to the roots of her hair but laughed regardless. "I want me a tall, burly guy who's maybe two or three years older than me."

"Mom, jeez!" Bernadette said in a shocked tone. Regardless, she knew her mom was only kidding.

Across from her, Luella snorted in amusement.

"Hell, I'll take any young buck that can keep up with this old wolf." Mildred gently nudged Maeve's ribs, then waggled her eyebrows at Bernadette.

They all burst out laughing. Bernadette loved her new people, and, judging by the way her mother had blossomed since moving to the MC, life with the MC and its community suited her too.

The trip into Rebellion passed quickly as they joked with one another. After they dropped off her mom, Mildred and Puppy, with Tom keeping a watchful eye on them, Bernadette let her thoughts return to her mate. Frank wanted to turn her so badly, and although Bernadette understood his desire and reasoning, she worried what the transformation would do to her. What if she couldn't cope with the shifts from human to beast? It was more difficult for a turned lycanthrope, more painful. Could she handle that?

"You're suddenly quiet," Luella stated as she navigated the turns on SR 800 leading out of Rebellion.

"Yeah," Puppy chimed in behind her. "What's eating you—besides Frank?"

Luella let out a loud guffaw at that.

"Frank wants to turn me."

Silence weighed heavily in the SUV.

"Damn. Your silence says it all," Bernadette added glumly.

"No, we love you, Bernadette, you know that," Puppy said. "It's just that becoming a turned lykoi is an important step—a huge one."

"And many humans who are turned have trouble coping with the transformation and the pain involved," Luella explained.

"I know. Frank has discussed this step with me at length since… Well, since last October."

"Ah, so you're not going into this lightly," Luella said. "You know what to expect."

She glanced over at Luella. "Yeah."

"Then what's the problem?" Puppy asked pleasantly. "I mean, the shifting and pain aside."

"That *is* what's bothering me—at least I think it is. I'm…well, I'm…" The answer to her true worry suddenly struck her and she gasped softly. "I'm afraid I won't be able to handle it and I'll disappoint Frank," she blurted out. She gripped the oh-shit bar as the SUV started through sharp downhill curves. "My fear of disappointing him is worse than the fear of the change and the pain."

"Oh honey," Luella said. "You do love him more than life itself, don't you?"

"Yes." Tears filled Bernadette's eyes, blurring her view of the winding road. "Every time I think about Frank, I'm so full of love for him it almost hurts. I don't want to disappoint him, and I certainly don't want to hurt him if I decide to stay human."

"Frank will understand if you decide to remain human," Puppy said.

A warm hand landed on Bernadette's shoulder. She turned to meet Puppy's sweet, understanding eyes.

She patted Puppy's hand. "But it means so much to him."

"Do what your heart says to do," Puppy told her. "If you follow your heart, you'll always make the right choice."

"What she said," Luella quipped.

Bernadette smiled, her soul lightening. She loved

Frank with every bit of herself, but she also loved her new family with total fierceness too. Finding Frank and his MC, his people, was the best thing that had ever happened to her.

And she wanted to be a part of them in every way. But could she do it?

* * *

Persephone sat on the edge of the hospital bed. The nurse had told her someone was coming to pick her up and would be there any minute now, but she didn't know who it was. Seph hoped it was Jack, but he'd said he had to work today. Last night she'd talked with him for only a few minutes, but after he'd left, the night nurse had told her the day shift nurses had said he'd been to see her, albeit briefly, when she'd been in and out of consciousness. Also, she'd overheard the nurses at the station across the hall. Arrangements had been made to leave two MC members outside her door at all times. Whenever she thought about the accident, she began to tremble. Why had the bikers targeted her?

Her thoughts returned to Jack again and her heart performed the weird jitter it did every time she thought about him. Then warmth spread from her lower abdomen into her pussy. What the hell was wrong with her? No man had ever affected her like this before, so what made Jack so different?

Vaguely she recalled the nurses urging her to stay awake, that going to sleep with a concussion was dangerous, but once she was out of the critical time frame, she'd been allowed to sleep without the nurses constantly waking her. One time, she'd roused just

119

enough to see Jack's concerned yet smiling face before she'd close her eyes and was out once more. However, an image kept rising in her memory, a picture—or was it remnants of a dream?—of a monster. She recalled opening her eyes after the crash—or at least she thought it was immediately after the crash; she couldn't be sure—and seeing this big, hairy, man-beast thing staring in the car at her. No, it must have been a hallucination, a nightmare created by the blow to her head.

It didn't matter. None of it did. By now the WHO team was probably on their way to retrieve her from the hospital and they'd be heading back to Detroit shortly after lunchtime. Maybe she could convince them to stop at the orphanage for a few minutes so she could visit with Sister Miranda. She certainly needed someone she could confide in and Sister Miranda always offered a kind ear and her amazing insight.

A slight knock drew her attention to the doorway. Luella and Bernadette stared back her, smiling warmly. Surprised, Seph looked beyond them into the corridor, seeing only a hulking biker and the busy nurses' station.

"How do you feel?" Bernadette asked.

"I'm good, but my face is a bit sore." Seph tipped her head to one side. "Where's my team?"

An uncomfortable silence descended on the room.

"Uhm, well…" Bernadette sighed. "Queen said there was nothing to investigate at Jack's place after all, so when another potential client called hysterical about something that had happened in their apartment, Queen decided they better head home."

Her team had left her behind? Her pride smarted, but she really didn't know whether to be hurt or not. She understood the need to reach potentially paranormal locations when the activity was hot, and that a client's safety was the most important point, but… For now, she decided she was fine with the team going on without her. At least for a few more days she wouldn't have to hide her abilities and dodge Queen's questions.

"But we're here to take you home with *us*," Luella said, pushing into the room. "It'll be two or three more days before you're ready to travel, I'm sure. Then, when you're ready, someone will drive you back to Detroit." She shot an amused look at Bernadette, then swept her gaze around the little room and the empty bed on the other side. "Do you have all your things ready?"

"What I'm wearing, my purse and"—Seph held up a white plastic Family Dollar bag—"what I bought the other day."

Just outside the doorway stood two new men with the posted guards, both wearing cuts with the Werewolves of Rebellion insignia. Seph didn't know their names, but she guessed one must be Tractor, Puppy's father. The other man, an enormous bald guy with a bushy, blond beard, she'd seen around the MC.

"You're sticking with us at the main house," Bernadette explained. "Frank spoke with Deputy Williamscot about the attack. No one except Jack saw what happened and he was too far away to identify the bikers. Jack told us they were wearing helmets with visors, but you identified the emblem on their leathers as the Wraithkillers."

"Yes."

"Until we figure out what's going on, or you go back to Detroit," Luella stated, "you go nowhere alone, understand?"

"Yes." Dammit. Tears filled her eyes, and her lower lip wobbled.

"Oh Seph. It's okay."

The bed dipped. Through a haze of tears, Seph looked over at Bernadette.

Luella tugged a couple tissues from a box on the mobile tray and handed them to Seph. "Here, these awful things are thin and rough, but they're better than using your shirt." She sat on the other side of Seph. "You've been through a lot and you have no idea why those jerks ran you off the road, so don't be ashamed to cry, honey. We're your friends."

The warmth and compassion the women had toward her proved to be Seph's undoing. A sob popped out of her mouth. She tried to stuff it back in with her fist clenched around the tissues, but it was no use. Cry after cry sprang from her like startled birds. Before she fully realized what was happening, Luella had pulled her into her arms and was rocking her as if Seph were a little girl. The aroma of floral shampoo and cinnamon pervaded Seph's senses as the big blonde soothed her.

"What the fuck's going on in here?" a deep male voice asked in the room.

"Beastman, watch your language in the hospital," Luella admonished. "Seph's confused and scared. Wouldn't you be if you were in her shoes?"

"Ach, woman. I was just worried something was wrong."

"Well, you don't need to go around the hospital dropping the F bomb like you're delivering roses."

"I didn't mean to—"

"Beastman, why don't you check to see if all the

discharge papers are signed?" Bernadette interrupted. "The sooner we can get Seph back to the MC, the more relaxed we'll all be."

"Yeah, you're right," the man rumbled. "Be back in a few."

Bernadette pressed a couple more tissues into Seph's hand. Seph pulled away from Luella. Embarrassed, she concentrated on wiping her eyes, then blowing her nose. She didn't know these people from Adam, but it was so easy to let them take care of her. It was strange, a little disconcerting, yet wonderful at the same time, as though she finally belonged to a family. She liked how it felt. It would be tough to give it up when she went back to Detroit.

"Don't be embarrassed," Luella said quietly by her ear. "We all need a good cry now and then."

Seph nodded and offered her a watery smile.

"Once you're at the main house with us, you'll forget about all this scary stuff," Bernadette said. "That place is always chaotic, but in a good way. But..." She shot Luella an uncertain glance.

"But we'll explain about sweetbutt night," Luella finished. "You might want to stay in your little room if public sex bothers you."

She jerked her head up and looked right into the woman's amused eyes. "What?"

"Like she said, we'll explain later," Bernadette replied, giggling.

The bald man stepped into the room. "She's all done and can go now."

"That big goof"—Luella nodded at the hulking figure—"is my old man, Beastman."

He winked. "Let's head out."

With trepidation, Seph let the women guide her from of the room and out to the black SUV she'd seen them in the other day. The two guards at the door rode up to them on Harleys and waited, the reverberations of the engines carrying over the neighboring homes. Beastman and Tractor waited on their bikes as Luella backed out of the space, then led the way around the hospital and out the exit with the guards bringing up the rear.

"Next stop is the clinic to pick up Bernadette's mom and one of the older ladies who lives in the MC community," Luella told her, meeting her gaze in the rearview mirror. "After that, we're going to the MC and starting dinner."

Seph smiled. Her belly growled. Food sounded awesome, and if she had her own room like she'd been told, maybe she could regroup and calm down. She wasn't sure why, but she sensed her life was about to change.

Chapter Twelve

After Persephone had gotten settled into her tiny under-the-stairs bedroom, Beastman showed her how to use the remote control for the tiny flat-screen TV that perched on a small, low dresser. The room didn't have a window, and the staircase creaked and moaned under everyone who passed up and down it, but Seph found the muffled noises comforting. The room itself gave her a safe feeling, and the quaint hand-painted pictures of berries, leaves, birds and little animals such as squirrels, rabbits and chipmunks along the upper slanted edges of the ceiling reminded her of a storybook cabin. Small, dark and shiny curio shelves with a few knickknacks of motorcycles and figurines of wolves lined either side of the walls where there was room, but the biggest one hung above the TV. The items on it consisted of a small alarm clock, a fat white candle in a glass holder with a little box of Rosebud matches next to it, a five-by-seven silver frame with a photo of what the farm must have looked like decades ago, and a chipped mug with strawberries painted on it that held a couple of number 2 pencils and some pens. Next to it lay a pad of paper.

Earlier, Puppy had brought her a plate loaded

with some sort of taco salad complete with sour cream, guacamole and tortilla chips. She also brought her a big glass of cola and a dessert cup of vanilla pudding with crushed Oreos mixed in it, covered in whipped cream. Seph ate like she'd been without food for a week. She'd settled on the bed to watch the Investigation Discovery Channel, then the next thing she knew, she was rousing from one of the deepest sleeps she'd had in a long time.

The dishes were gone. Hell, she hadn't even heard anyone open the door.

Here at the main house, she felt at ease. Here she had no worries of someone hurting her.

She thought about her team. She liked every one she worked with, but they weren't her family. Also, Queen was determined to crack her. Queen was aware Seph was different, and by now the woman had probably guessed Seph was a medium, but Seph's gift was draining—and frightening at times. Being a medium was the very last thing she wanted to do as a profession. That thought struck her hard. She needed time away from the team. Working for WHO had been taking more of a toll on her than she'd thought.

Besides, the only person she'd ever considered family was Sister Miranda. But the Werewolves of Rebellion were different. The idea of going back to Detroit pained Seph. Could it be she was ready to give up city life for a rural one? What would she do for a living? She had an apartment, albeit a shitty one, but it was hers until she saved up enough money for the condo she wanted. The flickering images on the TV drew her attention for a moment. Did she still want her condo? She blinked and rolled onto her side. So much had happened so quickly that Seph wasn't sure what she wanted anymore. Maybe she just needed to relax a couple days, then she'd be back to her old self again.

Flipping through channels, Seph paused on a movie, then surfed over to *The Big Bang Theory*. Reruns or not, she loved the show, but soon her thoughts strayed to Jack. God, she couldn't seem to keep him off her mind. He invaded her every waking hour. He probably had a girlfriend, and he obviously had a job that involved long shifts, so fantasizing about him was pointless. But she couldn't help herself. Each time she thought about the two kisses they'd shared, heat singed every inch of her skin each time she thought about them. "A good kisser" didn't even begin to describe Jack. She could only imagine what he'd be like in bed, thrusting into her, his hands all over her naked body…

Heat flared in her pussy and her heart rate sped up. Those kinds of thoughts would do nothing but leave her frustrated and aching. Firmly pushing Jack from her mind, Seph tried to focus on the sitcom.

* * *

Jack put his cell phone back in his pocket as he walked the path up to his house. He'd made sure Luella and Bernadette had picked up Persephone from the hospital without incident. He'd wanted to go to the MC immediately after work, but if he was going to be staying there for a while, he needed more than one change of clothes. He would pack a bag, then head straight over to the MC. The thought of seeing Seph, of spending some time with her, thrilled him so much he climbed the porch steps in two big leaps.

Inside, he quickly changed and showered before donning fresh clothes, then packing a bag for the next few days. In the kitchen, he glanced at the wall clock. The main house would be having supper right now. He'd been taught that interrupting a meal was rude, so he decided to wait half an hour before leaving. The house was cool and growing colder. Chilled, he decided to take the Keurig out and have a cup of coffee instead of making an entire pot.

After dropping his bag by the front door, Jack returned to the kitchen, took out the one-cup maker, then removed the box of K-Cups from a cupboard. He shut the cabinet and turned. The cupboard door creaked, then slammed with force. He startled and looked over his shoulder. What the hell? He'd just shut it, so how had it…? Wait, had he imagined it?

Dismissing the incident, he set the K-Cup on the counter and took a mug from the dish drainer. When he faced the Keurig again, the K-Cup shot across the counter and out into midair to land on the tabletop. It skidded to a halt on its side against the glass fruit bowl.

Jack froze. The hair stood up on his nape, along his bare arms and the tops of his hands. "Who's here?" he demanded gruffly.

Silence.

When a couple minutes passed without any further strangeness, Jack retrieved the pack and popped it into the Keurig. He finished setting it up and placed the mug under the dispenser. As the little machine heated the water and issued its gurgling noises with puffs of steam, Jack stood at the sink and stared out the window. His thoughts zipped straight to

Persephone. He wondered how she was feeling. Would she be anxious to return to Detroit, especially now her team had gone on without her?

She'd looked so vulnerable last night with her face bruised and the white hospital covers drawn up over her breasts, clutching the edge in her fingers as though the blankets were grounding her. He knew virtually nothing about her, but he decided he'd remedy that. Maybe tonight he could get to know her better. He hoped she'd want to know more about him too.

His thoughts settled on Seph's loveliness. Even with her face mottled with purple and blue, she was gorgeous. He hadn't noticed a ring of any sort on her finger, so he didn't think she was married or engaged. What if she had a boyfriend in Detroit? At that thought, jealousy and a fierce protectiveness seized him, stunning him with its intensity.

Holy fuck, what had this woman done to him?

The Keurig chugged out the last bit of coffee. Jack fixed it the way he liked and set the cup on the table. He pulled a chair out, preparing to sit, but something kicked it out from under him. The chair careened into the corner, striking the lower cabinets so hard the doors flew open. It landed on its side as Jack fell on his ass, banging his head against the edge of the kitchen sink as he hit the tile.

"Shit!" He scrambled to his feet, palming his throbbing skull, and looked from one spot to the next. "Where are you, fucker? It's easy to do shit to people if you're hiding, so that tells me that you don't have the guts to show yourself!"

A black cloud materialized between him and the

hallway. Ice-cold air wafted from the corridor and across the tile to swoosh over the table. Gooseflesh rose along Jack's body so suddenly and stiffly that his skin prickled painfully. His inner beast balked at the entity materializing, then rushed to the surface, wanting to attack the spirit. Jack kept his animal at bay and stood his ground, his heart hammering so hard he heard it in his ears.

The shape of a human finally formed. At first it looked like it was a silhouette cutout, but the more it solidified, the more vapors and twirling darkness drifted around it like strands of inky smoke. Eyes appeared, the same red eyes Jack had witnessed the night the window exploded. The entity raised a black, vaporous arm and pointed at Jack.

"What do you want?" Jack asked, his fear morphing into anger.

Something cold rushed through the kitchen from the living room, knocking over the broom propped by the pantry and sending the dustpan skittering across the tile. Lavender and citrus puffed over him in a big wave of fragrance that proved so real he could have sworn a woman had just strode by him. The gust ruffled his hair and the hem of his T-shirt. It struck the dark entity, and the black form dispersed, the tendrils of inkiness twirling and drifting in every conceivable direction until nothing remained. Gradually, the scent of lavender and citrus faded until it was gone too.

Jack stared at the spot where the bad spirit had been. So the female ghost did have some power after all. This certainly changed things.

Unwilling to remain in the house any longer, Jack gulped down his coffee, snatched up his duffle bag, grabbed his keys and leathers, then stalked to the front door where he stuffed his feet into his boots. With the door locked behind him, he headed to his pickup. The barn loomed off to his right. It was locked tight too, his motorcycle once more chained and beneath the tarp. He'd love to take his Indian, but the weather was still too cold, despite the brief warm hours during the sunny afternoons.

Leaving, he looked in the side mirror as the last traces of sun vanished into night. The house looked so peaceful.

He snorted. "Yeah, right."

Along the way to the MC, he stopped in Graysville at a tiny mom-and-pop store. Surprisingly, it was one of the few general stores that stocked Dos Equis, Frank's favorite. A six-pack of the beer was the least Jack could do for Frank's help regarding the attack on Seph and making sure that guards were posted at her room for her entire hospital stay. Besides, Frank was the MC president and a good man, his friend.

He slowed and pulled in to park near the front door. A motorcycle he recognized was parked next to the road. Inside, Phillip Andrews, Frank's second-in-command, stood at the counter buying beer and munchies.

"Hey, Jack," Phil said. "You heading over to the MC for sweetbutt night?"

"Nah, just staying there for a while."

"I heard about what's been going on," Phil stated. "Daffodil said she really likes that girl the MC took in. Said all the women seem to like her too."

"What are you doing out in the cold on your bike?" Jack asked. "You'll freeze your nuts off."

Laughing, Phil picked up the six-pack and a thin plastic bag. "I got to bullshitting with a friend of mine in Rebellion and didn't realize it had gotten so late. And yeah, I think both nuts are frozen." He winked, grinning from ear to ear. "But Daffi will thaw them out for me when I get home."

Jack cracked up. "You're terrible, man."

"And I enjoy every minute of it." Nodding, Phil headed toward the door. "See you round."

"Keep it between the lines, dude."

"Always."

Jack selected a six-pack of Dos Equis and, as an afterthought, he picked out a bottle of wine too. In the cooler, he found a small foam tray of three different cheeses, crackers and sliced summer sausage. He placed the items on the checkout counter, paid the woman, then headed out to his pickup.

Upon reaching his pickup, an all-too-familiar voice called to him.

"Jack! It's so nice to see you!"

The bottom fell out of his stomach. Fuck, not now, not *her*.

"What are you doing out tonight?" Tina asked, laying a hand on his shoulder.

Jack tried to act nonchalant. He shrugged off her hand, opened the driver's door and set the bag and six-pack on the seat, pushing them across it. "I'm headed to the MC."

"Jack, why won't you answer my calls?"

With strength he didn't feel, Jack faced Tina. The store lights washed her face in brightness, the sign flickering green over it from time to time as the neon blinked on and off. Blonde, blue-eyed, perky, a light sprinkling of freckles over her nose, Tina presented a pretty package that hid the manipulative, lying person she really was. The gold chain necklace and matching studs he'd given her for Christmas glimmered at her ears and throat. The sight of them made him ill.

He dragged his keys out of his front pants pockets. "Tina, I don't want to talk to you because you never take no for an answer. You always twist my words into meanings that suit what you want. We're over. I am not getting back together with you."

She pouted. "I thought we were friends."

"There's no being friends with you, Tina. You can't accept just friendship." He climbed into the truck, but she stepped in between him and the door so he couldn't shut it.

"I made a mistake." Her pupils dilated and she leaned in close to him. Jack cringed from her. At his reaction, anger marred her features. "Everyone deserves a second chance. Why can't you give me one?"

"Because I am no longer interested. You do nothing for me. Whatever I felt for you before was killed when I found you fucking two guys at the same time." He pushed her back and slammed the door shut. Starting up the engine, he jumped when she hit the driver's window with the heel of her hand.

"I'll win you back, Jack. I guarantee it!"

"Fuck off," he muttered under his breath. He backed out of the tiny lot, turned the truck around and headed down the hill.

It rattled Jack that Tina had suddenly shown up at the general store. She didn't live in that area, nor did she have any relatives or friends in Graysville that he was aware of, and driving SR 26 to Marietta was something only locals did because this end of it was a nightmare to navigate.

To distract himself, Jack turned on the radio, but he couldn't shake the idea that Tina was up to something. After he'd ended their relationship, several people had come forward to tell him what they knew about her, all of it not good. He often wished those folks would have told him the truth about Tina before he'd gotten involved with her, but he'd been in lust and doubted he would have believed any of it anyway. If Tina messed up his chances with Persephone... No, he couldn't entertain such a thought.

Besides, he had no idea if Seph had a special someone in Detroit. He knew nothing about the woman except that he wanted her—badly. Well, maybe tonight he could solve some of the mystery surrounding Seph.

Jack pushed the disturbing encounter with Tina out of his head and let himself anticipate the evening ahead.

Chapter Thirteen

Some of the women had told her about sweetbutt night, but it still didn't prepare Seph for what she witnessed as she emerged to go to the restroom. All children were removed from the main house and anyone wishing to scratch an itch could find a sexual partner. The moans and grunts that greeted her shocked her so badly it was a miracle her skin didn't catch on fire. Mortified, she hurried past a mostly naked couple on one of the big sofas, a guy thrusting into a willing woman against one wall, a woman astride a guy in an easy chair, and on a love seat, one guy kissing a woman while another woman gave him head.

Seph rushed to the tiny john just off the kitchen. She nearly knocked Puppy down in her effort to escape the sights and sounds. After Seph had relieved herself and washed her hands, she peeped out the door to find Puppy, Bernadette, Luella and a tiny blonde—she searched her memory for her name. Callie May?—regarding her with amusement.

"We tried to tell you," Luella stated with a grin when Seph finally stepped out.

"Do you want to stay in the kitchen with us?" the blonde asked.

Did she? The women were really nice, but Seph wasn't sure if she had much in common with them to just sit and talk.

"We were about to play cards," Bernadette said. "Come join us. Sweetbutt night will end in a couple more hours and things will be back to normal round here. Those of us who are in a relationship usually stay in our rooms or hang out in the kitchen or dining room if we don't leave the house."

Inching into the kitchen until she could see through the dining room entrance, Seph let her gaze wander over men and women who were either watching TV in the adjacent room or also playing cards. In one corner, it appeared about half a dozen men were engaged in a competitive poker game.

"The longer you're with us," Puppy added, "the more you'll realize we do many things that other MCs do, such as sweetbutt night, but not in the same way."

"Except for anything illegal," Beastman interjected as he entered from the dining room. He took a bottle of beer from the fridge and headed back across the kitchen. "We don't make, buy or sell drugs, nor do we dabble in human trafficking or any of those things."

Seph could only gape at the man as he returned to the poker table. Why were most of the men at this MC so large, especially Luella's old man? Damn.

"So," Callie May said, "do you want to play cards? I'll warn you that Luella cheats."

"What?" Luella sat back in her chair, her face a mix of mock outrage and humor. "I do not cheat! I'll have you know that everyone can see your cards."

The women all burst out laughing, the sound soothing Seph's frayed nerves.

"Well, I guess I can play—"

The door leading to the sun porch burst open and a gust of icy air blasted into the kitchen, stirring the discard pile and the tea towels drying on the oven's handle.

"Damn, that wind is cold tonight!" Climbing the two steps into the kitchen, Jack continued, "The weather reports keep calling for warmer nights, but I haven't seen one yet."

"Jack!" someone yelled from the other room. "Join us at the poker table!"

Jack caught sight of Seph. A huge grin crossed his face. "Evening, babe. Feel better?"

Speechless, she could only nod.

Without taking his eyes off her, he held out a six-pack toward the women. "Bernadette, is Frank around? I got him is favorite beer."

"I'm right here." Frank strode out of the dining room. "Take my place at the poker table. I'm tired of losing money." He laughed and accepted the beer. "Awesome, thank you, Jack."

"It's the least I could do."

"We were trying to convince Seph to play cards with us," Bernadette said, "but I think she's so weirded out by sweetbutt night that she might want to get out of the house for a couple hours."

Luella shot Bernadette a perturbed look. "Now *who's* cheating?"

"All I did was suggest that..." Eyes widening, Bernadette quirked one corner of her mouth. "Oh. Well, I didn't do it intentionally."

With a skeptical expression, Luella picked up her cards. "Right."

"We can ride around for a while," Jack offered. He held up a bag. "I even brought snacks."

"Okay."

"Grab your jacket," Jack said.

Elated to have the opportunity to spend time with him, Seph waved to the women and followed him out to his Dodge.

"Where do you want to go?" he asked when they were heading down the hill.

"I don't know anything about this area."

"I'd take you back to my place and watch a movie or something, but I had an encounter with this… Well, something weird."

She looked over at him, her curiosity piqued. "But the team said there was no activity at your house."

"It appears the spirits stayed hidden until they left."

"Well, like I said before, that's not uncommon." Ever since she'd been possessed by the female spirit, she'd been curious about the story she had to tell. "Why don't we go to your place and let me poke around the rooms, see what I can—"

"Sense?" he finished. "I'd forgotten you're a medium, *not* a medium."

At that, she laughed.

"You never told me why you didn't want Queen or the rest of the team to know what you are."

"My gift is frightening. Most of the time I see the spirits as they were in their previous lives, but there are the occasional ghosts that are different."

"That doesn't explain why you seem so determined to hide your ability from your team."

138

She stared at the lights of a distant farmhouse. "Some ghosts are scary, usually upset about something and very grumpy or disruptive. Then there are the entities. Those are evil. Those are the ones that scare the shit out of me, and interactions with darkness drain me, leave me weak and ill, and sometimes such creatures can attach to a person."

"Attach?" He turned the radio down, then glanced over at her before returning his attention to the road.

"Yes, like ghostly glue. It enables them to travel to other earthly regions." She shivered at the memories of some of her encounters, but grinned when he took it to mean she was cold and boosted the heater's temperature. "And as you experienced, spirits—the strong ones—can possess a living person. I don't want Queen using me as an investigation tool. I'm a person, not one of WHO's meters or energy detectors. Being a medium is draining and dangerous, but my ability seems to be supercharged. I eventually learned how to turn it off in day-to-day living, because I was seeing spirits everywhere. I couldn't even go to the grocery store without being stopped by half a dozen ghosts approaching me, asking me for help or to pass a message to the loved one they were watching over."

"Damn," he said. "That is intense."

"Try it sometime," she countered. "It's one thing to hear me explain and entirely something else to experience it."

"Then why investigate? That thing I saw tonight was evil."

"I investigate because it's who I am, I guess. I'm curious, drawn to it. Tell me what happened."

"It formed into a human shape. Black, like a

cutout. Then a gust of cold air that smelled like lavender and citrus rushed through from the opposite direction and hit the entity. It burst into ribbons of black smoke and disappeared." Jack braked for the turn into his driveway. "It's like there's good and evil warring in my home—but why? I built the place, so it's not like an old house with history that got remodeled and stirred something up. The structure itself is brand-new from the ground up."

"Sounds like you need do to some research on the property," Seph speculated.

"What do you mean?" He navigated the truck up the lane, splashing through iced-over puddles.

"Maybe the property has a history, like the Gettysburg battlefield is known for ghostly battles and the spirits of soldiers appearing to visitors." The security light by the path glared down on Seph's face. She squinted against the brightness. "Something might have happened on your land that has imprisoned these spirits."

"How do we go about getting that sort of information?" He parked the truck and shut it off.

"Leave that to me," she answered. "First, let me see what I can find now the team isn't here. Maybe if it's just me and you, whatever is in your home won't feel as threatened."

"Them? Feel threatened?" He snorted, grabbed the bag and wine, then opened his door. "I'm the one that had the hell scared out of me tonight."

Seph chuckled as he shut the door and rounded the pickup to her side. He helped her out and kept a firm hand at the small of her back on their way up to the front door. The urge to lean into him overwhelmed her, but she didn't want to come on too strong. After all, she'd be going back to Detroit any day now.

"It's cold inside," he said, unlocking the door, "but I'll have a fire going in the woodstove in a few minutes. Until then, keep your jacket on."

Jack walked through the house, flipping on light switches and turning on a lamp here and there until the home was aglow and comforting. He dropped the wine and bag on the sofa, then set to crumbling newspaper into little balls and placing them inside the woodstove, followed by a couple handfuls of kindling on top of it. In minutes, fire crackled through the thin sticks and he began laying small pieces of wood in the stove too.

As he worked, Seph wandered through the house. She liked the rustic look of the living room, the country-style kitchen and the simplistic decorating of the hall, bath and two bedrooms that showed a man owned the home. However, the kitchen had a dark aura surrounding the entrance to the corridor, as if someone had tried to stuff a gigantic cloud of soot down it and it had puffed out to stain the edges of the doorway. From the living room door then across the kitchen, a streak of white light was slowly vanishing. Without a doubt, Jack had seen something go down in the kitchen. No wonder he was rattled.

She stopped in the master bedroom, the memory of their possession still fresh in her mind, but she detected no energy. No ghosts stepped forward to speak to her. No evil lurked in dark corners or closets.

She spent a few moments looking at photographs hanging in simple silver frames in Jack's room, each one involving something with motorcycles and people who were obviously members of Frank's MC. In the hall, she found several that showed Jack with an older woman with the same eyes, and a couple were of Jack in his early teens with the same woman, but a tall man accompanied them then. Seph guessed he was Jack's father. It didn't appear he had any siblings. She smiled. At least they had one thing in common.

In the kitchen, she found Jack rummaging through the fridge.

"Pick up on anything?" he asked.

She shook her head. "Whatever is here has left or it's hiding."

He groaned, shut the refrigerator, then raked his hands through his hair.

"Don't worry, Jack." She'd seen clients suffer through this same thing on other cases. It bothered her even more with Jack. He was more than a client. If she wasn't careful, she'd end up with a broken heart. She had a home and a job in Detroit, so the broken heart had to be avoided at all costs.

"You probably think I'm goofy too," he said with his back to her.

"No, I don't. I keep telling you that I've seen this happen numerous times. What the team can't see or feel, I can. There may not be anything here right now, but the residual energy remains. Something was here because I see its residual energy in the kitchen."

"I can't live here if this keeps up," Jack said. "And who would want to buy a haunted house if I tried to sell it?"

"Jack, there's always an answer to any problem." She placed a hand on his shoulder, the heat of his body sending a shockwave up her arm. About to pull away, she gasped as he turned suddenly. Their gazes locked.

"Is there?" he asked.

Unable to make her tongue work, she could only stare up into his sand-colored eyes flecked with gold. It seemed to her she'd seen his eyes before…somewhere. The instant she tried to retrieve the memory, Jack closed the distance between them, invading her personal space.

"Jack," she whispered. "I don't think we should—"

"I don't care," he replied.

Before she could protest, he claimed her mouth.

Chapter Fourteen

Seph couldn't help herself. She melted into him, pressed herself to his body and let him kiss her senseless. Jack ravaged her mouth, bruising her lips, and robbed her of breath. His stubble grated over her skin. She moaned, wanting more of him, needing something—something besides the act of sex. What it was, Seph didn't know, but she sensed Jack was the only one who could solve this unnamable sensation for her.

He tickled the seam of her lips with his tongue, and she opened for him. Plundering her mouth, he deepened the kiss, winding his arms around her so tightly she couldn't have broken free if she'd wanted to. Why did she feel like she was home whenever Jack took her into his embrace?

A groan rolled out of him that stoked the fire burning in her loins. Desire rocketed through Seph. Her only thoughts now were to have him thrusting between her legs. Somehow she got her arms free and wound them around Jack's neck. He murmured his approval, breaking the kiss, allowing her precious air for an instant before he kissed her again and backed her up against the counter.

From the living room, a loud pop in the woodstove brought her back to awareness for an instant before Jack began kissing down her neck. At the firm, wet sensation of his mouth and tongue on her skin, all sounds, the cold kitchen and her worries vanished just as quickly as a snowflake on a hotplate. And oh what a hotplate he was! As Jack continued kissing and caressing her, his all-male aroma invaded her senses, something wild, primal and spicy. Heat poured from Jack, his breath heavy, hands rough and demanding where he'd slid them down her shirt, then up under it.

Seph glided her palms down his arms, reveling in the feel of the corded muscles. She tugged his shirt up out of his waistband, found a T beneath it and hurriedly yanked it free too, desiring only to feel his belly beneath her hands. The moment her palms connected with his skin, he tensed and a growl rumbled out of him that forced her to meet his gaze.

Staring directly into her eyes, he regarded her in a manner that rendered her both speechless and breathless. His eyes glowed gold. She gulped. Had one of the spirits possessed him?

"J-Jack?"

"Seph," he said, blinking the glow away. "I want you so badly it hurts, baby, but I won't make love to you if you're not sure it's what you want too."

Had she seen his eyes glow? Now she wasn't so sure. What she was certain about was how badly she wanted Jack.

"I need you," she said.

He jerked her against him, ripping a startled cry from her, and kissed her until she had to pull away to drag air into her lungs. When he thrust his hips into hers, pinning her ass to the counter's edge, something awoke deep within Seph that left her reeling from its intensity.

"Fuck, I have to have you," he groaned into her ear. "I want to feel your inner walls milking my cock."

She'd never had a man talk dirty to her. Not that she'd had a lot of sexual partners, but the few she'd had were all about making themselves happy and leaving her wondering why there was so much hype about sex. Everything about Jack, however, twisted her feelings, thoughts and sensations into a whirlwind of pure carnal need.

"I want to pound into you until you beg me to stop," he said. Somehow he popped the front clasp on her bra. Her breasts spilled free, and he cupped one in each hand. "I want to hear your cries and moans, feel your legs locked around my hips."

The instant his rough palms touched her breasts, the fire building in her pussy burst into a heat that spread up into her abdomen and down into her inner thighs. She couldn't think, only feel, and the one thing she wanted at that moment was Jack's cock inside her. Placing a hand on either side of his head, she drew him down to kiss her. Need arrowed through Seph. It suffocated her, rendered her a slave to it, pushed her to take the initiative as she'd never done with a man before. She wanted him, and she was going to have him, enjoy him and do it over and over.

Jack growled again, pressing into Seph, bending her back over the counter until her head bumped the upper cabinets. He punished her lips, his breath excited and hot over her cheek. She kissed him back with abandon, running her hands up and down his back, enjoying his hard muscles. He spun her around, eliciting a gasp from her, and began walking her backward toward the doorway.

"Living room," he mumbled against her lips, "not the bedroom, not after…"

She murmured her assent, her hands going to the button and zipper of his jeans.

Instead of moving toward the door, her butt bumped into the table. He tried shifting her to the side, but her hip got wedged between the table's edge and one of the chairs. He grumbled at the interruption and pushed her against the table, spread her legs, stepped between them, then laid her back on the tabletop. She pulled him down with her, the legs of the furniture groaning under their combined weight, and thrust her hips upward a couple times.

"Fuck…" he whispered against her throat.

"Yes," she whispered back, "fuck me."

The snarl he let out pushed gooseflesh over Seph's body. The deep, guttural noises of pleasure he made only inflamed her desire that much more. Everything about the man heightened her senses, shot lust through her veins, and revved her heartbeat so high it thundered in her ears. What would happen when they were one body?

He broke away from her, straightening. "Come on, baby, let's go in—"

She grabbed his hands and jerked him back down to her with strength she didn't know she had. His eyes widened in surprise an instant before his torso connected with hers, his hips nestling perfectly in the apex of her thighs.

She ground against him. "Fuck me," she urged.

"Damn, woman, you're insatiable."

"Jack, please!" If he didn't make love to her soon, she'd explode. The need throbbing in her folds was so intense it actually hurt.

She pumped her hips again. He thrust back. Rising slightly, he worked his cock free from his pants. Grasping him, she found his cock rock-hard, satiny-smooth, throbbing, hot. She let out a growl, the sound coming from low in her throat. He looked at her oddly.

"Baby?" he said. "Are you okay?"

"I'm better than okay," she replied. "Just want you so badly."

"Before we go any further, I should go get some protection."

The idea of using protection both sobered her and ruined the mood. She knew it was important, especially with a new sexual partner, but to feel him bare inside her…

She nodded. "Okay."

With a sigh, he rose, adjusted himself and headed down the hall to the bathroom.

Seph sat up and slid off the table. When her feet made contact with the tile, her knees nearly gave out. Wobbling, she steadied herself against the sink. Intense prickling assailed her skin, forcing a gasp from her. The sensation, like millions of bees stinging all at once, swept from the roots of her hair to the soles of her feet.

"Oh…damn…" She gripped the sink's edge so hard her knuckles ached, but within seconds, the fiery sensation vanished.

Sounds of Jack rummaging in a cabinet or drawer drifted down the hall. She started to go that way to help him look for the condoms, but a puff of icy air wafted over her from behind.

"You're a whore…"

The words were whispered into her right ear. She stiffened. Every hair on her nape stood up. Slowly, Seph turned, unsure what she'd see and finding nothing.

Her senses vibrated like a tuning fork. Without a doubt someone, or something, stood within a foot of her, but this spirit or entity was hiding its form.

"Whores must be punished."

More icy air puffed over her. She started to take a step toward the hall.

"Oh no you don't…"

A force cut off her windpipe. She brought her hands up to her throat to find nothing but more iciness. The entity lifted her off her feet. Eyes bulging, heart flailing, Seph struggled for air as the unseen assailant slammed her so hard against the wall that everything hanging on it rained down onto the floor in a clatter.

* * *

Jack couldn't find the rubbers. He could've sworn he had a couple stashed in the mirrored cabinet.

A thud from the kitchen, followed by a crash and the pings and clangs of things scattering across the tile, startled him. Frightened Seph had somehow gotten hurt, he lunged from the bathroom and rushed down the hall to the kitchen to find her pinned to the wall next to the stove. Seph frantically kicked her feet, which were several inches off the floor. She tore at her throat, eyes wide in pure terror.

"Seph!"

He leaped across the kitchen. Cold enveloped him. He pulled on Seph's hips and she fell into his arms, bearing him backward. The cold swirled over and around them. Seph dragged in air, her breaths ragged, high-pitched.

"Are you okay?" he asked.

Ice-cold settled over them, then a force struck Jack hard enough that it ripped Seph out of his arms and he flew backward into the refrigerator. Stuff on the top of it tumbled to the floor and the countertop. He shook off the blow, somehow managing to keep his feet under him, and faced the stove again. Bent over backward across the burners, Seph struggled to breathe, her hands at her throat again.

"Let her go, you sadistic fuck!" He grasped Seph's shoulders in an attempt to pull her free.

The energy pinning her there twined around them both.

"Release her!" Jack glanced over one shoulder, then the other. "I know you're here too! Wherever you are, help us!"

The aroma of lavender and citrus blew into the kitchen.

Seph met Jack's gaze, her eyes wide, frightened. She wheezed and thrashed as she struggled with the entity. Her eyes flared orange.

Frightened the spirit was trying to possess her, Jack yelled, "Please, help her!"

The sweet scent of lavender and fruit intensified. Somehow, Jack managed to pull Seph off the stove and stumbled into the living room with her. Together, they collapsed on the floor in front of the woodstove. They lay there, gasping.

Jack didn't stay on the floor with Seph for long. He heaved himself to his feet, then helped her up as she still sucked in ragged breaths and shook from head to toe.

"Grab your coat. We're leaving."

She staggered over to the sofa, where she collected her jacket and purse. Jack ushered her to the door, making sure he locked it behind him in case someone decided to pay him another visit with something worse than bags of weed.

He hurried Seph to his truck, got her strapped into the passenger seat, then sprinted around to the driver's side. In moments, he had the pickup pointed back down the lane. As he sped toward the MC, Seph cried softly across from him. Fury claimed Jack, awakening his beast, which he forced into submission. All he wanted to do was go back and rip the dark entity limb from limb, appeasing both himself and his animal.

But how did he fight something that was already dead?

* * *

When they reached the MC, Jack was relieved sweetbutt night had ended. The women were cleaning up the mess left by the poker players and putting away snacks.

"Want a drink, Jack?" Frank asked as they entered the kitchen.

"No, thanks."

Bernadette met Jack's gaze. Her eyes widened. "What happened?"

"Let me get Seph calmed down first," Jack said, "and myself."

"Could I please have a stout drink?" Seph asked as she settled in the chair next to Bernadette.

"Sure." Frank stepped back into the dining room. "Coming right up."

Jack moved behind Seph and placed his hands on her shoulders. She placed one hand, fingers trembling, over his, and his heart swelled at the action.

"The house?" Bernadette stated.

Jack nodded, once.

"Hang on," Luella said. "I want to hear this." After putting away a tub of chip dip, she walked into the living room. Ice clinked from the dining room as Frank made Seph's drink.

"What do you think is going on at your place?" Bernadette asked Jack.

"Between the shots fired at me, the weed planted in the house, Seph getting forced off the road, and now this," Jack said, "I have no idea if it's all tied together somehow, or what the fuck it is." He looked down at his hands on Seph's shoulders and realized he, too, was shaking. This angered his beast further, but he quickly quashed his animal's need for blood.

From the living room, Luella's voice rang out. "All right, you two. Sweetbutt night ended over 30 minutes ago. Get his dick out of your mouth, and you, put it back in your pants!"

Laughter from Frank and Beastman rumbled through the house. Someone grouched back at Luella, but Jack couldn't make out who it was.

"I don't give a shit if you lost track of time or not. The rest of us live here!" Luella snapped. "Go somewhere else if you're not done fucking!"

Footsteps approached the kitchen, then Beer Cans and a sweetbutt Jack didn't recognize entered. Beer Cans tossed them all an apologetic look, bid them good night, then led the young woman out to the carport.

"Luella is a force to be reckoned with." Beastman smiled from where he leaned against the doorframe.

"Damn right I am," Luella replied as she returned. "Members live here as well as their children. Why a few people can't seem to understand that sweetbutt night has strict hours is beyond me. Those two"—she gestured toward the sun porch where Beer Cans and his woman had exited—"are found fucking everywhere at any time of day or night. If they don't start obeying the sex rules for the MC, they can stay out of the main house." She fixed Frank with a pointed look. "Well?"

"Agreed," he said, handing Seph her drink. "I'll have a talk with Beer Cans, don't worry."

She nodded and sat at the table. Beastman moved to stand behind her and began lightly rubbing her neck.

"We'll be back tomorrow" Puppy strode into the kitchen with Callie May. Each woman had a garbage bag full of aluminum cans. They went into the laundry room to dispose of the items in the recycle bins stored there.

"I'll help Puppy finish the cleanup in the morning," Callie May chimed in once they reemerged.

Luella waved good night to the young women. "See you in the morning."

They called out their farewells as they left, the door shutting firmly behind them.

"I'm out of here too." A teen girl exited the dining room, juggling a wad of dirty plastic forks on top of a stack of used paper plates. She tossed them in the trashcan.

Jack couldn't recall which Stellarmi girl she was, but then he had trouble keeping track of all the young wolves in Frank's MC, especially the big Stellarmi family.

"Mom said she'll be late coming up to help with the spring cleaning, Luella," the girl continued. "She has a dentist appointment first thing in the morning, but she'll come straight here once she's done."

Luella nodded and waved to her.

Once the sun porch door shut, quiet finally settled over the kitchen.

"Now that it's just us here," Luella began, "did I miss anything?"

Looking up at Jack, Seph said, "No, I don't think so."

He shook his head. "Bernadette was just asking what I thought was going on out there, but I'm at a loss."

"Are you sure you're okay?" Frank asked Seph. "Bruising is starting to appear on your throat."

"I'm fine"—Seph placed a hand over her throat—"really."

Every time Jack thought about what had happened, he wanted to kill. His beast surged to the surface, demanding blood. He had to keep it under control or he'd let his composure slip and scare Seph worse than she'd been when the entity had attacked.

He couldn't let that happen, couldn't allow her to see he wasn't fully human.

"I think the house needs a cleansing, whether magical or religious," Bernadette stated. "But we need to know what we're dealing with so we know what route to take."

"If someone will drop me off at Rebellion's records office," Seph said, "I can do some research. I think the spirits are tied to the property, not the house."

"Good idea," Luella stated.

"Also," Frank added, "since this is all tied to a club member"—he inclined his head toward Jack—"I think it's time we set up a meeting with Crow. It's bad enough we have another paranormal matter to deal with, we don't need shit from another MC added to it. I really don't feel Crow has any knowledge that some of his boys have gone rogue. The man has worked hard to keep the truce secure between the Wraithkillers and the Werewolves of Rebellion. If it were some of my men who were out stirring shit, I'd want to know about it."

"Although I'm not sure why," Beastman said, "I agree with you. I don't think Crow knows what's going on, either."

"I think you're both right, baby." Luella patted her husband's thigh. "It could be that Crow becomes a strong ally for us."

Beastman leaned down and kissed his mate on top of her head. "Call me paranoid, but after the shit Bloodbath caused between us, the Wraithkillers and the River Rebels, I'm really hoping this isn't another attempt to drag us into a gang war."

"We need answers," Jack added. "I agree with Frank. It's time to start asking questions."

"You look tired, Seph," Bernadette observed.

"I am." Standing, Seph looked at Jack. "Grab us something to drink and meet me under the stairs." With that, she bade everyone good night and left the kitchen.

"Lucky bastard." Beastman offered Jack a grin so big Jack caught a flash of his gold molars.

Jack picked up Seph's tumbler, then headed for the liquor cabinet. He caught a smug expression that Bernadette tossed at Luella and wondered what that was all about. Shrugging it off, he said, "I'm hoping that's the case."

His friends laughed behind him as they hollered their good nights.

In Seph's tiny room, Jack waited until she'd kicked off her shoes and crawled onto the bed. When she was settled with another drink, he started asking her general questions about her interests and got her to talking. Finally, he asked about her life in Detroit, and she told him how she was left on the doorstep of an orphanage when she was only a couple hours old. Stunned, he lay on his side facing her as she told him about her life in the orphanage, how Sister Miranda had become a mother figure to her, and how she began to see, sense and communicate with spirits when she was about three years old, beginning with the head nun who had founded the orphanage over a hundred years ago.

In return, Jack told her about being an only child, that he'd been close to his parents, but after his father had died and his mom had moved to Florida to be with her sister, he'd decided to focus on his love of motorcycles and had drifted from town to town before finding the Werewolves of Rebellion, where he felt he truly belonged. He even told her about restoring the Indian. She seemed genuinely interested in how he'd rebuilt the bike, even asking him questions about the process.

She'd drunk the scotch Frank had poured her and half of the one Jack had made, and now lay batting her eyes as she fought sleep.

"Are you going to make love to me?" she asked.

"Yes, but not now."

She pouted, then to Jack's surprise, two fat tears, one in the corner of either eye, formed and plopped onto her pillow.

Horrified, he asked, "What's wrong?"

"I thought... I mean, I..."

"Good God, woman, I want you. Believe me!"

"You do?" She blinked several times and, thankfully, no more tears fell.

"Yes, very much," he said. "I want you so badly I think you've given me blue balls."

She giggled like a young girl, whether from the alcohol or his comment, he wasn't sure, but he loved the sound of her laughter.

"You've had a rough night," he said gently, "and you're still recovering from a concussion." He stroked a light finger over her throat bruised with honest-to-God fingerprints from whatever had tried to choke her. "When we're finally together, I want you to be healed and lucid."

She frowned at him and he chuckled.

"Baby, right now you're about three sheets to the

wind." He smoothed the backs of his fingers over her upturned cheek. "You're not a drinker, are you?"

"Not really. Mostly an occasional wine cooler."

"Wine coolers?" He chuckled again. "That's pretty much Kool Aid."

She grinned weakly.

Jack set her glass next to the scotch bottle on the little bedside stand, then rolled her over so he could spoon her. For now, holding Seph, having her safely in his arms all night, was the best feeling he could imagine.

"Sleep, baby. I'm not going anywhere tonight."

She let out a contented sigh and relaxed into him.

Despite his worries, Jack found himself drifting off too.

Chapter Fifteen

A couple days later, Bernadette sat at her writing desk with her laptop open. She'd tried to write a few more pages of her new manuscript, but her thoughts kept straying to the latest chaos plaguing the MC. Jack had invested a lot of money, time and dedication into building his new home. Everyone had been so happy for him when he'd finished his place that they'd had a big pig roast right before Thanksgiving to celebrate.

Now he was in danger and Seph was too.

Frank had set up a meeting with Crow, who had agreed to talk with him. That worried her just as much as the evil in Jack's house did. What if the meeting went awry and someone got trigger-happy or brave with a concealed knife?

She didn't want to entertain such thoughts, but it wasn't out of the realm of possibility. All she had to do was remember Bloodbath and the Claiming and Maiming. She shivered.

Rising, she flicked one hand at the laptop and the lid lowered. She wandered downstairs for a snack and a cup of coffee. Alone in the house—a rare occurrence—she prepared the coffeemaker and set it to brewing. Luella and several of the women had taken

Seph, who wanted to research Jack's property, and left for Rebellion to run errands. Bernadette had decided to use the quiet time to work. But her mind wouldn't cooperate. She kept thinking of Frank.

What if she got pregnant and something untoward happened to him? How would she function without him? How could she raise a child, or children, without his guidance, especially if they inherited his lycanthrope genes? As she stared out the kitchen window at the side lawn growing greener with each passing spring day, she fretted more and more about what she should do about the next step in their relationship. The love she had for him increased every day, the depth of the emotion often overwhelming and simultaneously wonderful.

Bernadette turned from the window and gathered items from the fridge for her lunch. She put a turkey sandwich, some coleslaw and a few grapes on a plate, then, with the coffeemaker chugging out its last few drops, she paused it and poured herself a cup. Finished, she headed back upstairs. She had to get some work done while she could.

Back in her room, she motioned toward the laptop, her energy lifting the lid again. She set the plate and coffee next to the computer and settled on the chair once more.

As she munched, her thoughts abandoned her work and instead strayed to children. She enjoyed the little ones who scampered in and out of the main house. Several resided in the community too. As a matter of fact, she'd enjoyed holding one of the new additions to the community the other day and had hated relinquishing the baby to his mother when he had started wailing at feeding time. The infant had smelled like baby powder, a little sour milk, Dreft laundry detergent and that special baby smell only a woman could appreciate. The warmth of the child, his soft gurgles and squeaks as he'd awakened in her arms, the wrinkles and dimples in his hands, wrists and elbows had filled Bernadette with a need she'd never experienced before. Ever since, the desire to procreate, to start a family and build upon it over the next few years had consumed her every free thought. And she welcomed it.

Regardless, worries about beginning and raising a family with Frank plagued her as well. What would it be like to have lycanthrope children and know she'd have only a short time with them before she left this world? They'd go on to live very long lives without her.

The root of her upset struck her, the sandwich suddenly tasteless in her mouth. She couldn't bear having lykoi children and not being with them, not enjoying their lengthy lifespans. If she were lucky, she'd live to be over 80 before she passed, but her children—providing they inherited Frank's DNA— would live decades longer. There were stories about other lycanthrope clans with individuals who were well over 300 years old. Hell, if the rumors were true, their own Mildred was approaching 200.

Could she be happy remaining human, then one day having her lykoi children care for her aging body and deteriorating mind before she left this world?

The thought rattled her right down to her bones.

Was she willing to one day pick up and move to another clan should outsiders start asking questions about her longevity or Frank's?

If it meant keeping her family safe, yes.

The answer she'd been seeking suddenly landed on her as if it were an asteroid. If she wanted to be with her family, see them grow into mature lycanthrope people, and enjoy her mateship with Frank as long as possible, she had only one choice.

Frank had to turn her.

* * *

They'd passed through the front gates with little fanfare, but upon reaching the Wraithkillers' actual compound, Jack found himself staring up at another set of gates, these ones taller, broader, heavier and with guard towers. On each guard tower stood two men with AK-47s at the ready should there be any trouble. His Indian purring smoothly beneath him, he sat between Frank and Beastman on their Harleys. Phil waited on Beastman's other side. Steven, a prospect, Sledgehammer, Beer Cans and Tractor idled behind them. Finally, Crow's guards gave them the okay to enter the Wraithkillers' compound, and the big doors slowly swung back.

Frank, Beastman and Phil led everyone just fast enough to keep from duck-walking their bikes across the last couple hundred yards to the clubhouse. The compound was impressive, and from what Phil had once told him, the place had been upgraded—a lot. Although a run-down farmhouse sat off to the side several yards away from the clubhouse, which was a huge, converted barn, it was obvious by the menagerie of farm equipment from Allis-Chalmers tractors to discs and hay rakes, that the property was still a functioning farm. Between two outbuildings sat about a couple dozen motorcycles of various makes and models.

Pulling up next to Frank, Jack shut down his machine along with his comrades. Two tall, lanky men both packing guns in shoulder holsters and knives on their belts motioned for them to follow. Once Frank and his head men approached the guards, more Wraithkillers moved in behind their group and flanked them as they were ushered into the MC.

Jack had to admit the clubhouse was quite impressive. Where stalls should be now stood offices, living quarters and a gambling room. The design was still barnlike, but more rustic with a definite motorcycle theme right down to the nude and half-naked women sprawled across the leather sectional that encircled a big fireplace in the center of the building. Heat blasted from the hearth, and many of the men wore only their cuts without a shirt. Other sweetbutts lazed around in booty shorts and various bras, some with rhinestones and metal studs.

To the left, several Wraithkillers played either pool at one of four tables or threw darts. Jack stayed alert when several of the members threw hostile looks their way. Some even stepping in front of the sweetbutts who were ogling them hungrily. Lycanthrope men were taller and heavier built than average human men, so it wasn't unusual that they drew the women's attention, something that always caused bar fights.

As they headed toward the bar, they passed another seating area where an orgy of sorts was in progress. Although sweetbutt night at their MC was public sex, it was done in a discrete manner out of respect to nearby lovemakers. The display on the sofas a few yards away even made Jack a little uncomfortable. He'd never seen so many bare asses and wet cocks in one spot in his entire life.

The bar distracted him, though. Impressed, he allowed himself a moment to admire the craftsmanship and uniqueness of it. Several high stools lined the oaken counter. Also oak, the liquor shelves boasted booze from the cheap stuff to some very expensive scotch and bourbons. Crows and ghosts had been wood-burned into the shadowboxes holding the specialty liquors.

From behind the bar, an ornate door opened, and a dark-skinned, raven-haired man greeted them. "Welcome to my club. Frank, it's good to see you."

"Crow," Frank said. "It's been a while."

"Why don't you and your head men join me in my office?" Motioning to the bartender, he added, "Drinks on the house for the rest of Frank's men. Anything they want, got it?"

The bartender, a small, wiry dude, nodded and waved to Jack and the others.

"That one"—Frank pointed at Jack—"needs to join us. He's part of what's going on."

"Good to know," Crow said amicably. He whistled shrilly, the sound brief.

Three men emerged from what seemed like pure shadows, but upon closer inspection, Jack's lycanthrope eyesight picked out several poker tables in the dark corner to the right of the bar.

"Phil. Beastman." Frank jerked his head toward Crow, who had turned to go back into his office.

Jack followed Frank and Beastman into the room with Crow's men bringing up the rear. Inside, a luxurious office with another fireplace, a medium-sized table that looked handcrafted with matching leather-padded chairs, and a multipaned window presented the image of a businessman more than the president of a biker club. Jack wondered where Crow had gotten the money. Although they knew the Wraithkillers dealt in meth and weapons, the MC could be functioning on mineral or gas rights money, too. It seemed that nearly everyone in the tri-county area had jumped on the money bandwagon.

Crow sat at a desk crafted out of the same reddish wood. He slid his penetrating gaze over each of them, then flashed a wide, toothy, startling white smile. As Jack studied the Wraithkillers' president, he couldn't decide if the man was Native American, Samoan, Asian or... He kept his face placid as he pondered the stirrings of an old memory, something his mother had once told him about a race of lycanthropes who could take on the persona of other races mixed into one, so they were dark, mysterious-looking and incredibly dangerous.

One guard stood next to Crow. The other took a spot by the door.

"My second-in-command will be here shortly," Crow finally said. "So, tell me, Frank. What's going on?"

Jack wanted to launch into what had happened to Seph, but bit his tongue. It wasn't his place to talk and protocol had to be maintained.

"It seems four of your men ran someone off the road, nearly killing the person," Frank replied. "A police report was filed."

The guard next to Crow straightened and placed his hand on his weapon. Crow shot a stern look at the guy, who reluctantly stood down.

"How do you know these men were mine?" Crow asked stiffly.

"The woman who was forced off the road in a rental car told the police the men wore cuts with a strange emblem," Frank explained, his tone direct but respectful. "Her description matches the Wraithkillers' patch. They also wore black-visor helmets, which"— he sat back and placed a boot heel on the opposite knee—"struck me as odd, but it's clear that whoever they were, they wanted to make sure they couldn't be identified."

"Who was the driver? One of your old ladies?" Crow asked. "Or a sweetbutt?"

"No," Frank said. "No one tied to my MC. She's a visitor."

"Fuck." Sitting back in his leather chair, Crow placed his arms on the rests and met Frank's gaze without flinching or blinking. "This is unsettling news."

Frank jerked a thumb backward at Jack. "This is Jack Henessy. He saw the bikers run the woman off Drunk's Curve, but he was too far away to identify the motorcycles. If he hadn't reached the woman when he did, she probably would've died, Crow."

It was killing Jack to stand by quietly while Frank handled the discussion, but Frank had a knack for talking to people so they didn't feel threatened. Jack had to play it cool and let him do the work.

A knock interrupted them.

"Come," Crow hollered.

Jack recognized the man who entered the room—

Crow's second-in-command, Firewater. Although average height, the guy was built like a tank and was known for being a retired professional wrestler. He kept his coppery hair pulled back in a long ponytail, wore a full, bushy beard that was almost orange in comparison to his hair, and sported a sleeve tat done all in black and gray for each old lady he'd been with over the years. Halfway up the man's right bicep, a new woman's face was in progress. The guy must switch out his old ladies as much as he did his underwear—both aspects disturbed Jack.

Barrel-chested and thick-armed, Firewater crossed the room to stand at the other side of Crow. "Boss?"

Quickly, Crow filled him in on the news.

Red eyebrows raising in skepticism, Firewater shot a glance at Frank. "We're taking the word of someone's old lady or sweetbutt?" he grumbled.

"No," Crow interjected. "The woman was a visitor to Frank's MC."

"Well, fuck," Firewater said. "After what happened with Bloodbath, this doesn't look good."

"Exactly," Frank added and leaned forward, both feet on the floor. "I felt you should know what happened, Crow, and if we can keep each other informed about anything anyone notices, we might be able to head off another... Well, for lack of a better word—attack."

Nodding, Crow braced his elbows on the armrests and steepled his fingers. "It seems as though someone wants our MCs to be at odds."

No, Jack didn't think that was the case.

"Your man thinks differently?" Crow, fingers still steepled, pointed at Jack with them.

Frank looked over his shoulder at Jack.

"I didn't say anything," Jack said.

"You shook your head," Crow replied. "Just barely, but I caught it."

"I'm sorry." In one step, he stood even with Frank's chair. "I'm sorry, Frank. I was just thinking."

"No, no," Crow said. "Go ahead and share your thoughts. Our clubs have shared a truce now for nearly a year. Neither I nor Frank wants it destroyed, do we?" He looked pointedly at Frank.

"Go on," Frank urged.

"I'm not sure why," Jack began, choosing his words carefully, "but I get the sense someone has a different agenda in mind." Slowly, he told Crow about the planted pot and the shots taken at him. "I can't put my finger on what it is, but I just have this feeling right here"—he fisted one hand and patted the spot just under his breastbone with it—"that tells me there's something else going on."

A long moment passed with Crow staring at Jack so hard that Jack wondered if the man had zoned out.

Finally, Crow blinked and looked at Frank. "Actually, I think your man is on to something. We're not rivals, Frank. Our clubs aren't competing for drug runs or distribution areas, and the Werewolves certainly don't deal in weapons. So that leaves me wondering why some of my men would want to stir shit." He sighed and placed his arms flat on the rests again. "This doesn't make sense."

"What if someone in the club has a vendetta?" Firewater suggested.

Crow glanced up at his second-in-command. "For what reason? Why would he go after a visitor to Frank's club? That doesn't make any sense, either."

"No," Frank said, "it doesn't, but Firewater has a point. You never dreamed Bloodbath was a plant. The River Rebels have been a thorn in everyone's sides, including local residents and the pigs."

"Fuck me sideways," Crow groused. "I don't need a group of stupid fuckers stirring shit. The last thing I want is the pigs looking our way when things have been running so smoothly the last few months."

"If anything else should happen," Frank told Crow, "and as long as it isn't a life-or-death situation, I'll inform you first. I'd appreciate it if you would do the same for me."

Crow rose and held out a long-fingered hand. Frank stood and gripped it.

"Agreed," Crow stated. "I'll have Firewater look into the matter without rousing any suspicion among my members. Keep an eye on your women, Frank. If someone targeted a female visitor, they might try it again with one of your old ladies or sweetbutts."

"We will. Thank you, Crow."

"Nah, thank you. We might not always see eye-to-eye, Frank, but you've never stabbed me in the back. I respect you, so let's keep this truce going. I think it serves both our clubs well."

"Thanks for seeing us, Crow."

Frank motioned for his men to leave.

Following Frank, Phil and Beastman, Jack wrestled with a combination of satisfaction that they had the Wraithkillers temporarily on their side and frustration that they knew no more now than they had when they'd entered Crow's office.

Chapter Sixteen

Later that day, Persephone had been combing the property records all morning for a clue to the problem at Jack's place. Nothing before 1814, when Rebellion was founded, provided any hints as to what had happened, on Jack's place. The only records after that year were of a Rennert man who had purchased the property from the government in 1890. He'd built a couple cattle barns on the land where Jack's buildings now stood and had used it to run cattle until 1931. Then his nephew had inherited the place and also used it for livestock. Later, in the mid-1980s, relatives of the Rennerts had gone in and leveled off a spot to set a house trailer on, where an elderly mother of one of the Rennert cousins had lived for five years. After she'd passed away, the trailer was used as a family hunting retreat for about 20 years before it was abandoned. Seph found a brief newspaper story in *Rebellion's Light* about some teenagers who had set the Rennerts' old, dilapidated trailer on fire, but could find nothing more until she discovered the information about Sam's purchase of the land.

When she'd checked with the records keeper about any surviving relatives of the family who had handed the property down the line, she was told the last of the Rennerts had moved away shortly after the old woman had died.

It seemed Seph would have to return to the house and try to contact the spirits there. After the attack, though, the idea of doing so rattled her, something that didn't normally happen to her on cases. She was accustomed to dealing with the dead or otherworldly spirits, but this entity was full of so much hatred and fury that Seph worried she wouldn't be able to fend it off. Dark spirits tended to use manipulation and trickery. The entity in Jack's home possessed very strong raw energy, energy it seemed able to wield quite well on the physical plane.

She rose and wandered through the records office to the entrance where Tom and Beer Cans stood just outside the door. The men flanked her as she traveled down two flights of marble-tiled stairs to the front steps of the courthouse. She descended those too, then picked out a vacant bench to wait for one of the women to meet her. Tom and Beer Cans stood talking a few feet away but kept flicking their attention to her.

The day had warmed considerably, and, sitting on the sun-heated wooden seat, Seph pushed up the sleeves of her windbreaker and unzipped it. After the cool atmosphere in the hospital, then the cold nights at the MC and Jack's place, she welcomed the sunshine's warmth and comfort.

People hurried back and forth across the square, dodging traffic. Seph let her thoughts wander to Jack as they were prone to do of late. Their erotic encounter in his kitchen never failed to fluster her. Just the thought of his kiss, let alone his hands all over her, or his hot, hard cock in her hands, sent her blood to racing, and thrumming began in her pussy. Then, later in her little under-the-stairs hideaway, it had been wonderful to fall asleep in his arms. When she'd awakened the next morning to find him gone to work, she'd never felt so alone in her life.

But it was time for her to return home.

The thought straightened her spine. Why did the idea of going back to Detroit strike her as such a foreign one?

And who said she had to go back?

That thought actually forced Seph to suck in a startled breath, and she realized she had no desire to go back to the noise, crime, crowds, her dinky apartment or the urban environment.

But she didn't have the funds to move her things down here to Rebellion. And what would she do here? Wait tables? Answer phones for one of the local businesses for minimum wage? She stared across the square at the Taco Bell and groaned. Hell, even though her wages with WHO didn't provide her the high life, they kept her bills paid. She could put a little away each payday toward her condo down payment, and she had some pocket money until the next pay period arrived. Could she live in Rebellion happily while barely earning enough money to subsist?

The idea of scraping by week to week frightened her. She'd done so before she'd found her place with WHO, but this was a new world to her, a new environment, a different way of living. However, she'd watched the way the MC women functioned as a team, had listened to their plans for planting vegetable and herb gardens. She could certainly learn how to live here, couldn't she?

"Persephone!"

She looked over her shoulder. Bernadette and Puppy waved to her as they approached.

Seph stood and walked toward them, meeting them on the corner. Behind her, Tom and Beer Cans kept pace.

"Did you find anything that might help Jack?" Bernadette asked.

"Not a darn thing," Seph replied a little glumly. She quickly explained about the Rennert family and how the property had been handed down through various family members. "That's all I could find. I feel like I'm letting Jack down."

Balmy spring air tossed Puppy's ponytail around her neck. She looked thoughtfully at Seph for a moment, then said, "Just because there isn't anything recorded doesn't mean something didn't happen there."

"That's true." Walking with her friends, Seph spotted the SUV parked in front of the courthouse's side entrance. "I was thinking I might have to connect with the…"

"I know you're a sensitive of some kind," Bernadette stated with a soft chuckle. "You know I'm a witch, right?"

"I've heard people talk."

"Well, she's a good witch," Puppy threw in, "so don't worry."

Tom and Beer Cans joined the two Wolves waiting astride their Harleys parked behind the Suburban.

"I've dealt with many strange things in my line of work," Seph told Bernadette and Puppy, "and I've met

173

a couple other witches, but what I do is… well… dangerous."

"So is witchcraft," Bernadette said with conviction. "Maybe the two of us can work together to solve Jack's case."

"Now that's an idea." Upon reaching the SUV, Seph waited as Carol slid over on the backseat so she could get in. "It might take the two of us to solve this case, Bernadette."

With a nod, Bernadette clambered in the front seat with Puppy climbing in next to her. Luella started the SUV.

Whether or not Seph figured out the case at Jack's home, she had to wonder if she was just a fling in his life. When it was all said and done, she knew only what Jack had told her about himself and that the MC members all seemed to like and respect him. Regardless, what did she and Jack have to base a relationship on?

Most of all, would he even want her to stay?

* * *

"I still think this is a bad idea," Jack said.

He stood in the driveway with Bernadette, Seph, Frank and Beastman. The sun had set about 15 minutes ago and so far the temperature hadn't dropped too much, for which Jack was thankful. Peepers croaked nonstop in the water-filled ditches and in the marshy spot below the pole barn, their frog song almost overwhelming when the wind blew toward the house. Nodding to himself, Jack welcomed the racket. Whenever peepers sang, spring had officially arrived.

174

"You didn't have to come out here too," Bernadette said, looking up at Frank.

"Until we find out who has targeted Seph and Jack," Frank said, "I'm a part of this."

With a hand on the back of Seph's neck to keep her calm, Jack added, "It might be that the same person or people who have been pissing me off of late have turned their attention to you as well."

"But why?"

"We don't know," Frank answered, "and that's the reason we met with the Wraithkillers and told their club president what's going on."

"We had a problem last year with the Wraithkillers," Bernadette explained. "It was caused by an MC that has recently moved into the area. Frank doesn't want another gang war targeting the Werewolves of Rebellion."

"War?" Seph pressed closer to Jack.

He drew her to his side. "Our MC is peaceful, and the Wraithkillers are trying to be peaceful too, but there are one-percenters, such as the River Rebels, who can and will cause trouble." He pointed her in the direction of the path and they began walking toward the house with the others following. "But I think there's another factor involved in the strikes here at my place, and on you, and that worries me more than the spirits in my house do."

Jack didn't like this at all. He couldn't be with Seph 24/7. He had to work to pay his bills. And although at least two guards were always with her, they couldn't protect her against such things as a bullet or even—he gulped and willed his heartbeat to slow—something like a car bomb, which could take out more than one of them. He hoped it didn't escalate to such extremes.

Bernadette stared over at him with wide, worried, green eyes. Frank was right to accompany her tonight.

"Frank, I appreciate you and Beastman helping us out this evening," Jack said. "I just hate it that this stupid shit"—he gestured toward his house—"is affecting the MC too."

"I would've been here regardless," Beastman rumbled next to the porch steps. "Besides, Luella would've kicked my ass if I hadn't."

They all laughed, but Jack knew Luella well enough to know that if Beastman had refused to come with them, she probably would have picked the man up and thrown him here.

"Well," Seph said, glancing around, "where's this lady you said would help us?"

"Scary Mary," Bernadette told her, "and she should be here any—"

"I'm right here."

Jack jumped with the rest of them.

"Damn it, woman," Beastman growled. "I wish you wouldn't do that!"

A robust woman moved out of the shadows created by the trees in the front yard. She strode into the security light casting its glow over the front porch. Jack had seen the black woman at the MC a few times when she'd met with Bernadette, but he'd never had any one-on-one dealings with her. He'd heard the rumors, though, but based on what he knew from Bernadette working with her, the woman, although a powerful witch, practiced only white magic. Scary Mary halted next to their group, her long salt-and-pepper locs swinging around her shoulders, a hand-rolled cigarette with a red ember between two fingers. The aroma of cloves reached Jack.

"There's much negative energy here," Scary Mary announced. She focused on Seph, her eyes inky in the feeble light. "You're a medium, aren't you?"

Seph nodded.

Motioning to Bernadette, Scary Mary said, "Come, child. We'll need to provide some security for her."

About to ascend the steps to the porch, Jack paused when Seph stopped.

"I need to delve into what's on the property," she said to Jack. "Like I told you earlier, the only residence here was a house trailer, so something must've happened on the land itself to bind spirits here." She moved away and stepped off the path. "Follow me, but try to keep quiet."

"Let's cast a protection ward first," Scary Mary said. "Bernadette."

The witch stood in front of Seph, and Bernadette stood behind her. They held hands, enclosing Seph between them. The two women closed their eyes and said something in a language Jack didn't recognize but that sounded a lot like Latin. Finished, they released each other's hands, and Scary Mary withdrew a plastic zippered bag from one of her skirt pockets. From it, she withdrew a handful of its contents and pitched it over Seph. The scent of sage filled the air. A brief flash lit up the little area around the women, and what looked like ashy embers floated on the air to wink out as quickly as they'd appeared.

The display unsettled Jack a bit, but upon

thinking about it, he rationalized that if he could deal with a malignant spirit that had tried to kill Seph, a little flash and some sparkles was nothing in comparison.

"Fucking magic," Beastman whispered next to Jack. "It makes my fur stand on end."

"With good reason," Frank whispered back. "But now it's different between lykoi and witches."

A snort erupted from Beastman. "Not true. It's only with *certain* witches, such as her."

"I suppose you're right," Frank replied.

Jack knew the history of lycanthropes and witches, how over the centuries witches cursed people to become werewolves and how, over time, so many werewolves came into existence that they formed clans and began having cursed families. But if Bernadette trusted Scary Mary, he would too. Anything to keep Seph safe.

* * *

The magic would have rattled anyone else, but Seph had dealt with the paranormal for so long that the ward Bernadette and Scary Mary cast didn't bother her at all. In fact, she welcomed it. If the malevolent spirit was any indication of what she was about to encounter, she'd need all the protection she could get.

Glancing at Jack, who gave her a smile of encouragement, she walked out into the front yard with Bernadette and Scary Mary flanking her. She consoled herself with the knowledge of the ward there to protect her and opened her mind while simultaneously keeping an image of white light around herself as a precautionary measure.

Dark energy pervaded the area. It emanated from the earth, thrummed through the trees and pulsed up their roots. An inky form arose from the ground to take a humanoid shape several yards in front of her. To her right, Scary Mary sucked in a sudden breath, one that said she also sensed or saw the entity.

Seph walked slowly toward it, but stopped within a dozen paces of it. "Who are you?"

Instead of answering, the figure developed red, glowing eyes, embers from hell.

"Who are you?" she said more forcefully. "Why are you here on this property?"

The silhouette darkened considerably, becoming almost solid, yet ebony wisps of what looked like oily spoke twirled around the top of its head, at its fingers and around its feet. The thing actually blinked as it regarded her.

It was sizing Seph up.

"What do you want?" she asked with a firmness she didn't feel.

Images of total control, of someone bound hand and foot, prostrate at the feet of a man Seph couldn't fully see, bombarded her mind. The one bound struck Seph as feminine.

"Is the one you have tied at your feet?"

"Yes..."

"Is she the female ghost who is also here?"

The entity remained silent, but Seph interpreted its refusal to answer as a yes.

"What did she do to deserve punishment?" she asked.

Betrayal struck Seph with such force she staggered back a step.

179

"She was a whore…"

The women each placed a hand on one of Seph's shoulders to brace her. Finding her footing, she resumed her spot in front of the spirit.

"Who are you?" she asked again. When the spirit said nothing, Seph tried a different tactic. "Who is the woman who betrayed you?"

"Wife."

"Your wife betrayed you?"

"Adulterous whore…"

"So why are you here now?"

Again, nothing came from the entity. Clearly it had secrets, ones that would shed much light on the situation here at Jack's home.

"What you're doing here is wrong," Seph stated. "You're not welcome here."

"He awoke me… Found that infernal machine… Now you're here, another whore just like she was…"

A wave of energy shot toward Seph in the form of a smokey cloud. Her feet left the ground. Then, just as suddenly as she'd gone airborne, the air rushed from her lungs and she lay gasping for breath as she blinked up at the stars. On either side of her, Bernadette and Scary Mary heaved in ragged breaths. The men rushed to them. Except for the use of "fuck" over and over, the rest of the men's words were jumbled and confusing until Seph came back to herself enough that she could sort through the chaos.

"Persephone!"

The croaking peepers penetrated her consciousness. She finally focused on Jack's face above hers, his eyes worried, deep lines of anxiety furrowing his forehead and bracketing his mouth.

"I'm okay," she said and sat up. She looked over at Bernadette, who Frank was helping up. On her other side, Beastman grasped Scary Mary's hands and hefted her to her feet.

"I thought you cast magic to protect yourself?" Beastman asked Mary.

"We did, but it was to safeguard against possession, not an energy strike." Mary got her bearings and shook dirt out of her locs. "You okay, Bernadette?"

"Yeah, just shaken," she replied. "Persephone?"

"I'm fine too," Seph answered. As if she weighed nothing, Jack lifted her and set her on her feet.

"What the hell just happened?" he asked her.

"Right now," she began shakily, "all I know is that the entity wants to maintain control and that he's pissed off at his wife, who I'm assuming had an affair."

"Who are they?" Frank questioned.

"I'm not sure, but I think the entity's wife is the female ghost here." She looked up into Jack's eyes. "I think her interference when he strikes is what has him more pissed than usual."

"Ah," Mary said sagely, "the entity fears it's losing control over her."

"Exactly." Seph looked over at Bernadette and Mary.

"But what's he...?" Jack shook his head. "What are they doing here?"

"The dark one wouldn't answer many of my questions, so we don't know much more than we did before."

A gentle breeze wafted over the lawn. Crisp

spring air swirled around them, along with the aroma of citrus mingled with lavender.

"She's here," Jack said.

"No." Seph shook her head. "She only passed through. The dark one is keeping her away from us."

"Persephone is right," Scary Mary agreed. "I felt the woman spirit pass us." She dipped her head toward Seph and smiled grimly. "One thing I can add is that the entity is particular nasty and it's determined to keep control. The energy that came from it was so strong I couldn't miss it."

"Neither could I," Bernadette agreed.

"So what do we do?" Jack asked.

"Go home and have a six-pack or two?" Beastman suggested.

Frank backhanded him across the chest.

"Sorry." Beastman rubbed the place Frank had struck, then stared at his feet.

Amused, Jack snorted and looked over at Seph again.

"I need to investigate a little more"—she threaded her fingers with Jack's—"but I don't think it will do any good tonight. The dark spirit will be on guard to keep me from talking to the woman."

"I think she's right," Bernadette said.

"Agreed." Bobbing her head, Scary Mary produced a coffin nail from a skirt pocket.

"Let's head to the MC, then," Frank said. "Mary, would you like a ride since your place is over the hill from us?"

"As nippy as that air is," she replied, "I'll take you up on that offer."

As Seph wandered back to Jack's pickup, his arm

loosely draped around her waist, she knew she couldn't leave these people and go back to Detroit. Somehow she had to figure out a way to make a living here and remain close to the Werewolves of Rebellion, whom she'd begun to consider her family.

But first she had to help Jack solve the haunting of his home. Cold pushed at her back, an iciness that said she'd better leave before the evil here decided to wreak havoc tonight. Shivering, she leaned into Jack's embrace, knowing she'd do anything to help him and keep him safe.

Chapter Seventeen

Bernadette finished her last bite of pound cake. Luella had baked two cakes that afternoon, then sliced them up for the evening snack and brewed a strong pot of coffee. Although Bernadette was learning more and more about cooking and recipes, she didn't think she'd ever have the knack to take a few simple ingredients and turn them into something scrumptious like Luella could. Where Bernadette was a magical witch, Luella was a culinary witch.

"I think your pound cake is my favorite dessert, baby," Beastman said as he placed his plate and fork in the sink. He kissed her, then patted her on the ass. "Finish up in here and let me give *you* some dessert."

"I swear," Luella grumped but smiled the entire time, "your appetite for sex is worse than your appetite for food. It's a wonder I can walk at all."

His deep laughter filled the kitchen. "Don't be long, babe. Those dishes will be there in the morning."

She huffed and began washing them. "That's easy for him to say. He's not the one who has to look at them in the morning."

"I'll help you," Seph said.

At the table across from Seph, Jack glanced up

sharply, then quickly focused on gathering the cake crumbs on his plate with his fork. At the distraught look on Jack's face, Bernadette almost burst out laughing. It was clear he had other plans for the remainder of the evening. The wait would only make him appreciate his time with Seph even more. She grinned. If he got his way, Bernadette won the bet.

Seph rose with her dishes and placed them in the sink. She then moved to Luella's other side and began rinsing the plates, cups and utensils.

"Frank?" Bernadette said.

He set his coffee mug down. "Hmm?"

"I want to talk to you."

A puzzled frown marred his brow. "Okay. I'm done here." He handed Luella his dishes.

Butterflies exploded in Bernadette's belly. Although she was determined to tell him her decision, the idea of being turned still frightened her silly. Maybe she should wait and reserve a table at a restaurant, then give him her news, make it a celebration? As she crossed the living room to the stairs, she shook off the thought and stepped over a prospect's legs where he sat sprawled watching TV. The best place to give Frank her decision was in their private room, a safe, comforting place for both of them.

Upstairs, she threw open their bedroom door and flipped on the overhead light. The aroma of Gain laundry detergent hung in the air. She looked over at the bed. Luella had stripped their bedding and had remade their bed with clean sheets, and even swapped out the comforter for one of the alternates they'd laundered a few days ago. Mentally, she made a note to thank her best friend for her thoughtfulness.

Frank shut the door behind them. "This is about turning you, isn't it?"

Anxiety clenched her gut. "Yes."

"And what have you decided?" He shrugged out of his cut, followed by his shirt and stood bare-chested in front of her.

She took a moment to appreciate him—her man and lifemate. The idea sent tingles to her crotch. The thought of more than mere decades with him pleasuring her with that amazing physique shot more heat to her pussy. She tried to open her mouth and tell him what she'd decided, but words failed her. She wanted to live as long as she could in the embrace of Frank's love, watch their children have children of their own, and she even wanted to be around when her grandchildren gave her great-grandchildren and even great-great-grandchildren. The idea of the new people who would be brought into their family left her anticipating the names and personalities that would accompany each new soul.

"Sweetheart?" he urged. "Just say it. I won't be upset with you."

Bernadette took a moment to admire him as he was probably worrying that she was going to refuse being turned. His brilliant tat sleeve always enthralled her, the artwork incredibly realistic. She loved the lifelike wolf draped over his shoulder. The wolf then blended into the diamonds and sapphires midway down his arm and transformed into leaves and thorns and finally barbed wire that encircled his wrist. She never tired of looking at his flat, taut belly and broad, thick chest. Meeting his concerned gaze, his dark, dreamy eyes full of hope and worry, she allowed herself to meld with his soul. Frank was a good man, a fair, just man. One who had the responsibility of not only the MC, but also his clan and the entire community below the main house.

She found she was looking forward to creating their first child together. With Frank at her side, their children would grow up to be wonderful, caring people.

Her fear vanished.

"I've decided I do want you to turn me," she whispered, her words shaky. At his surprised expression, she rushed on. "I know by letting you do so means there's no going back for me. I want to see our children grow into adults. I want to be with you for our very long lives and be here to see our lineage progress for as long as possible."

She almost laughed at his expression as it changed from surprise to delight.

"Are you sure about this?" he asked. "I mean, *really* sure? Like you said, once turned there's no going back to being purely human."

"Positive."

Before she could say anything else, he crossed the distance between them so fast she gasped. He kissed her hard, robbing her of breath, then just as suddenly, he released her lips and wrapped her in his arms.

"God, I love you," he said. "You have no idea how happy this makes me."

His words rocketed happiness through her, followed by intense warmth. She squeezed him back as hard as she could.

"So what do we do next?" she asked. For the second time that night, butterflies erupted in her belly.

"I know it's painful, so I really don't want to be somewhere the people in the house will hear me."

"Don't worry," he mumbled into her hair. "We have a ritual of sorts that we do, something that helps the process. It won't take the pain away, but you'll have comfort." He stepped back and held her at arm's length, gripping her shoulders. "I'll ask you one last time, Bernadette—are you positive you want me to turn you?"

"Yes."

He nodded, moved away from her to pull his shirt back on, then motioned for her to follow him. "We'll have to"—he made air quotes—"wake Beastman and Luella."

Laughing, she followed him out into the hall and down it to the couple's bedroom, where Frank knocked on the door.

"Yes?" Luella called. "Door's open."

Frank poked his head inside and announced their news. "I need you as a Witness for Comfort," he said. "Beastman, you'll be the Monitor."

"Dude, I'm really happy for you," Beastman said loudly, "but can't it wait until after I get my dick wet?"

The sound of a slap fired through the open door.

"Ow!" Beastman roared. "I was half kidding!"

"Get your hairy ass dressed and let's get going," Luella ordered.

Bernadette placed a hand over her mouth, hiding her smile, but when Frank turned around, he was chuckling. He shut the door, then drew her into his arms.

"Turning you needs to be out in the woods," he

said. "Normally, we'd just disrobe here, but since we have non-clan members living among us, we try to be a little more discrete. Not everyone is comfortable seeing naked people walking around. There are some still scared from the Claiming and Maiming too."

Unsure how she'd feel about her friends seeing her naked, she began to tremble.

"Aw, sweetheart," he soothed. "Don't worry. Lycanthropes have no judgment of the physical form. Besides, your body is exquisite."

The door opened. Luella beamed at her and Beastman scowled.

"I'm sorry for interrupting you," Bernadette said.

"Nah, it's okay." He glowered at Luella. "But someone is gonna have to make it up to me."

"Oh, for the..." Obviously exasperated, Luella looked up at her mate. "How about a blowjob, followed by the 69, then an extra-long fucking session?"

He grinned, his bushy, yellow beard bunching at the corners of his mouth. "Well, that's a good start."

Frank burst out laughing. "Let's get going."

* * *

Jack smiled as Seph snuggled against his side. There wasn't a lot of room on the single bed, especially with his bulk, but it made for a good excuse to cuddle. He had put a fiver in the movie money jar in the kitchen, then he and Seph had chosen an action movie to watch. She'd insisted that she liked action films, so he wasn't going to argue.

"That was a good movie," she said.

"Yeah, I really liked it." He started channel-surfing. "What else would you like to watch?"

"It doesn't matter."

She lay as if she were watching TV, but when her hand landed on his thigh next to his crotch and the heat of her palm penetrated his jeans, he couldn't keep his dick under control. It swelled until it pressed painfully against his zipper.

"I want you, Jack."

Had he heard her correctly? He swallowed, hard.

"Make love to me?"

His raging hard-on had become unbearable. He tried not to think about it, but the moment she palmed his groin, all reason fled his brain. "There's…not much…room in here," he managed to squeeze through his tight throat.

"As long as I'm close to you," she said, "I don't care."

She moved away and sat looking at him, her eyes sleepy, hair tousled, skin flushed.

Jack rose and immediately cracked his head on the low, slanted ceiling. She giggled, then slapped her hands over her mouth.

"Sorry," she mumbled through her fingers.

He chuckled, rubbing the offended spot. "No, you're not."

She giggled harder. "No, not really."

"If I'm taking off my clothes, then so are you." He grinned down at her.

Slowly, she stood and began unbuttoning her blouse. He couldn't take his eyes off her fingers. As each button fell away to reveal her pristine white bra beneath, he couldn't imagine not having Seph at his side. He had to figure out a way to keep her here with him. She'd admitted she had no family, so what did she really have to go back to in Detroit? Besides, with her abilities, she could open her own paranormal investigation office or even work with the police departments in the area on cold cases.

"You're not taking off your clothes," she said, jarring him back to the present.

"I was lost in thought," he replied.

"About?" she asked and unhooked her bra.

When her breasts spilled free, all his thoughts evaporated. With a low growl, he shucked his shirt, unfastened his jeans and peeled them off along with his socks and underwear before Seph had even finished pushing her slacks all the way down her legs.

She snorted in amusement. "Eager?"

"Woman, you have no idea how badly I want you."

"Then show me."

He helped her pull off her jeans, panties and socks, then drew her to his body. The contact of her warm, silky skin against his was almost enough to make him come. Fuck, she was all soft curves and silky planes. He couldn't wait to sink his cock into her hot core.

"Oh," she whispered, looking up into his face.

That did it. The complete trust in her eyes coupled with the raw desire in them was his undoing. Jack claimed her mouth, ravaging her lips. He molded her to him, her curves pliant against his hard body, her upper thighs smooth, warm, tantalizing. His cock throbbed where it lay sandwiched between them. He deepened the kiss, wanting to devour her and absorb every tiny part of her sweetness. This woman had captured his curiosity, his inner wolf and his human side. He couldn't bear to lose her.

He broke the kiss. "Wallet."

"Wh-what?" She blinked rapidly, her eyes clearing of lust.

"My wallet. In my pants." He sucked in a much-needed breath. "Protection."

"Oh." She smiled and climbed onto the bed.

Lycanthropes were immune to sexually transmitted diseases, so he had to keep up pretenses so she wouldn't suspect anything out of the ordinary or ask questions. Fumbling through the pockets of his jeans, he finally found his wallet and retrieved the condom stashed there while mentally cursing that he had only the one. Hell, in this house, every bedroom drawer was probably brimming with rubbers for the humans, so if Seph was up to more than one round, he'd find one of the guys and bum some condoms.

When he turned to face Seph, he nearly swallowed his tongue as he sucked in a big breath. She lay on the bed, the pillows propping her up, legs splayed and her bare cunt presented to him. He devoured her with his gaze, unable and unwilling to move, wanting only to appraise every square inch of her beautiful body, to admire her glorious clit, pink, swollen and glistening as Seph waited for him. She smiled languidly and slid one hand down to her pussy where she parted her folds.

"Fuck, woman." Jack gulped noisily. His inner beast surged to the surface, forcing him to close his eyes so Seph wouldn't see the unholy glow he knew was shining in them due to the heat and prickling in his eyes. "I'll try not to be"—he gulped again as a tremble raced through his body—"too rough with you."

"I like it rough."

"F-f-fuck," he whispered. He spoke to his wolf, forced it to obey, and when he was sure he could look at her without revealing himself, he opened his eyes. He swept his gaze over her nakedness. Even with her bruised temple and throat, she was still gorgeous. "You're incredible, Seph. Beautiful."

With quaking fingers, he tore open the condom wrapper and sheathed himself. Even to his own hands his cock felt like a steel rod. He hoped he didn't hurt her.

He sat on the edge of the bed. Above them, someone ascended the stairs, each step creaking beneath the person's weight. From the little television, the theme music to *Law and Order* began to play.

"I really like your shoulder tattoo," she said. "It suits you."

He looked over at the interlocked kings, queens and aces playing cards interlocked with a larger jack right in the center of his upper arm all done in black ink. It had hurt like hell, but the tat had turned out amazing.

"Come here." Seph held her arms out to him.

Jack didn't need to be told twice. He settled between her thighs and began kissing every part of her that he could. He began with her lips, trailed across to her earlobes, then down the cord of her neck to her collarbones and on into the valley between her breasts. He loved her tits. They weren't huge, nor where they small. Her breasts were more than a handful, firm yet

193

pliant. He latched on to one of her pale nipples, and she rewarded him by arching her back, pushing the fleshy globe farther into his mouth, clenching his hair in her hands.

"Mmm…" he groaned and flicked the nub harder.

She cooed and arched farther. He sucked on her nipple until the tip turned into a tiny stone. Wiggling beneath him, she managed to slide herself down until his cock was nestled in the apex of her thighs. Fuck, he wanted her so badly, he feared he'd hurt her. Needing to distract himself, Jack eased himself down to her mound.

"Mmph," she breathed, tugging on his head. "Want you."

"You'll have me, baby, don't worry." He nuzzled her folds with his mouth, eliciting a startled squeal from her. He grinned and did it again, receiving the same delightful reaction. "If I don't distract myself," he told her, "I may not last long."

"Don't care…" She sat up slightly, threading her fingers into his hair.

Instead of allowing her to draw him back up her body, Jack plunged his tongue into her pussy. Seph stiffened, her entire torso and hips rising off the mattress. He chuckled, slid his hands and forearms under her ass so he could grasp the curve of her hips, and jerked her soundly to his face. He pushed his tongue in and out of her rapidly and ground his face into her folds, her musky odor intoxicating him.

"Oh…my…" Her words died on a squeaky note.

He pushed his tongue in and out of her opening, imitating the action of sex. Squirming, pleading, moaning and gasping, Seph writhed against him until she began a thrusting motion in time to his pumping tongue. The more excited she became, the muskier her scent and the more her juices flowed. He paused to give his tongue a break and sucked on her clit.

"Jack!"

He sucked harder.

"Fuck," she squealed.

He flicked the nub, then drew back slightly to look at his work. Her clit, red and swollen with arousal, stood at attention slicked with his saliva and her fluids. Leaning forward, he took it between his lips again and sucked anew.

"Oh...oh...oh..." Seph thrust faster.

He sucked harder still.

"Jack...I don't know how much more I can take."

"Come for me, baby," he mumbled against her.

"I don't think I can..." She gasped and shuddered. "I'm right there, but can't—"

He shoved his tongue into her core again. She let out a strangled cry, stiffened, then began bucking convulsively.

Chapter Eighteen

Bernadette shivered in the cold. She placed her clothes with everyone else's on the end of the pier, then took Frank's hand and let him lead her behind Luella and Beastman. Luella looked like a white goddess in the starlight, her long blonde hair hanging down her back in a sheaf of white gold. Although Beastman wasn't her type, Bernadette had to admit he'd been hiding an impressive body beneath his baggy jeans and big T-shirts and flannels.

Their friends led them around the edge of the pond. Moonlight gilded the ripples caused by the breeze. The cold, squishy lawn beneath Bernadette's feet had already begun to send chills up her legs. She shivered.

"Don't worry, sweetheart," Frank said, his voice low. "You'll be warm in no time."

She nodded and focused on the three-quarter moon rising over the tree line.

"It's okay," he said. "The hard part will be over very soon."

"Frank?" Luella said over her shoulder.

"Yeah?"

"Shut up. You're scaring her."

He tightened his grip on Bernadette's hand. "Am I?"

"Yeah, a little," she said.

"I'm sorry, sweetheart."

He drew her to his side, and she took comfort in his warmth.

Beastman went into the trees first, then Luella, Bernadette and Frank. They walked for what felt like hours to Bernadette, but she knew it could only have been five or ten minutes. Although the moon was bright and the spring leaves still tiny, there was little light and Bernadette marveled at how well the others could navigate in the darkness with their lykoi eyesight. Would hers be as keen as theirs once her transformation was complete?

Sticks poked the soles of her feet. Little rocks bruised her heels. The wind gusted up from the creek where she often met Scary Mary when it was warm enough to have an outdoor magic lesson. Now, naked as the day she was born, Bernadette started shivering until her teeth chattered. Every hair on her body tightened painfully. Normally she would have enjoyed the crisp air tinged with wet pine needles, but now the cold was pure agony.

"Here we are," Beastman rumbled from somewhere ahead of her.

Frank brought her to where Beastman stood in a clearing, the moonlight filtering softly through the opening. Two large rocks stood like sentries on either side of the area. Luella climbed onto the top of one and stood with her arms at her sides. On the opposite rock, Beastman did the same. Somehow, with her friends standing naked in the moon's glow, the severity of the situation settled over Bernadette. This

197

was real. It was happening to her. When it was over, she'd never be the same physically.

For an instant, she almost called the whole thing off, but she pushed her fear aside and thought only of Frank and the beautiful gaggle of children that was in their future. She wanted this, wanted to be with Frank as long as possible.

"Ready?" Frank asked, startling her.

"I…I think so."

He smoothed one hand down her neck, then over her chest and one breast. "Stay calm, sweetheart. You're about to become a part of me through a bond that is impossible for humans to comprehend. You'll be one of the few to experience such a bond."

He gripped her hand and tugged her into the center of the clearing. There, she looked up at the billions upon billions of stars winking brightly and the luminous moon reflecting the sun's light. Frank palmed her pussy, and she sucked in a breath that blared her shyness to the trees.

"Don't fight it," he told her. "Beastman and Luella each fulfill a role. We need two witnesses to confirm your willing transformation into a lycanthrope. Luella is also to offer you comfort when the timing is right. Beastman is the Monitor, the one who will help me keep you corralled to a specific area once you've turned. That way you won't get lost in the woods."

"Okay." The word shook from her mouth.

"I know you're cold, but it won't be much longer."

"We're ready, Frank," Beastman called from his perch. "We'll start shifting the moment Bernadette goes into transformation."

"It's time," Frank said.

Looking into his eyes, she nodded.

He drew her into his arms, kissed her, then stepped back. Staring up at the sky, the moonlight washing him in silver, he stood quietly for a moment before stiffening with a low moan. He pitched forward, landing on his hands and knees. With back bowed and arms rigid, he let out a low, steady growl as the change swept over him. Bernadette stood awestruck as she always did whenever he transformed into a werewolf. His body twisted, bones shortened and lengthened, fur covered skin, fingers shifted into paw-like hands. His ears disappeared to reappear as pointed ones higher on his head. A muzzle took shape where his nose and mouth had been. In minutes, Frank had taken the full form of his lycanthrope counterpart. He rose to his paw-feet and faced her as a very large, ebony-furred beast.

She'd never feared Frank before, but in that instant, a tiny primeval part of her whispered "run." Instead, she stood her ground, her entire form quaking, and cursed the biting wind. Frank stalked toward her, his eyes glowing amber.

She flicked a glance at Luella to her right, standing tall, slender and beautiful as though she were a Greek goddess. To her left, she caught sight of Beastman, his presence huge and almost foreboding.

She returned her attention to Frank and jumped as he took her into his furry arms. She knew he'd been changing into a werewolf long enough that he shared the beast's mindset and controlled it, but until now, she'd never allowed him to embrace her in his full wolf form, for he'd warned her that his inner beast could still overpower him at times and take over when it was excited. She tried not to be frightened, but when he suddenly bent her neck to one side and bit down on her shoulder, terror bloomed within her along with intense pain.

She screamed.

* * *

As she'd lay next to Jack watching the movie, Seph couldn't stop the arousal that kept growing in her. No man had ever affected her the way Jack did, and by the time they were halfway through the movie, all she could think about was spreading her legs for him and letting him fuck her until she couldn't breathe. The need for sex with him overpowered her, rendered her helpless and shackled her in its steely grip. She didn't understand why it was so powerful, so overwhelming, but she had to have Jack—and oh how he did not disappoint!

Now, with Jack laving her pussy and sucking so deliciously on her clit, Seph couldn't seem to stop bucking. Wave after wave of intense sensation pierced her core and washed through her body all the way out to her toes and fingertips, leaving them tingling with acute sensation. Jack kept lapping at her until her orgasm finally faded and the roughness of his tongue shot pain through her over-sensitized pussy.

"Oh! Oh! P-please stop, Jack. Oh!"

He eased her down onto the mattress and lay with his head on her belly as she panted and gasped. What had come over her to make her want to make love with abandon? Sure, she'd wanted him for days, but this— this was something primeval.

"Now that I've gotten a grip on myself," he murmured, "I can make love to you without hurting you or coming too soon."

"I don't know if I have"—she gulped in air—"another orgasm in me."

He laughed, the deep sound of it enfolding her in its embrace. "Honey, I'm just getting started."

"Wh-what?" Incredulous, she raised her head to look down at him.

"You heard me."

He shifted between her legs and settled himself farther up her body so his cock lay firmly against the lips of her pussy.

"I'm drained," she said, but was already aroused. How was that possible? She shouldn't want him again so quickly, but the need to be one with him was already consuming her in its searing fire.

"Do you still want me?" he asked. "I mean, I can stop now—"

"No! I want you. I don't know how after that bone-melting orgasm, but I do."

"Good, because I mean to have you."

With that, he shifted abruptly and pushed into her, filling her, stretching her. Seph's eyes widened. Holy hell, she wasn't going to be able to accommodate him! Regardless, something awakened within her and she pushed upward with her hips and, despite the length and breadth of him, she impaled herself on his cock. This time his eyes widened. He drew in an abrupt breath. If possible, he hardened within her even more, his cock so fucking steely it felt like a hot piece of pure metal inside her.

She had to move, had to have him fully seated inside her. She thrust her hips.

201

A growl unlike anything she'd ever heard before rolled out of him. She darted her gaze up to his eyes. There was no denying it. His eyes *were* glowing. Oddly enough, the glow didn't frighten her. Instead, her lust for him exploded. She had to move, had to make him move. Something stirred in her mind. It rushed up to the surface of her consciousness and butted its presence into the spot directly behind her eyes. It frightened her, yet at the same time, it seemed so natural, but just as quickly as that part of her awakened, it slid back into the deep recesses of her mind, leaving her to pure sensation and the incapacitating need to have him fuck her senseless.

He lay balls-deep inside her. The infernal itch had reawakened in her core and was quickly turning into something that was both wonderful and infuriating in a way she could not label. A fiery sensation erupted on her skin, followed by a maddening stinging that swept over her body.

"Mmm…Jack…fuck me into the mattress."

He snarled, the glow in his eyes brightening, and began thrusting into her so hard he scooted her up the mattress. He paused for an instant to place a pillow between the top of her head and the wall, then began thrusting again in earnest. The sensation of his cock firmly inside her, forcing her inner walls to accept him, the head of his dick hitting her cervix, created a hunger in Seph that frightened her. She couldn't get enough of him, wanted more of his cock, had to have him deeper, harder, faster.

"Oh…fuck…" she cried.

"Fuck is right," he growled into her ear. "I'm going to fuck you until you beg me to stop."

"Jack... harder..."

He rammed in and out of her like a madman. Someone rapped on the door and hollered for them to quiet down because they were trying to watch TV, but she ignored the voice, and Jack pumped into her harder still. The bedframe groaned beneath them. Jack pushed as deeply as he could go and held still.

"No!" She slapped his ass. "Keep going."

"I don't want to come yet."

"Jack, *please*!"

He began pummeling her again. Each time his cock fully entered her, Seph felt as though she was truly one person, one soul with Jack. She had to have him deeper. Fuck, she couldn't control herself. She wiggled her ass farther down into the mattress and wrapped her legs around his driving hips.

"Oh, God...Seph..." He kept thrusting. "Want to fill you up, baby. Got to have you. Make you mine..."

At his words, the stinging swept over her skin again. For a long minute all she could do was hang on to Jack, clasping him so hard around the hips her legs protested, but eventually the horrible tingling passed. Once it was gone, she returned to meeting him thrust for thrust.

He paused and sucked one of her nipples into his hot mouth. She cried out, her insides pulsing with need, but her orgasm still taunted her at a distance.

"I need..."

He released her nipple and switched to the other one, the roughness of his tongue torturing the hard nub.

"Oh... I need...."

He raised up to look at her. "What, baby? What do you need?"

She tossed her head from side to side. "I don't know…" She pushed him back with strength that shocked her, and he withdrew from her body, falling backward against the wall so hard the plaster buckled. Before he could move, she launched herself into his lap, settling her cunt down over his still-hard, wet cock.

She rose up and down several times as Jack gripped her hips, guiding her motions, but even at this angle, he still wasn't deep enough and thrusting hard enough for what she craved. She looked directly into his eyes. "Just…fuck me as hard as you can."

"Get on your hands and knees," he ordered.

The idea of doggy style thrilled her. She scrambled across the bed and presented her ass to him. Another feral growl rolled out of Jack. The instant he placed the tip of his cock against her opening, the horrible stinging assailed her skin again, even the palms of her hands and the soles of her feet. She wailed at the combination of pain from the god-awful needling and the abrupt, slick intrusion of his cock. He pumped into her several times, then held still. Seated fully within her, he held that position for a moment, withdrew, then did it again, the head of his cock hitting her cervix so firmly she cried out. He slid from her, then drove home a third time.

"I don't want to hurt you, Seph."

"Fuck me!"

He grabbed her ass, digging his fingers into her muscles, and shoved himself into her over and over as fast as he could, nearly driving her into the wall. She lowered herself so that her head was buried in the pillow and one shoulder braced against the wall, ass in the air, legs splayed and let him take her. This was where she was meant to be—his cock buried to the hilt inside her. If she had her way, they wouldn't come out of this room for days.

He shoved into her—hard. The plaster against her shoulder cracked. Buried balls-deep in her again, Jack held that position for a long time. Stinging returned, pebbling Seph's skin with its heat. She cried out. He kept thrusting into her until the rounded part of her shoulder broke through the wall. At the crunch, Jack withdrew and flipped her over.

"Let me see your shoulder." He sighed in relief. "It's fine. I don't know how you don't even have any scrapes on it."

"Jack, I'm fine. I just want you. *Please!*"

Jack looked down at her with a strange expression, as though he was genuinely shocked. "Are…are you okay, baby? Your eyes look…are you sure I didn't hurt you?"

She clasped him by the hips and drew him back into her. With another growl, he began pumping into her again, his eyes rolling back into his head.

Why couldn't she quench this insatiable need and why couldn't she come again? She was right on the verge of shattering, but every time she thought she'd orgasm, that damnable heat and stinging would cover her entire body. She held on to him, ankles crossed above his ass, arms flung over her head, tits bouncing with the intensity of Jack's hip motions. Gradually, he scooted her back up to the wall until her head bumped it several times. He leaned over her and hoisted her hips up so that the backs of her thighs lay over the tops of his.

Jack braced one of his shoulders against the plaster and banged her until more hollers of "Fuck!

Could you guys keep it down in there!" penetrated the door along with a couple thumps on the stairwell wall. He kept pummeling her core, and she relished every hard stroke. Something cracked above Jack where he leaned over her, but with his shoulders in the way she couldn't see what it was, then the little curio shelf tumbled down, landing on the stand next to the bed. The pictures and knickknacks bounced in all directions and glass shattered. Jack didn't even hesitate.

"I'm going"—a deep snarl burst from him—"going to come, baby!"

He stiffened, his cock buried to the hilt, the head of it planted firmly against her cervix.

He leaned back slightly, his muscles straining, a sheen of perspiration coating his body and face. The instant Seph saw his face, her orgasm struck her with force. She screamed. The instant she screamed, Jack stiffened further. He began thrusting shallowly, and Seph reveled in the sensation of his throbbing cock as he pumped his essence into her. He growled low in his throat. She rode out the sensations crashing through her and flung herself over the precipice into pure euphoria.

Still fully inside her, he grinned down at her.

"You're incredible, Seph."

"So are…" She frowned. The stinging sensation returned a million times worse. Pain seared her body. She stiffened, crying out.

He slid free of her. "Seph? Baby, what's wrong?"

"Oh my God! The pain!"

She rolled into a ball. Pain…pain…intense, bone-searing pain… The stirring in her head returned, and this time it shoved Seph aside, taking over. Freedom!

But the pain surged back, shoving the stirred thought away. Once the pain was gone, she would flee. She would run and run and run… The pain ebbed.

Her mate let out a surprised shout, but she had to run, had to be free. The bedroom door reared up to meet her, but it was nothing to deter her as she crashed through it and ran through the house full of startled people. Another door barred her exit, but she shoved through it too and ran into the darkness.

Freedom at last!

Chapter Nineteen

Bernadette lay on the cold, wet ground. Tremors racked her body. The cries and throaty groans of Luella and Beastman on their perches reached her as they transformed. She couldn't stop the trembling, which grew steadily worse with each passing second. A mixture of intense heat and fiery needle sensations swept across her skin. One instant she thought she was going to burst into flames, and the next the stinging hit her so hard that it sucked the breath from her lungs.

A seizure gripped her, forcing her to flop over onto her back. Cold kissed her ass and shoulders as she looked up at the star-ridden sky. She stiffened and bowed until she truly thought she'd snap in two pieces. Another seizure flipped her over on her side facing Frank where, still in werewolf form, he lay on his side watching her, his eyes glowing amber in the moonlight.

"Hang in there, sweetheart," he said, his speech guttural. "It'll be over soon."

A gust of cold wind cooled her overheated body. It ruffled the tufts of fur protruding from Frank's tall, pointed ears, and just as she noticed the very details of each strand of fur, the whiskers around his muzzle, the way she could pick out the individual flecks of color in his irises, the maddening sting returned.

She let out a shriek as the stinging transformed into a pain that attacked her very bones. Two heavy thuds trailed her scream, the impacts coming from the big rock perches. How was it possible that she could be in such misery and yet be aware of what was going on around her too? But the instant the thought entered her head, even more intense pain riddled her body, wiping out everything except the agony. Fire blazed through her nerve endings. Her bones were melting, oh heaven help her they were truly melting! There could be no other explanation for the mind-numbing pain.

Something snapped. The sound penetrated her consciousness like a bullet ripping through flesh. At first she wondered what it was, then, upon another loud crack, she abruptly realized the noises stemmed from her as her bones reformed into her lycanthrope counterpart. For whatever reason, the knowledge arrived before the discomfort registered in her brain. The scream she let out morphed into a howl that shocked her.

Bernadette held up one hand. The fingers of it lengthened, the palm grew broader, and pads just like a dog's appeared on each digit, followed by wicked-looking, shiny claws poking from each one. This was really happening. She was becoming a werewolf.

Something awakened at the back of her mind to surge to the forefront of herself. It pounded against her mind, asking for freedom, needing to run, run, run…

A whine next to Bernadette told her that Luella had settled beside her. How she knew the whimper, she didn't know, but she understood Luella would comfort her, help her through this ordeal.

More misery rumbled through her body as if it were a freight train bearing her toward a massive crash. The second half of herself leaped up in her mind and, too weak to fight it, Bernadette let it take over.

She stood on all fours for a few moments, swaying and nearly falling flat on her muzzle, but Luella jumped to her side and braced Bernadette with her tan, furry body. Bernadette stood panting, her tongue lolling out of her mouth, nerve endings afire, body still singing with the ghostly remnants of the painful transformation. She stared up at the not-quite-full moon and the urge to run claimed her. She rose to her feet, her stance awkward, and took off at a half gallop. Luella kept pace with her.

Aromas bombarded her wet nose. She could see into every inky nook and cranny of the forest. The heat signatures of chipmunks, mice and birds littered the area. Within a cluster of briars lay three deer, their bodies glowing like rubies deep within the brambles. Their scent, wild and musky, called to her and she found herself salivating. Before she could stop herself, the beast within her forced her to wheel and she headed straight for the deer. Next to her, Luella issued an excited sound that told Bernadette's beast she reveled in the bloodlust too. They crashed into the undergrowth, each of them descending on a doe before the animals had fully leaped to their feet.

The coppery scene of blood filled Bernadette's sensitive nose. A red haze settled over her vision. She tasted raw venison, her human side repulsed by what she was doing, but her beast shoved her aside and shredded the doe. She smelled and tasted the animal's waning fear as its life ebbed out of it, the kill heady on her tongue. Across from her, Luella ripped out another doe's throat and blood from it splattered over Bernadette's heavy coat. They luxuriated in the kill, ate their fill, and lay next to each other basking in the primal moment that Bernadette knew only a fellow lycanthrope could ever understand. It was a curse, but it was also freeing. It was frightening and yet exhilarating. Until now, she'd never felt so free and unhindered. However, the power and intensity of her lycanthrope side could easily get out of control. Thankfully, she had Frank and her friends to guide her through this new part of her life.

A howl reached them. Bernadette raised her head, twitching her ears one way then the other to determine the actual location and the identity of the call. Her mate. He wanted her to return.

Luella reared up on her knees, blood dripping from her muzzle. She looked at Bernadette, her eyes glowing silver. She chuffed at her, then said in garbled words, "Frank is calling for our return. Are you ready?"

Attempting to speak, Bernadette suddenly realized it was something she'd have to learn to do when in lykoi form. Instead, she issued a growl and bobbed her head. Together, they walked out of the brambles, the briars tearing at their fur, and exited into the flat area that heralded the slope from which they'd descended. Bernadette climbed the hill with her friend and they found their mates where they'd left them in the clearing.

Another howl reached her—this one unfamiliar. Bernadette's beast tensed, listening, on guard yet intrigued. Howling, eerie and full of fear, sliced through the woods a second time. A foot away from her, Luella chuffed several times softly.

Beastman answered her in similar chuffs, but deeper and more cautious, then said, "There's a non-clan lycanthrope in the woods."

Somehow, the approaching howls seemed familiar. Bernadette listened carefully. The essence of the owner spoke to her. Could it be she? If so, how?

The males stood in front of them. In moments, another werewolf appeared. A coal-black female with amber eyes glowing starkly against her fur.

Persephone. Bernadette had been right, but how could Seph be a werewolf?

The newborn lycanthrope stumbled into the clearing and fell onto her side to lie there unmoving. She heaved in and expelled out big gulps of air.

Frank began morphing back into his human self. When he'd finished, he looked at Bernadette and said, "Stay here."

Beastman and Luella began to transform back into human form too. Their shifting triggered Bernadette's. Again, the pain tormented her. As she regressed into human form, Luella took her into her arms and hummed and rocked. Finally, after what felt like hours to her, Bernadette lay against her friend's side, gulping in big breaths of air as tears slithered down her cheeks, then trickled into her now-human ears. Cold wind kissed her skin and she shivered.

"You did really well for your first transformation," Luella soothed her, then kissed her on the top of the head. "Really well."

Hugging her, Bernadette said, "Thank you, and thank you, too, for being a wonderful friend."

The smile of pleasure Luella offered her chased away the last lingering traces of pain.

"You're not going to believe who this is," Beastman grumbled in the darkness.

"Who?" Luella asked.

"It's Persephone," Bernadette answered.

Looking from him to Bernadette then back to Beastman, Luella said, "What? Seriously?"

"You heard her," Frank replied.

"How did you know?" Luella asked Bernadette.

"I'm not sure," Bernadette stated, "but I just knew." She shrugged. "Somehow it seems…natural or fitting. It's hard to explain."

"Well," Frank added, "it looks like our clan is growing. It's obvious Persephone is Jack's true mate."

"I'm glad." Luella stood and began wiping clumps of mud off her body but only succeeded in smearing the deer's blood into it. "I really like her and I think she'll fit in with us perfectly."

"I do too." Rising onto shaking legs, Bernadette tried to get her balance, but fell to her knees. "Maybe we can be there for each other since we're both new lycanthropes."

Frank went to her side and helped her to her feet. "She'll need your help more than you'll need hers. My guess is that she had no idea she was a lycanthrope."

"Poor thing," Luella murmured.

"Jack's coming," Beastman said. "I hear him about 200 yards up the path."

* * *

At the pond, Jack caught Seph's scent and tracked her into the woods. He followed her trail over fallen logs, around rock outcroppings and down the slope to the creek. Along the way he found the remains of a rabbit and some bloody fluff of a squirrel. Now things were making sense—the insatiable need to be with Seph, his overpowering protectiveness of her, the unbelievably strong sexual desire he had for her. She was his one true lifemate. That was why she'd been insatiable during sex. Her inner wolf had been trying to surface. It needed to come forth so that they were fully mates tonight.

Elated to have her as his mate, Jack paused to get a grip on himself. Oh, how he loved her! The thought struck him as thought someone had hit him over the head with a brick. Yes, he loved her. Destined mates didn't always fall in love until after they'd been mated, but with Seph, he'd fallen for her the instant he'd seen her. His inner beast had known, had recognized her. How could his human half not recognize her as such? He snorted.

Maybe he should transform and find her through his beast? No, she was already frightened out of her mind. If he showed up as a werewolf, it might be too much for her human side to comprehend on top of what she'd just gone through.

Voices drifted through the woods. Jack followed them until he emerged at the ritual clearing to find Frank and Beastman naked and kneeling next to Persephone, who had returned to human form and lay shivering, bloody and mud-smeared. Several yards behind them in the center of the clearing stood Luella and Bernadette. He smiled. So Bernadette had decided to let Frank turn her.

"Did you know Persephone was a lycanthrope?" Frank asked.

214

"Not until a few minutes ago." Jack kneeled next to Seph. She lay crying softly. His heart ached for her. She had to be frightened out of her mind.

Gathering her into his arms, he sat with her across his lap, his ass getting wet through his jeans. "It's okay, baby. I've got you."

"I'm a monster!" she wailed.

"No, no, you're not." He hugged her close. "Your parents were both lycanthropes. They must have left you at the orphanage to protect you. A werewolf in a city is a dangerous combination, and if you were in the city, you wouldn't run into your mate, so you'd never change and you'd never be the wiser."

She cried harder.

"You know what you have to do, right?" Beastman asked him.

"Yeah." He shushed her and stroked the hair out of her face, but she kept her eyes closed and buried her face in his shirt.

"Join me and Bernadette," Frank offered. "We haven't consummated our mateship yet since she shifted. Maybe if Seph does the final step with Bernadette at her side, it'll help Seph ease into acceptance of what she really is."

"Are you sure?" Jack asked, genuinely surprised by the suggestion. "It's *your* mating ritual."

"Hey, our clan and MC has been through everything together; why not this too?" Frank smirked.

Nodding, Jack eased Seph off his lap and stood to pull her to her feet. She swayed and leaned heavily against his side.

"Baby, we have to make love," Jack told her.

She stared at him with pure fear, her eyes wide,

pupils engulfing all but a miniscule ring of orange-gold iris.

"What?" she gasped. "Now? Here? In front of people?" She shook her head violently. "No way. I can't!"

"We are all werewolves," he explained calmly. "Even Bernadette is now. She was human and asked Frank to turn her. Now they must make love to finalize their official mating as lycanthrope mates."

She shook her head again.

"Hey, it's okay," he soothed. "Bernadette is going through the same thing you are right now. Her being with you will be a form of comfort." He kissed her. "Besides, I want you forever, Seph. I love you, love you more than you can ever comprehend. I want to be your mate, your man, your protector, companion and partner in everything. We're destined mates, so if you fight it, you'll find it will bring you back to me no matter how hard or how far you run. The same goes for me. I could never stay away from you."

More tears slithered down her bloody cheeks. "I…I love you too!" She lunged into his arms and threw hers around his neck, sobbing against him.

"I take it that's a yes?" Beastman said in a mischievous tone.

Frank swatted Beastman across the chest.

"Ow! What is it with everyone slapping me of late?" Beastman stalked over to Luella and stood waiting in the moonlight with her.

"Come into the clearing with me, baby," Jack murmured in her ear. "We'll consummate our love as lifemates, then head back to the main house where we can make love all night."

She leaned heavily against him, trembling so hard that it forced emotion to wedge in Jack's throat. "And I'll answer as many of your questions as I can."

She stepped back and offered him a watery smile. "I really do love you."

"I know you do, babe. I feel it emanating from right here." He chuckled and placed a hand over her heart, her skin hot beneath his palm. Desire flashed through him and settled in his cock.

He led her over to the clearing. The others waited as he disrobed. He tossed his clothes and boots over in a pile out of the way. "We'll make this quick so that we all don't freeze our asses off in human form." Already so hard he thought his cock would snap, Jack turned her around and pushed gently on her back. "On your hands and knees, sweetness. The consummation must be symbolic of our lycanthrope selves."

With hesitation, Seph looked over at the others.

"It's all right, honey," Luella said gently. "We're all friends here and there's no judgment, no perversion. Each mated couple goes through a mating ritual. Beastman and I did it a few years ago in this very same spot in the same way you will. We're all friends within a clan who will stick together through everything, who share a bond that humans can never understand, and who will all live very, very long lives together watching each other's families grow and expand down each individual line."

For a moment, Jack thought Seph would bolt, but after she listened to Luella, a calm settled over Seph's face. She looked over her shoulder at him.

"You're *all* my family now?"

"Yes," he said.

The others echoed his answer.

She dropped to her knees, as did Bernadette a few feet away, then fell to brace herself on her forearms, her ass in the air, the lips of her sex glistening in the moonlight.

Jack's knees nearly buckled. Seph was his—his! His one true mate, the lifemate he would have as his helper, wife, lover and the mother of his children. He straddled her hips and sank his cock into her pussy. The moist heat of her enveloped his cock and, before he could contain himself, he started rocking into her, eager to spill his seed into her body and officially make her his forever.

* * *

Bernadette sympathized with Persephone. This was scary, and although their situations were different, it still comforted her that Seph was going through the same thing she was. Although Bernadette was a turned werewolf, she could only imagine the shock Seph was in right now to learn she was a natural-born lycanthrope.

She dropped into position and Frank lined himself up behind her. Luella and Beastman climbed the rocks once more to serve as witnesses. Self-conscious, Bernadette closed her eyes, wishing the heat of her embarrassment would go away, but it pebbled her skin, momentarily protecting her from the chill wind's bite. The instant Frank settled the head of his cock against her opening, her shyness evaporated on the breeze and heat erupted in her pussy. Her beast surged to the front of her mind, eager to have him enter her, to consummate their mating and fuck her into the earth.

Unable to restrain herself, a low growl rolled out of her and she wiggled her ass.

"Have mercy, woman!" Frank muttered.

A few feet away, Seph issued a deep, needy growl too.

Bernadette glanced over at Jack and Seph. The image of him seated balls-deep inside Seph, his face a mask of pure pleasure, heightened Bernadette's arousal. The picture of them joined as one body was so erotic, so enticing.

Suddenly, Frank fully entered her body. The abrupt invasion prompted another growl from Bernadette. Her beast thrilled at the connection with her mate. Frank's cock, hard, hot and stretching her, wasn't deep enough. She had to have more, so she lowered herself onto her forearms, shoving her ass farther into the air and simultaneously impaled him deeper.

He issued a throaty grunt behind Bernadette. She knew that sound and smiled at what was coming—Frank was about to fuck her silly. He gripped her hips, drew back and shoved home again.

"Oh!"

He withdrew and shoved into her a second time, harder.

"Mmm, yes!"

Next to her, needy half-wolfish, half-human noises tumbled out of Seph. Behind Seph, Jack had begun a serious of snarls in time to his thrusts.

"You're mine forever," Frank yelled and began pounding into Bernadette's ass.

"Mine, Persephone," Jack hollered. "Mine forever!"

"Oh, oh… ah…" Bernadette welcomed Frank pushing into her over and over.

Fuck, he felt so good inside her, hitting her cervix, forcing that spring deep within her core to tighten, tighten, tighten… Frank fucked her so hard, his thrusts so rapid that she folded her forearms in front of her and braced her head against them, unable to do anything other than let him have her body. The aroma of mud and crushed spring grass invaded her nostrils. She breathed in deeply and let the sensations of her man spearing her with his cock roll over and through her.

Unexpectedly, her beast reared up and pushed Bernadette aside in her mind. A prehistoric lust seized Bernadette, and the orgasm that took her in its grip forced a howl from deep within her chest that both thrilled and shocked her. The beast returned power to Bernadette, allowing her to steep herself in the clenching and unclenching of her pussy as Frank pummeled her. Growl after growl from him melded with his thrusts.

"Oh… my…" A second orgasm claimed Bernadette. Her knees gave out and she fell flat against the thawing ground, but Frank hiked her hips up, her thighs against his knees and continued fucking her. She cried out over and over, the pleasure rendering her helpless.

Finally, he sucked in a big breath, halted his thrusting and stiffened, his cock pulsing and throbbing. Heat filled Bernadette's core, inspiring one more final orgasm that wrung a strangled cry from her, leaving her weak but fulfilled as she'd never been before.

He coaxed the last few drops of himself into her, then fell over her body, warming her as he panted into her neck.

* * *

Seph glanced over at Frank and Bernadette as they collapsed to the earth, exhausted. This was crazy! She was in the woods with Jack fucking her while two other people watched and another couple climaxed next to her and Jack. What was she thinking? How could she be doing this?

But the moment the lightning-quick thoughts entered her brain, the beast within her tossed them aside and gloried in how Jack's cock felt so damn good inside her. He stretched her with every thrust, the tip of his cock pounding against her cervix in a mixture of pleasure-pain. He thrust into her as if he were possessed, the pat-pat-pat of his hips against her ass echoed across the clearing—and she wanted even more.

Seph pressed the side of her face into the grass, the scent of mashed leaves and mud heavy in her nose, and offered her ass higher. A long, low snarl burst from Jack that further inflamed her need. How was it possible to want someone so much?

If that spot inside of her grew any tighter, any hotter, she would explode into flames—fuck, it felt so amazing!

Before she could stop herself, she shouted into the earth. "I'm yours, Jack, forever and always!"

He stopped suddenly, his pelvis mashed to her ass, cock buried to its hilt, body so tense his trembles shook her hips. Then, with a shout to the trees, Jack came—hard. He surged into her, pushing her across the ground a few inches. At the same instant, the dam within Seph burst and her orgasm crashed through her so forcefully she could do nothing but sag, a strangled whimper slipping from her lips. Jack held her up, pumping into her. Heat bathed Seph's channel, and the last vestiges of sensation rippled from her core to spread out to her fingertips and toes. Jack thrust a few more times, his movements short and quick as he milked the last of himself into her. Exhausted, he fell to the side, then drew her to him, spooning her as they lay gasping for breath.

Across from them, Seph met Bernadette's gaze. The sensation of finally belonging somewhere, of having a secure mooring in her life instead of feeling as though she were adrift, descended on her in a heavy blanket of comfort, and although the knowledge of what Seph was terrified her, somehow it made a weird sort of sense that she couldn't put into words. Relaxing against Jack's body, she grinned at Bernadette, who smiled back just as warmly. Seph closed her eyes.

Home. She was finally home.

Chapter Twenty

She'd wanted to ask Jack a million questions about being a… Werewolf. She was a werewolf. No matter how much it shocked and disgusted her, Seph was unable to think straight, even too exhausted to walk back to the house. After Jack dressed, he swung her into his arms and carried her up the trail to the pond. The others strolled quietly with him.

Seph relaxed and enjoyed Jack carrying her. She listened to the women talk behind them as Luella explained a few things to Bernadette about being lykoi.

Abruptly, Bernadette said, "You owe me 50 bucks and you have a month of laundry duty."

"Yeah, yeah, yeah…" Luella groused. "Like I don't do most of the laundry anyway."

"Now wait just a minute!"

Luella laughed. "I'll pay up in the morning."

They paused to gather their clothes at the pier, but Jack continued up the slope and into the house.

A few prospects were gathering up the destroyed screen door. Jack stepped inside and into the kitchen, where he sat Seph on a chair. Through the doorway, she had a view of her little under-the-stairs room, its door gone and only a bit of wood hanging by one hinge. A sweetbutt helped Beer Cans clean up the debris. The young woman plugged in the vacuum cleaner and turned it on.

Seph looked up at Jack. "What happened?"

"You happened," he said, chuckling. "When your wolf took over, you went through both doors."

She slapped her hands over her mouth, speaking through her fingers. "I'm so sorry!"

The others entered the kitchen.

Frank laughed. "What you did won't be the first time something like that has happened, so don't worry about it."

"Congratulations, you two," Beastman said. "We're all heading upstairs to our rooms to wash up."

"Good night," Luella and Bernadette called as they followed their men into the living room.

A memory surfaced suddenly. A creature staring into the wrecked car at her, the beast she'd seen after she'd been forced off the road. Seph blurted out, "It was you!"

Jack looked at her sharply. "Me?"

"You were the werewolf at my car wreck."

He nodded. "I had to shift so I could rip the door open. It was jammed and I was worried if you had a serious injury I wouldn't be able to get to you in time."

His explanation made sense, but just as the knowledge penetrated her brain, she recalled the small animals she'd killed. Seph gasped and told Jack what she'd done.

"It's okay, baby. It's part of your lycanthrope nature."

"But I ate so much!" She grimaced, then lunged

224

for the sink where she stood heaving, but amazingly, nothing came up but bile. "How could I have digested so much... stuff so fast?" she managed between dry heaves.

"It's part of your new metabolism," he explained and turned on the faucet. He ripped a paper towel sheet free of its dispenser, wetted it, then smoothed it over her neck where he'd moved her hair aside. "It takes a huge amount of energy to maintain werewolf form and all the abilities that go with it, so a feast like that is burned off super-fast. In the morning you'll want to eat the refrigerator and everything in it, but once your system adapts, the only time you'll feel that sort of hunger is when you're in the form of your beast."

She straightened and blinked up at him. "I'm so tired."

"That's normal too."

He pulled her into his arms and nestled her head against one of his pecs. Despite her horror and revulsion at herself, she welcomed the warmth and support he offered her.

"We'll gather some clothes for you and shower in the main bathroom. You're covered in mud and blood."

She glanced down at herself. "Holy shit, I'm naked!"

He started laughing, his mirth growing until he had to lean against the sink for support.

* * *

Jack escorted Seph to the main bathroom off from the living room, then hurried back to her under-the-stairs hideaway to grab some clean panties for her and also a set of pajamas Luella had lent her.

When he returned to Seph, she sat on the toilet lid, her head and shoulder against a tall cabinet, eyes closed.

"You okay?" he asked, concerned.

"Mmm-hmm. Just so tired."

After starting the shower, he disrobed, then helped Seph into the tub. Once he'd entered, too, he jerked the curtain around them.

"Oh…the hot water feels so good…" she purred.

He leaned back, his shoulder wedged into the corner of the wall and admired her as she slowly washed herself off. Seph let the water rush over her body, the mud and blood running down her smooth skin in rivulets to snake across the pristine white bottom of the tub and into the drain hole. She grabbed a bottle of shampoo from one of the recessed shelves and poured some blue-green goo into one hand, then returned the bottle and began lathering her hair. Heady eucalyptus and citrus filled their little space. The aroma opened Jack's head, also relaxing him.

She rubbed grit and dirt from her face and hair, increasing the bubbles and foam already flowing down her neck and onto her breasts. Jack let his gaze wander over her delectable body. Seph was his, really his. He kept telling himself that fact, but his brain just couldn't believe it. The willowy, raven-haired beauty in front of him, her breasts pert, nipples upturned as she stretched her arms over her head, raven hair glistening where it lay plastered to her back was truly and completely *his*. And she loved him! She'd confessed her feelings in front of witnesses.

Elated, he drew her against his body, the bubbles squishing between them.

Her tawny eyes flew open and she smiled weakly. "What are you doing?"

His cock, already hard and eager, bobbed between them. He moved closer, pressing it into her lower abdomen. "What does it feel like?"

"I don't have the strength, babe," she said breathlessly.

The use of her endearment fueled his desire, but the way her pupils dilated with lust sent his pulse to pounding.

"Want me?" he asked.

"Are you kidding?" She let out a chuff of amusement. "Even so tired I can barely stand, all I can think about is having your cock inside me."

He lifted her, and she wrapped her legs around his waist, his cock sliding into her core.

"Oh, heaven help me," she whispered, eyes falling shut. "I can't get enough of you, Jack."

The heat of her felt so fucking amazing. He stood with her under the shower spray as it rinsed the last of the shampoo from her long tresses. Satisfied the soap was all gone, he turned with her, desperate to have her and pressed her to the back wall, her core already gripping his cock rhythmically.

"You must know something," he said, preventing himself from thrusting. "Now that we're lifemates, you can get pregnant at any time, more easily than a human, I mean."

"Shut up and fuck me," she whispered into his ear.

Gooseflesh washed over his skin. "And you said you didn't have the strength."

She chuckled lightly, but upon his first thrust, her laughter turned into moans. He suddenly realized he was tired, too, but his beast wanted her one more time before they slept, so he made love to Seph pinned to the wall, her legs about his hips so that her pussy split wide to accommodate him. He braced her body with a hand on each of her ass cheeks and set up a slow, languorous rhythm. He wanted to suck on her breasts, bite her earlobes, withdraw and push her farther up the wall to taste her slick, pink cunt, but right now his wolf had to claim her one more time to make sure this wasn't all a dream.

In and out, his movements slow, sure and firm, Jack enjoyed every grip and clench of her inner walls. She was lava silk around him, and he wanted to fuck her so hard they broke the tile, but he couldn't, not now. If he did, someone would discover them in the morning naked in the bottom of the tub, asleep. No, he'd enjoy this slow fuck, then take her to bed. Maybe they could make love again after two or three hours of sleep.

Seph threw her head back, her skull whacking the tile. She began thrusting against him. Hunger for her held Jack prisoner. He wanted to thrust so hard, but he had to be easy with her right now. Her inner walls fluttered around his cock, then she stiffened, rubbing her pussy hard into his pelvis, her core clenching him so hard it forced a grunt out of him. Tingling erupted at the base of his spine. It rushed into his balls and up his rod, burning delightfully until he had to prevent himself from thrusting into her more forcefully than she was able to handle right now. He surged into her several times, barely keeping himself in check. Seph cried out, whining excitedly into his neck as she rode out her orgasm, then abruptly bit down on his trap muscle. Jack growled at the pain, both loving it and cringing from it. Her action made him desperate to leave his essence all over her body, marking her so every male who looked her way would know she belonged to him, but that would be for another time.

He pumped his seed into her, hoping in the back of his mind that it would take root. He wanted children, wanted many of them as well as a very long life with his mate.

"Oh…!" Seph bucked hard against him, then went lax.

Elated she'd come fully before him, he milked the last of himself into her, then stood holding her to the wall, both of them panting into the other's neck.

"I love you, baby," he said.

"Oh, how I love *you*," she replied.

Happiness filled him until he thought he'd shatter from its intensity. "Let's get out and dry off."

Once he put her down, he shut off the water, then swept a fluffy towel up and down her body.

Moments later, he thanked Beer Cans for pinning a blanket over Seph's bedroom doorway.

"No problem, dude," Beer Cans said and clapped him on the shoulder. "Congratulations on your beautiful lifemate."

"Thanks." Practically floating into the tiny space, he finally came to terms with the fact his life was about to officially begin with Seph. He settled her in bed, then lay down and drew her into his arms. Although he figured he'd lay there for a long time just enjoying having her in his arms, sleep descended swiftly on him. With a last thought of how much he loved Seph, he succumbed to exhaustion.

* * *

So much information and newness about her life careened through Seph's head that she couldn't make sense of any of it. The following morning, she sat at the kitchen table as Jack dressed in her room. Luella set a cup of coffee in front of her.

"Thank you," Seph said.

"Hungry?"

"Starved." Seph looked up at her. "I might start chewing on the table any second now."

Laughing, Luella opened the refrigerator and took out eggs and a packet of bacon. "I imagine Bernadette will feel the same way when she comes downstairs."

The big door on the porch opened, then slammed.

"What happened to the screen door?" Puppy asked as she entered.

"Long story," Luella called, "but we have a new lycanthrope to add to the family."

Puppy walked in and waved at Seph. Then said, "Wait. You?"

Luella giggled as Seph nodded, her cheeks warming.

"Well, I'll be damned. Jack's your lifemate, right?" Puppy asked.

"Yeah," Seph replied, her cheeks flaming hot now. She didn't understand her embarrassment but figured it was largely due to being a part of a family that she didn't know much about, although she thought the world of them. New territory, she decided.

Puppy patted her shoulder. "Welcome to the family, really. I'll help you with your transition any way I can."

"Thanks."

Looking over at Luella, Puppy said, "I'm going to get started working upstairs this morning. I'll wash down the balcony wall. I'm glad we're almost done with spring cleaning."

"Me too," Luella replied. "Did you think to bring our mail up?"

"Shit, I forgot."

"I'll go get it," Seph offered, suddenly needing to get away by herself for a few minutes. "I need to clear my head so I can think straight after last night."

Puppy shot Luella a questioning look.

"I'll tell you later," Luella answered, "but know that Bernadette let Frank turn her."

"That's wonderful!" Leaning down, Puppy kissed Seph on the cheek. "And if you really want to get the mail, take my car. The keys are in it. I drove up because it's raining."

"Thank goodness," Luella said happily. "I was so tired of this last cold snap."

"I'll be back in a few minutes." Seph snatched her jacket from its peg on the sun porch, then hurried outside to the only car parked on the carport that morning. She got in it, turned on the ignition, then backed up and headed the vehicle down the drive toward the community.

The rain pattered hard on the windshield. Seph found the wipers control without any problem and flipped on the headlights, illuminating the early morning gloom. She puttered through the community, passing Maeve on her roofed stoop where she stood brooming off the steps. She waved to the older version of Bernadette and headed out to the orchards.

Although it was raining, the orchard brimmed

with spring. Tiny, bright green leaves lined all the branches with red and pink buds just starting to open here and there. Smiling, Seph realized she'd be here to see the cherry and apple trees in full bloom. It had to be a stunning sight.

The realization she wasn't going back to Detroit forced her to think of Queen. She missed her boss's friendship, but now she had no reason to return to the city other than to collect her belongings. She'd call Queen and tell her she wasn't coming back to her job or her apartment, that she'd fallen in love and was staying in Rebellion with Jack Henessy and his MC. Queen might try to talk her out of it—after all, Seph had known Jack only a very short time—but she'd explain that if it didn't work out with Jack, she'd return. It wouldn't be the truth, but there was no way she could tell Queen she and Jack were werewolves. Her boss was an open-minded woman who had dealt with a variety of spirits, even demons, but werewolves might be pushing Queen's limits.

As she exited the orchard to the sprawling hayfields on either side of the lane, Seph made a mental note to telephone Sister Miranda too. She needed answers about her parents, answers the nun might or might not have, but Seph had to ask.

Upon reaching the gate, she found it already open and stopped between the two brick pillars, leaving the car idling. She walked over to the row of mailboxes and checked each one until she found the one with the words *Main House 33718* stenciled in white across its flap. She opened the box and removed a stack of mail wrapped in a newspaper. A few envelopes slipped free and landed on the gravel at her feet.

The sound of a vehicle starting up seemed distant in the pounding rain. She snapped her attention to a point down the road behind her, wondering if there was a nearby house and someone was leaving, but more mail fell to the ground. She scrambled to collect the letters accumulating at her feet.

The vehicle slowed as it approached. Perhaps it was someone from the MC preparing to turn onto the lane. She was about to go and move Puppy's car, but the vehicle stopped directly behind her. A crack of thunder startled her, followed by two car doors opening. She spilled the rest of the mail to the ground. The cloying scent of sour cigarette smoke wafted to her, her new sense of smell balking at how strong the aroma seemed to be. About to snatch up the mail then look for the source of the smell, she squealed as something pierced the side of her neck. Someone jerked her against their body. She struggled, her inner wolf trying to surge forward, but an intense sense of helplessness fell over her. She couldn't move, couldn't function, couldn't even speak, then blackness descended.

* * *

How did she get back on her hands and knees with Frank's cock deep inside her? Bernadette frowned, but the feeling of him seated in her body proved too damn enticing. She moaned and thrust back. A groan greeted her efforts. Wait, this was too real. This was…

She fluttered her eyes open to find Frank staring into them, a sleepy smile on his face as he lay between her thighs, his cock buried to the hilt in her.

"Mmm, what do you think you're doing?" she asked, both aroused and amused.

He thrust into her, forcing her eyes to roll back in her head. "What's it feel like I'm doing?"

"Not fair," she whispered. "I haven't brushed my teeth yet."

He thrust again. "Neither have I."

"But I'll asphyxiate you with my horrible green morning breath," she protested.

"So we'll suffocate each other with green morning breath," he countered and thrust again.

"Fuck, I want you." She hooked her heels behind his knees.

"That was the plan."

She giggled, but as Frank began thrusting in earnest, her giggles transformed into sighs, cries and throaty moans. He paused in his motions. Grumbling in protest, she waited as he rose onto his knees, sitting back on his haunches, knees splayed, and pulled her ass between his thighs. Oh, how she loved this position! It gave him complete control of her body and he could drive his cock into her at an angle that pushed her toward insanity. Frank tugged her a little closer, planting himself as deeply as he could go. She cried out with need.

"Please, Frank…"

"I love you," he said. "You have no idea how happy you made me last night."

"I love you too," she said on a moan.

She placed her hands on his thighs and held on as he jackhammered his hips. Each time his cock hit her deepest point, her pleasure ratcheted up another notch. She looked up at his wide, powerful shoulders, the muscles flexing in his chest and arms as he pounded into her. The vision of all-male strength shoved her over the edge. She fell off the pleasure point and stiffened as wave after wave of pure euphoria rocketed through her, then the orgasm intensified so that she began bucking against him, needing him deeper, needing him to empty his seed into her.

Frank tensed, then jerked her ass hard to his crotch, holding her still as she kept shrieking her pleasure. His cock jumped and pulsed inside her, spurring her orgasm to clench just a little harder. She squealed, then fell lax as he spurted inside her, then fell over her body.

"Now that's how we should say good morning every day," he said between pants.

"You don't hear any complaints out of me, do you?" she asked.

He laughed.

She rolled over on her side and scooted her bare ass into his lap. "I know a lot about the lykoi from living here for nearly a year, but killing the doe and eating like I did last night really bothers me."

"On the way out of the woods last night, Luella explained to you how the lycanthrope metabolism works."

"I know, but…wow."

He chuckled again. "Just be glad it's burned up the way it is, if you get my drift."

"Ew!" She turned and glared at him.

He chuckled harder, then hugged her. "Are you ready to start our family?"

She sighed happily. "Anytime you are."

"Good, but wait until you're pregnant *and* in lykoi form. You think the doe feast was excessive."

235

Wiggling until she was on her back again, she stared at him in horror. "Are you serious? I'll weight 800 pounds!"

"No, no…just 799."

"Frank!" She stared over at him in horror.

Laughter exploded from him.

"It's not funny!" She slapped his hip.

"You keep forgetting the super-high-metabolism thing," he managed to gasp out.

She rolled onto her side again. "I don't want to talk to you anymore."

"Then let's make that baby."

His cock poked her in the ass, and before she could utter a word, he'd parted her cheeks and pushed into her pussy again. She cried out and shoved her ass back into his lap, eliciting a delighted grunt from him.

"I could"—he thrust hard—"stay like this all day," he groaned.

"Just make me come," she gasped.

"How many times?"

"However many you want," she said on a breathy moan.

Chapter Twenty-One

Jack finished dressing, then took his toiletry bag into the main bathroom where he fished out his toothbrush and paste, then brushed his teeth. He hadn't eaten breakfast yet, but he didn't want to greet Seph by killing her with morning breath, so he'd brush his teeth after breakfast too.

Finished, he left the bathroom and tossed the toiletry bag onto her bed as he passed the doorway. He entered the kitchen but frowned when he found only Puppy and Luella chatting over coffee and scrambled eggs.

"Where's Seph?" he asked.

The women looked at each other, then at him.

"She needed some air, so she took my car to the gate to get the mail," Puppy told him.

"It's been a good 15 minutes, though," Luella said carefully. She slid her gaze toward the sun porch. "She should've been back by now, especially with it raining so hard."

"The guys who leave for work at the ass crack of dawn leave the gate open," Puppy reasoned, "so maybe Seph thought she had to lock the gate. You know what a pain it is to lock when it's wet."

Jack poured himself a mug of black coffee, then reached for the condiments on the lazy Susan to fix his brew. "I'll give her five more minutes, then I'm going out there."

"There's scrambled eggs and bacon keeping warm in the oven," Luella said.

"Thanks." He quickly made himself a plate of food and had it scarfed down so quickly that Luella raised both eyebrows at him in surprise. He shrugged sheepishly and slipped his plate and fork into the always-present dishwater. After washing his plate and putting it in the drainer to dry with his fork, he gulped down his coffee.

"You're gonna either burn the hell out of yourself with the coffee or inhale the mug," Luella admonished him. "Seph will be back any second, so calm down."

But he couldn't calm down. Something was wrong—dreadfully wrong. He sensed it, felt it in his very bones.

He clunked his cup down on the counter. "I'm driving down there to check on her. Since her beast has awakened and mated, there's no telling what she might feel or react to."

Puppy placed a hand over her mouth, her big brown eyes wide with worry.

"You're right," Luella said gravely. "Until she can control her wolf, she's unpredictable."

He hurried outside to find a hard, cold rain falling and rushed around to the front of the house where he'd parked his truck. He climbed in, cussing the cold water dripping through his hair and down into his shirt collar, and grabbed the keys under the floor mat. In seconds he mashed the gas and barreled too fast down the hill.

The moment he saw Puppy's car parked at the gate, the driver's door standing open, his suspicions were confirmed. Barely setting the parking brake and putting the truck in neutral, Jack bailed out of it. He checked the car, finding nothing out of the ordinary save for the open door and the idling motor. Hopefully the rain hadn't already washed away all scent of her. He accessed his lycanthrope senses and barely caught a whiff of Seph. At his feet, her sneaker imprints led from the driver's door past the gate pillars where he paused, his gaze tracing her footprints heading to the row of mailboxes. The hard rainfall had already washed away the bulk of her physical trail. He followed it to the main house's mailbox and a pile of soaked, muddy mail.

His wolf smelled two human males, one of which reeked of stale cigarette smoke. Water trickled into Jack's eyes and dripped off the tip of his nose as he studied the ground. He picked up the mail. There, two heel marks gouged the muddy roadside and ended at the edge of the asphalt.

Seph had been dragged.

Fear detonated in Jack's heart.

* * *

Seph awoke with a raw throat and a nasty aftertaste at the back of her mouth. Tingling ravaged her feet and hands. She found herself on a sofa facing a woodstove. A fire crackled in it. Where had she seen that woodstove?

Recollection hit her—she was in Jack's house. Frowning, she struggled to sit up and realized her hands and feet were tied with cord. The memory of someone grabbing her rose in her mind. She gasped and wrestled herself into an upright position. The front of her had dried from the fire's warmth, but her backside and hair remained damp from the rain.

"So you've come to," a soft, girlish voice stated to Seph's left. "Sometimes people have bad reactions to designer drugs, so I was beginning to worry Benny had used too much of it on you."

Seph turned toward the female's voice. She blinked away the heavy sleepiness that threatened to claim her again and tried to focus on the girl. She blinked again. No, she wasn't a girl, but a woman in her late twenties whom Seph had never seen before. She racked her brain trying to place her as one of the Werewolves' sweetbutts or even a member of the MC's community, but didn't recognize her.

"Wh-why are we at Jack's place?"

As the drug's effects faded, Seph began to take in details about the woman. She wasn't very big, smaller even than Puppy. Long blonde hair hung to her very large breasts straining against a Pink jersey T-shirt with gold-sequined sleeves. Black leggings showed off the woman's trim hips and slender legs, the outfit ending in rain boots with a pink-and-gold paint-splatter design. Seph couldn't focus on her eyes enough to tell what color they were—blue or maybe green? The woman would be pretty if it wasn't for the haughty and slightly manic expression on her face.

A tall, lanky guy dressed in biker garb pushed between the woman and the kitchen doorframe where she leaned with a cup in one hand. He held an open bottle of beer and settled himself in the chair off to one side of the woodstove. A sneeze over by the TV drew Seph's attention to another guy, who sat in the recliner, lighting, then puffing on a cigarette. A big cloud of gray-white smoke lifted over and encircled his seat. The chemicals in the cancer stick assaulted Seph's lycanthrope senses and she wrinkled her nose.

"Fuck, Smokey, go suck on that thing on the porch, would you?" the woman barked. "Those things stink."

"Bitch," he said. "It you weren't paying me so much, I'd slap you through the wall."

"We both know it's more than the money," the woman purred and air-kissed at him

He paused next to her and cupped her crotch. The blonde rolled her eyes back in her head and ground a couple times against his hand.

"Yeah, you're a hot piece of ass, Tina, I'll give you that. But the money you're paying me will stick around longer than you will." He kissed her, then stalked around the sofa past Seph to the front door. As he left, she tried to see the emblem on the back of his cut—a Wraithkiller. She snapped her attention over to the man called Benny. He grinned at her and raised his beer in a little salute. The black-and-white patch over his left pec revealed the same insignia of a witch that looked part ghost. Why was this woman working with the Wraithkillers? Was she one of their sweetbutts? No, that couldn't be right, because sweetbutts didn't wield the power this woman seemed to possess.

The door slammed behind Smokey.

"Tina?" Seph managed to croak from her still-raw throat. "I have no idea who you are."

"I'm surprised Jack hasn't told you about me,"

the woman replied as if insulted. "I'm Jack's girlfriend."

At first, the announcement made no sense. Seph studied the little blonde for a long moment. "Girlfriend?"

"Why, yes." Tina laughed, the sound carrying a sharp edge, as though Seph had struck a nerve. "Jack broke up with me months ago, but I know he wants me back. Then you showed up, distracting him. I may have messed up, but everyone deserves a second chance, right? But now Jack has messed up too."

"Jack messed up?" Although she was trying to wrap her mind around Tina's claims, none of them made any sense other than the fact this woman was obviously an old girlfriend—a crazy one.

"He screwed up by getting involved with *you*," Tina said, her tone implying that Seph was stupid. "I made a mistake by fucking these guys in the back of my car, and now Jack has fucked up by dating you. Jack and I are even, so he'll have to take me back."

The weight of the situation bowled Seph over. Tina was delusional, and Seph was bait to draw Jack here. The two Wraithkillers might hurt him. And once Seph's usefulness was gone, what would happen to her?

"Planting weed in his house didn't work," Tina explained. "I thought if I bailed him out of jail for possession, Jack would realize how much I love him and I'd win him back, but for some reason, even with the law showing up here to investigate, nothing came of it." She shrugged. "Then I decided to rid myself of competition, but you survived driving off that cliff." Sighing, she waved her free hand in the air. "And of course, being the wonderful guy that Jack is, he had to save you. So then I tried scaring him, but I should've known he wouldn't scare easily. And when Smokey—the dumbass—almost shot Jack off his bike the other day, I knew I had to try something different so that these two morons"—she jerked her head in Benny's direction—"didn't kill him." She smiled smugly. "And here we are."

"What makes you think he'll come out here?" Seph croaked. "He has no idea where I've gone."

"Oh, he'll know, trust me. And after he takes me back," Tina added happily, "Smokey and Benny can have you."

Benny chuckled and waggled his eyebrows at Seph. She wrinkled her nose in distaste.

"See?" Tina crowed. "Everyone gets something, even you." She waved her cup at her. "You obviously like bikers, so when Jack takes me back, you'll get two bikers for the price of one." She turned and disappeared into the kitchen. "You'll thank me too. Smokey fucks like a hero."

Fear pooled in Seph's belly. How was she going to get out of this without getting hurt? Worse, what if something happened to Jack? She didn't think she could live without him.

"Did you send the text?" Tina called from the kitchen.

"Yep," Benny hollered. "Sent it when you told me to."

Tina appeared in the doorway again with the same mug. Steam puffed from the rim of the cup. "Great! Now we wait." She beamed at Seph.

Another wave of fear passed through Seph. She

didn't know which was worse—dealing with a deranged woman, or fending off big bikers who believed Seph was their prize.

Benny leaned forward in his chair, the now-empty beer bottle clutched loosely in the fingers of one hand. "You and me are gonna have lots of fun, baby." He swept his gaze over her. "Always did prefer brunettes over blondes. I bet you give amazing blowjobs."

Repulsed, Seph closed her eyes and fell back into the couch. The thought of sex with anyone other than Jack disgusted her. Tingling moved from her bound hands and feet up through her arms and legs, but as it spread, the tingling shifted into stinging. Her eyes flew open. Was she about to transform into her beast? The instant the thought entered her mind, her inner wolf surged to the front of her consciousness.

No, no, no! She couldn't transform. Not now, not here! She couldn't control her beast, had no idea how to make it obey her, and the thought of hurting or killing someone terrified her more than what Tina and her henchmen had planned for her.

"Got a text back," Benny said, jarring Seph back to the present.

"What did he say?" Tina asked.

The door opened and shut. Smokey walked around the sofa to stand between the woodstove and Seph. He stared down at her with lust in his eyes.

"Asked who was texting him," Benny answered Tina.

"Text back that we have his girlfriend and to meet him at his house," Tina ordered, "but don't tell him who we are and make sure he knows the police can't be involved or his bitch will be killed."

The gleeful way Tina spoke pushed a needle of unease down Seph's spine.

"Done," Benny said.

Tina sat on the end of the sofa and glanced down at Seph. "Now we wait."

"I want her," Smokey said. "What's the point of taking a new bitch if I don't like the way she gives head or puts out?"

"I'm first with her!" Benny protested.

"You were first with Tina, remember?" Smokey shot back.

"He does have a point," Tina told Benny.

"Fuck." Benny sat back, then threw the beer bottle against the stone platform beneath the wood burner. The glass shattered and tinkled across the flat rocks.

Before Seph could utter a protest, Smokey hauled her up off the sofa by her upper arm. "Come here, baby."

Pressed to Smokey's body, Seph held her breath against the odor of stale cigarette smoke that clung to him.

"We're gonna go to the back of the house and have some fun." After nuzzling the side of her neck, Smokey cupped one of her breasts. "Not as big as Tina's, but still nice and firm." He chuckled. "We'll be back later."

Benny glowered as Smokey swung Seph up into his arms.

"Have fun," Tina said, laughing.

The stinging sensation swept over Seph's skin and heat followed in its wake. If this guy raped her, she'd never be able to look Jack in the eyes again. She was Jack's mate, dammit! But what could she do to fight this jackass?

He strolled through the kitchen with her. A puff of cold wind wafted over them. With it came the aroma of citrus and lavender.

"Throw some wood in the stove," Smokey yelled over one shoulder. "It's damn cold back here."

"Okay," Benny said.

The sound of something heavy thumping on metal and the noise of wood clunking against wood followed them down the hall.

The aroma of citrus and lavender followed them to Jack's bedroom. Hell, no! She couldn't be taken right there on Jack's very own bed.

"You smell good, baby," Smokey said as he entered the room. "Like…oranges and lavender mixed together. Some of the sweetbutts at the club just smell like old beer and sour sweat." He nuzzled her hair, his beard catching a few strands and pulling. "I love it when a woman smells good."

He tossed her on the bed. Seph bounced a couple times, then tried to roll away.

"Oh no you don't." He grabbed her feet and yanked her to the edge of the mattress. "Trust me, you'll like this."

"I have a…" She couldn't think of a word to replace lifemate, so used the only other one she could think of. "A husband."

Smokey straightened and pulled a large penknife from his pants pocket and opened the blade.

The sight of it silenced her.

"You married that asshole, Jack?" he asked.

She nodded, once.

"Tina will shit a brick if she finds that out. Oh well. You're mine now."

He sliced through the cords binding her feet, but before she could kick him, he'd yanked her pajama bottoms down her legs, then straddled her thighs, pinning her knees to the edge of the mattress.

"Get off me!" she snarled. Both repulsed and furious, she startled to wiggle.

"That's it, baby," he said, obvious pleasure roughening his voice. "I love it when a woman fights me. Makes it more exciting."

The stinging across her body intensified to painful proportions.

"*Get off me!*"

Smokey laughed and began unfastening her jeans.

Chapter Twenty-Two

Jack rushed into the sun porch and up the two steps into the kitchen. Everyone looked suddenly at him, all eyes wide, mouths ajar.

"Fuck, what happened?" Luella asked where she stood with her hands in the dishwater.

The brief tune of "Smoke on the Water" playing loudly in the kitchen came from his phone. Jack could only stare at the display. The texts taunted him. His legs nearly gave out, forcing him to lurch to the side, where he came to rest against the refrigerator.

"Shit!" From the table, Beastman leaped to his feet and made it to Jack's side in two huge steps. "Dude, what's wrong? You've gone white as a sheet!"

Jack's beast reared up with fury, insisting that he allow it to take over and find Seph. Trembling with a mixture of fear for his lifemate and anger that someone would kidnap and threaten her, he dropped the cell phone.

Catching it in one massive hand, Beastman spun it around on his palm and read the display. "Fucking hell!"

"What?" Luella, Puppy and Bernadette all said at once.

"What is it, Beastman?" Frank rose from the table and handed Luella his dirty dishes.

"Someone has kidnapped Persephone," Beastman answered. "They want Jack to leave the pigs out of it and meet them at his place."

"Who?" Frank asked, his tone steely.

"No idea," Jack managed to say.

"If you ask me," Beastman said, looking Jack directly in the eyes, "we need to handle this with fangs and claws."

Jack shifted his attention over to Frank. "What does our president think?"

"Beastman has the right idea," Frank said, "but we go in as men first, then shift if the need arises."

"Agreed." Jack got his strength back and stood up, but Beastman kept one hand on Jack's upper arm. "I'm betting there's at least four involved in this. That's how many that ran Seph off the road."

"We're going too." Luella dried her hands on a tea towel.

"No," Frank stated. "All she-wolves stay here."

Also standing, Bernadette looked at Frank. "But—"

"No, Bernadette," Frank said firmly. "We don't know what we're dealing with and there's already a pissed-off spirit in Jack's house."

"*But* my magic might be useful," she insisted.

"I agree with Bernadette," Luella stated firmly.

"Me too," Puppy echoed.

"I said *no*." Turning back to Beastman and Jack, Frank added, "We'll take Phil, Tom and Tractor as backup. Make sure everyone is packing."

"Let's go." Jack spun on his heel and headed back

out to his truck. Although thankful he had such a good MC and clan behind him, even the women wanting to help, he worried Seph could be hurt in other ways. He opened the driver's door, rain pounding down on his head, and leaned the seat forward. Removing a .9 mm from a holster fixed to the back of the seat, he quickly checked the weapon and reassured himself the clip was fully loaded. If any of the men involved in this touched her... His beast lunged behind his eyes, desperate for blood.

He drove too fast, slowing only when he came to the community, then once he was past the homes, he mashed the gas and sped to the highway. Behind him, Beastman drove his pickup with Frank riding shotgun while Tom and Tractor followed in Tractor's SUV. No doubt Frank had already called Phil to meet them at the end of Jack's lane.

Rain bashed against the windshield. Even with the wipers going full speed, it was still difficult to see the pavement, which pissed Jack off all the more. He wanted to get to his place as quickly as possible, but the inclement weather slowed him down. If he didn't reach Seph in time, if something happened to her because of the fucking rain limiting visibility...

The familiar sensation of a shift flowed over his skin, even tightening each hair follicle on his head, heralding a full shift, but Jack forced his beast to bend to his will and prevented himself from transforming. Driving his pickup in a deluge was dangerous enough, but a sudden shift into lycanthrope form while driving would end in him wrapping his truck around a tree. No, he had to keep a level head, had to remind his inner beast that being dead wouldn't help his lifemate.

But fuck, he wanted to taste the blood of his enemies on his tongue!

Who would want to take Persephone from him? Who could possibly be so low as to…?

Tina.

"Fuck!"

The revelation took him by surprise and he nearly drove straight through a hairpin turn. He let off the accelerator, his heart thrumming painfully, and managed to guide the pickup around the bend without mishap.

Tina was the only person who had a vendetta against him. For Tina's sake, he hoped his suspicions were wrong.

* * *

Through her wiggling to get away from Smokey, Seph somehow managed to move so she could drive her knee into his gut, forcing him to release her. He let out a sudden "dung!" and rolled to the side, drawing his knees up. She scrambled to the head of the bed and stood with her back pressed to the wall. The photograph frames hanging there poked her in the ass and shoulders. He rose, one hand cupping his belly, then faced Seph. With a leer, he began unbuckling his pants. He stood eyeing her up and down as the wind threw rain against the windowpanes. Water ran down the glass in wide rivulets. Thunder rumbled somewhere in the distance, the illumination of the lightning bolt flickering over the man. Silver glimmered in his slicked-back hair and beard.

"Aren't you cute," Smokey sneered, his gray eyes

darkening with lust. "You might as well enjoy this, baby. No place for you to run and not much you can do with your hands tied."

She stood her ground, waiting for him to make a move.

Nonchalantly he stepped up on the bed, his belt buckle jangling against his open fly. He took one step toward Seph, the bed dipping under his considerable weight.

He closed the distance between them. Terrified, Seph did the only thing she could think of—she kicked like a Rockette. The heel of her foot connected with his chin. His head snapped back and, windmilling his arms, he fell over backward and off the bed, landing in a heap.

"You bitch!" Utter fury filled his voice.

Dread and fear shot through Seph. This was it. She was done.

Smokey rolled over and scrambled to his feet. "You'll pay for that. We were just gonna have some fun, but you had to be a bitch about it."

"I told you I already have a man. I'm married. What you plan is rape."

"Doesn't matter now." Ice laced his voice. "I'll use you until there's nothing left."

He leaped across the bed at her. Seph tried to dance away from him, but he hooked her by the ankles and jerked her legs out from under her. She slid down the wall, bringing the photos down with her. One glanced off her brow bone. Pain flared in her face and she gasped. Smokey dragged her across the mattress, the covers bunching under her hips.

"Let me go, asshole!" she shrieked, kicking and

flailing her legs. One foot met with the nightstand, shooting pain up her leg. The lamp toppled over and glass crunched.

He held her down by planting one hand on her shoulder and leaning over her, simultaneously half pinning her bound hands with his torso. "I'm going to fuck you and you're going to like it."

"What the hell is wrong with you?" she screamed. Pins and needles coursed over her body, forcing every hair on her head and body to stand at attention. "You're a disgusting excuse for a human being!"

Thunder boomed overhead. Cold wafted over the bed, bearing the same perfume as before.

"You smell so good," Smokey crooned. "I'm going to enjoy fucking you so much. Hell, might even make a night of it right here in this bed."

Somehow, he managed to scoot his jeans over his hips using his free hand. He wedged himself between her thighs and yanked on the waistband of her panties, the ripping material loud in the room. He pulled again and this time the leg band gave way.

Settling farther between her thighs, he began to chuckle. "Bet you fit my cock like a glove."

The tingling faded to be replaced by unbearable stinging, as if her skin were on fire. Panic aroused Seph's inner beast. If Smokey didn't get off her, she'd kill him. She didn't want to kill him, feared ending the life of another human being, but this was self-preservation. She belonged to Jack and couldn't bear the thought of returning to him soiled by this nutjob.

The stinging increased. Heat flashed across her skin.

"Damn, you're hot, baby," Smokey said as he kissed her neck. "Working up a sweat for me, huh?"

At his words, Seph's wolf jumped higher within her. It wanted out—now.

Lavender and citrus swirled over the bed.

"Mmm…gonna fuck you now, baby…" He positioned the head of his cock at her pussy.

Seph tensed, panic nearly suffocating her, but her wolf pushed her aside. Red fell over her eyesight. She looked up at Smokey and growled. The sound came out low, rumbling and pissed off.

He stiffened and raised his head to look down at her. "What the fuck was that?"

Unable to control her wolf, Seph could only scream in pain as the transformation into her counterpart took over. The stinging grew to unbearable proportions. The heat of the shift penetrated her bones until snapping and pops signaled even more pain.

Vaguely, as if from far away, part of Seph heard a shout.

"What the fuck is happening?"

A man's frightened cry sliced through the room.

This time, she was aware of a few things. The flash of lightning illuminating the room, the broken lamp in the corner, its bulb free of its shade, the man in front of her with his pants around his ankles, his cock shriveled, his face a mask of horror and disbelief.

The aroma of lavender and citrus penetrated her senses. It was sweet, comforting, and her wolf recognized the odor. Why was it familiar to her inner beast?

No, she couldn't dwell on an odor.

She had a throat to rip out.

* * *

Rain thrashed the landscape; everything lay saturated or ran with water. Jack wanted to shift into his wolf, but until he knew the situation inside the house, he had to restrain himself. He'd waited at the end of the lane where he'd parked his pickup until the others joined him. Phil, only a minute or two behind them, pulled onto the edge of the road.

He jogged up to Jack and the others, water running through his hair and saturating his cut. "What the hell's going on here?"

Quickly Frank filled him in on the situation.

"Fuck," Phil said. "This could go really bad if we're not careful."

"I like bad," Beastman rumbled. "I didn't have any bad in my Fruit Loops this morning, so I'm making up for it."

Despite the worry wedged in Jack's gut, he smirked at Beastman. Leave it to the blond giant to lighten the mood.

"Use your animal senses," Frank advised. "We don't know how many men might be positioned around the area watching for us."

"At least the rain will mask any noises we might make," Tractor said, his inky eyes scanning the woods lining Jack's driveway.

"Yeah, as well as any sounds from anyone out here with us," Tom stated.

"We have to save Seph," Jack said, whirling on Tom.

"Easy, dude." Tom met Jack's gaze with sympathy. Rain bounced off his head, plastering his hair to his skull and running in streams down his unshaven face. "I'm just pointing out we have to be doubly careful because this downpour works against our lykoi hearing and sight."

Jack wilted. "You're right. I'm sorry, man."

"It's okay," Beastman said in his awkward manner of soothing someone. "I know how I felt when the Wraithkillers grabbed Luella because they wanted that crate of guns."

Beastman patted him on the shoulder until Jack thought he might be trying to drive him into the ground like a fence post. He stepped slightly to the side to avoid another pat. "Thanks, Beastman."

"Let's go," Frank ordered. "We'll move through the trees. Quietly. If you have to shift, only half shift. Don't let your bloodlust take over."

In minutes, Frank came upon a guy sitting in a white van about halfway down the drive. He motioned to Beastman, who waited until a flash of lightning occurred and thunder crashed, then he darted across the lane to skirt the van on the other side. Before Jack could reach the vehicle, Beastman had jerked the guy out of the driver's seat and flung him into the bushes where he landed in a heap and lay still.

"Tie him up," Frank told Tom. "I'm sure there's something in the van you can use."

"Leave him in the rain," Beastman added.

Frank looked at him quizzically.

"That dude stinks. Probably hasn't washed his nasty ass for days," Beastman explained and wiped rain out of eyes. "A little water will do him good."

Jack laughed and jogged down the lane, puddles splashing under his boots. Beastman caught up with him. Tom skulked through the trees to Jack's left and Frank to the right. Movement in the entrance of the barn forced Jack to grab Beastman and halt suddenly. Together, the pressed their backs to the side of a strange car parked in front of the house. He motioned at Frank, who nodded. To Tom, Frank indicated the pole barn and they circled behind it, entering from the backside. In moments, the cries and shouts of a man reached Jack and Beastman.

Satisfied, Jack said, "We'll go in through the back door."

Beastman bobbed his head once. Waiting, Jack prayed for another lightning display. It took several minutes, but when the clouds cut loose, he whacked Beastman on the shoulder and the two sprinted as fast as they could past the house and around it to the back stairs leading up to the small deck.

Once they were halfway up the stairs, the window next to the back door exploded. A man flew through the air, screaming. He hit the ground and lay groaning, unmoving.

Leaning over the railing, Beastman looked down at the guy sprawled on the back lawn and asked, "Is stupid part of your DNA? Dude, you never piss off a newly turned she-wolf."

Upon seeing the man's jeans bunched around his boots, bare ass pointed to the sky, Jack knew what had happened. "Seph!"

Dread pooled in his belly and nausea erupted in his belly. He prayed Seph was all right and pounded up the remaining steps. The back door was locked, so he hit it with his shoulder. The frame crunched inward. Beastman pushed the door open.

The instant Jack entered the hall, he stopped. The master bedroom lay in ruins. Photos had been ripped from the walls, the bedcovers lay all over the room, the lamp rested in one corner, winking on and off.

Screams from the front of the house galvanized Jack into motion. The roar of a she-wolf rent the air. He rushed down the hall, framed photos littering the floor.

"Hope you can calm her down," Beastman hollered behind him. "She might twist your head off too."

"I'm about to find out," Jack said as he ran through the kitchen.

Chapter Twenty-Three

Bloodlust claimed Seph. Her inner beast demanded more. She'd wanted to kill the asswipe who had tried to rape her, but somehow she'd managed to quell her wolf. There were others who had to pay for what they'd done to her. They'd also pay for taking her away from her lifemate.

As she stood in the living room towering over the humans clustered there, the other man stumbled away from her and fell over the pile of firewood stacked on the stone platform. He landed against the woodstove's iron side, then let out a scream that should have awakened the dead. The aroma of seared skin drifted to Seph. She salivated. Fried jackass. Her favorite dish.

He rolled away from the stove, his face and hands ashen from contact with the superheated metal. Still screaming, he leaped over the sofa, then launched himself at one of the windows. Glass shattered, a thud followed, then another thud, and finally sobbing muffled by rainfall somewhere out in the yard.

"Wh-what are you? Get away from me!"

Seph faced the person. The female. A human female. The one who wanted to take Jack away from her.

Red settled over her vision a second time. She advanced on the woman.

"No, no, no, no…!" The female backed into the corner next to the television.

Seph's wolf enjoyed the aroma of fear emanating from the human female. She crossed the room in three strides, snatched the woman under the armpit, then shook her like a dirty rug. Both her rain boots flew off. One landed on the carpet a few feet away. The other catapulted through the air to land on the coffee table. Screams and pleas from the woman to stop, to not kill her, only further excited Seph's beast. She dropped the female into the corner, then clasped her by one of her ankles. She'd take the rival out into the woods, toy with her for a bit, then kill her. Death was the only way to prevent this little wisp of flesh from separating Seph from her beloved Jack.

She hauled the female up from the floor, banging the woman's skull against it a couple times just for the enjoyment of doing so. Turning, she took a step toward the door, but it swung open and two men rushed inside.

Recognition hit Seph. They were lycanthropes too. The one…Frank…he'd been there as witness to her mating to Jack. Her wolf relaxed. She vaguely remembered the other man, a tall, dark-haired male, his hair and clothes glued to his body by the rain.

"Seph!"

She looked behind her to find her mate with Beastman beside him.

"Don't kill her," Jack said. "You'll never be able to live with yourself if you do."

Not kill her? How could she not kill the human?

This deranged female would only return to wreak more havoc, hurt Seph's lifemate, possibly hurt the clan.

"Seph," Jack said gently, "put her down. I'll make sure she never bothers us again—I promise."

She tried to speak, wanted to say she had to kill the female and why, but all that came out were grunts and garbled sounds.

"Please, baby." Jack approached her and looked into her eyes. "That woman isn't worth it. She's seriously fucked up in the head and needs help."

"H-h-heeeelp?" Seph finally managed to say with her thick, long tongue.

"Yes. Don't let your beast manipulate you, baby. It should serve you, not rule you. Fight it. Do the right thing. You're still human."

Panting, she held the female up by her foot, the woman's other leg out an acute angle. Upside down, the woman sobbed and blubbered some sort of nonsense. Tears leaked from her eyes, and snot dripped from her nose to land on the carpet.

Elated to be a little stronger than her inner animal, she let go of the woman, who landed in a heap, limbs akimbo. Tina. Now Seph remembered. The one who was screwed in the head, the one who thought Jack still wanted her. The one who had given her to the bikers so they could abuse her. What a sad little human.

Seph's inner beast still wanted to taunt the female. She leaned over, her head inches from the woman's, and growled as she licked the side of Tina's face. The odor of urine punctuated the air and a wet spot appeared on the carpet beneath Tina's hips.

* * *

"What is it, child?" Scary Mary asked when Bernadette opened the sun porch door to find her mentor standing in the rain.

"How did you—" She motioned for Mary to come inside.

"I feel it too," Mary stated firmly and shook water out of her locs. "I was drawn here. Something is unbalanced, and now it's become a matter of pure evil versus good. I know I'm supposed to help you, but with what?"

"I...I don't know." Bernadette quickly told her what had happened to Seph. "I don't know how to explain it, but I know Seph needs me—needs us—and for the last half hour I've been thinking about going to you to see if..." She sighed in exasperation and scrubbed her face with one hand. "Frank said none of us were allowed to go with them to help. If I disobey his orders—"

"I'm here now. And when it's a life-or-death situation that our magic can handle, your lifemate and MC president can kiss my black ass."

Luella appeared in the doorway above the two stone steps leading into the kitchen. Laughter burst from her. "Now that's what I'm talking about. I'll help any way I can."

With a hand on Bernadette's shoulder, Mary squeezed. "That young girl needs us. We'll figure out what needs to be done, but just in case, we should gather a few things to vanquish a demon."

"Is that what the entity is?" Luella asked.

"He wasn't at first," Mary replied, tossing Luella

a glance, "but his hate and thirst for control has turned his soul into one."

"If we have any ingredients here you can use," Luella said, "help yourself."

"Much obliged. Come, child." Mary brushed past Bernadette and stepped up into the other room. "Let's get started, then haul our asses out to Jack's place before it's too late."

"Puppy," Luella called, "I need you to man the fort while we're gone."

* * *

As soon as Seph calmed, the change back to human form consumed her. Jack caught her in his arms as she buckled in pain, then held her until she finished the transformation into her beautiful human body. She lay gasping and trembling in his embrace. He kissed her on the forehead several times.

"Are you okay, babe?" he asked, his lips still pressed to her skin.

"I…I think so," she panted.

"I'll call Deputy Williamscot," Frank told Jack. "He'll come up with a story to cover our asses." Shrugging, Frank grinned and took out his phone. "Even if the Wraithkillers involved here tell everyone they saw a werewolf, who will believe them?"

"I'll go outside and tie up the one in the front yard," Tom said.

"There's one under the stairs out back too," Jack said.

"Got it."

The door opened and shut quietly.

"Did he…?" The words wouldn't come. Damn, he feared the worst and couldn't voice the question to find out if Seph was okay.

"He didn't rape me," Seph stated. "He tried, but that's when I shifted."

Relieved, he hugged her tightly. "Your inner beast protected you, thank God."

Phil pulled the crocheted afghan from the back of the sofa and draped it over Seph. She smiled her thanks.

"If you need someone to talk to," Phil said softly, "my Daffodil can help you. She'll understand how you feel."

"Thanks," Seph replied.

"Yeah, thank you." Jack conveyed his gratitude through his eyes.

The scent of lavender and citrus swirled in the room.

Jack looked around. "She's here."

"I didn't recognize that scent in my human form, but I smelled it in the bedroom and…"

Jack shifted so he could look down into Seph's face. "And what, babe?"

"It smelled familiar to me. My wolf knew the odor, but I don't know why I recognize the scent in lykoi form."

About to say she'd eventually figure it out, Jack grunted as something ice-cold hit him, bearing him backward and spilling Seph to the carpet. He found himself staring into the red-coal eyes of the entity as it propelled him across the floor and pinned his back to the front door.

Frank, Beastman and Phil uttered startled yells.

Jack scrambled to his feet and turned toward his mate. Crying out, Seph tried to get to her feet too, but the entity hurtled toward her. It struck her hard and she flew backward to impact with the back of the sofa, then flipped over it, the afghan falling away from her body, and landed on the stone platform. She cried out in pain.

Blind fury claimed Jack. His beast pushed him aside and red fell over his vision.

* * *

Agonizing pain penetrated Seph's body. With her face pressed to a flat stone, she moaned and tried to sit up. Discomfort radiated from one elbow, a hip and a kneecap. The woodstove bathed her in its heat. She'd landed too close to its hot metal surfaces, but she'd been luckier than the Wraithkiller she'd tossed into it.

Cool air drifted over her backside and the soft citrusy, flowery perfume penetrated her senses. It comforted Seph, and once again, familiarity rippled through her mind.

"Let me possess you, Granddaughter," a woman whispered in her ear. *"If we work together, we can defeat him."*

The perfume grew stronger, as if Seph had just spritzed the scent all over herself from a bottle.

Cold wrapped around her and pulled her to her feet. A force pushed her to bend over the woodstove. Heat blasted upward from its surface.

A snarl from behind Seph told her Jack had shifted.

"Grab her!" Beastman yelled.

Hands took her by the arms and waist, tugging her backward, but the entity proved much, much stronger. The amount of energy it was drawing from everyone's life forces fueled it with plenty of power.

"Stop," she yelled. "You're all giving the entity too much energy!"

"Let me help you," the female voice whispered.

"Do it," Seph answered.

The dark spirit pushed Seph's face closer to the metal. Heat radiated upward, drying out her eyes. Two more inches and her face would be scarred for life. Fearful of moving her feet and losing her balance, Seph couldn't shift her body to get a better stance so she could pull back from the stove.

The furious growl that burst from Jack as he threw the sofa aside to reach her forced Seph to shout, "Don't! Stay back, Jack!"

His confused snarls created a wedge of regret in her gut.

"Let me handle this," she said. "It'll be all right."

"You sure about this?" Frank asked, his words guttural.

"Yes. Take Jack outside, and one of you just stand in the front door"—she pushed her head up as the entity tried shoving it down—"and keep watch in case things take a turn for the worse."

Jack protested with a serious of snarls, growls and pissed-off half howls.

"Out, Jack!" she screamed.

She didn't have a chance to hear what happened behind her. The female spirit claimed her body, fully possessing her. Coolness settled inside her, but it soon blended with Seph's self. Images flashed through

Seph's mind—an unhappy married woman who took a lover, her true mate. Her mate wanted to take her away, then a baby turned her world upside down. After she had the child—Seph's mother—she gave it to a local coven and arranged for them to make sure the baby was taken far away to a place where she could never be found by Malachi.

Her grandmother gave her the strength to stand and shove the black entity aside. He rushed her again, but this time, with her grandmother's help, Seph struck him with their combined energy. The entity hit the wall by the kitchen door. Ectoplasm appeared on the paint and slid down in greenish-silver streaks. Slowly the entity solidified until a corporeal male ghost stood before Seph. A man in his late forties regarded her with malice in his light blue eyes. He looked just like any old-fashioned farmer except that he was well muscled beneath a tattered, gray tunic. His wool pants clung to trim hips and led down to heavy leather work boots.

"You adulterous bitch!" he yelled viciously. He reached for something on his belt and produced a wicked-looking bowie knife. "I'll gut the bitch you've possessed."

"After all the beatings I took from you"—Seph startled at the words coming through her from the female spirit—"I would have left you anyway! And you will not harm my granddaughter. The two of us together have the power to vanquish you."

"You are my wife, Etta!"

"In name only," the words burst from Seph's mouth. "I found my mate, and my inner animal knew it. I had no control over it, Malachi. It's the way of the lycanthropes. Our one true lifemate calls to the other in a way you never understood. You could have done the right thing by letting me go with Anthony, but no. You took the coward's path and murdered him in his sleep." An image of a sleeping man filled Seph's head. Malachi leaned over him and shoved a handcrafted blade composed of silver through his heart as he slept. "Then you used me as though I were a whore because you wanted a male child—and to no avail. You hid Anthony's Indian in the outbuilding, hoping no one would ever find it, but Jack did find it, restoring it, and therefore waking you. Now it's time for you to finally burn in hell!"

"What the fuck are you doing here?" Frank shouted from the porch.

Female voices sifted into the living room from outside.

Malachi smiled. "Good. More energy for me to eat."

He rushed Seph, but Etta threw up a wall of force that stopped him in his tracks.

"Let us through, Frank!" Bernadette said.

Pushing through the men, Bernadette and Scary Mary entered the house.

"Oh look," Malachi sneered. "Some spicy witch energy for me to feed upon."

The women sprinkled something around them on the floor. The instant the last of it hit the carpet, Malachi lunged at them but hit an invisible wall and reeled back. Instead, he turned and leaped at Seph, but again, Etta threw up an energy barrier, forcing him back.

Bernadette and Scary Mary started chanting

words Seph didn't understand. At first, Malachi laughed, the maniacal sound overwhelming the entire house. When the men tried pushing into the room, Mary pointed a stern finger at them, halting them, but didn't stop chanting.

Shoving past Beastman and Frank, Luella entered and handed Bernadette a lemon with springs of what looked like lavender inserted into a hole carved into the fruit. As Bernadette kept chanting, she held the lemon and Mary stuffed big grains of salt into the hole, then followed it with sage that she took from a plastic bag removed from a pocket in her voluminous skirt.

Furious, Malachi rushed the salt ring over and over, crashing into the barrier each time.

"He's so filled with anger that he's doing exactly what they want him to do," Etta whispered in Seph's mind. *"He's weakening himself."*

Finally hopeful that this spiritual battle was going to end, Seph could only watch, spellbound.

With her other hand, Mary removed a tiny glass vial and emptied the contents into the hole carved into the lemon. Still uttering the same mantra, Bernadette and Mary leaned toward each other until their foreheads touched. Both now held the lemon, Bernadette's hand on the bottom, cupping the fruit, and Mary's over its top, mashing the lavender sprigs down, their fingers forming a fleshly ball around it.

White light speared through their fingers, illuminating their faces. Suddenly Mary straightened, turned, and placed the lemon into Seph's hands.

Etta rejoiced in the gift, and before Seph fully realized what she was doing, she threw it at Malachi with all her might. The fruit struck him dead center in the chest. The explosion of energy flung Seph backward and she landed on her ass in the center of the room. Malachi screamed and shrieked. Flames consumed him, melting him, drawing him down into the carpet where he vanished in a cloud of inky smoke that also vanished. Only a burn mark on the floor and the rotten-egg odor of sulfur remained.

Seph glanced over at the women who had fallen against the men's feet. Frank helped Bernadette up, and Phil and Beastman lifted Mary and Luella to their feet.

A brilliant light in the shape of a narrow column appeared in the kitchen doorway. Seph squinted against it. A striking raven-haired man stepped forward dressed in old-fashioned dungarees, his clothes dated from the early 1900s. Etta saw him and joy filled Seph. She separated from Seph's body. Suddenly exhausted, Seph forced herself to remain sitting up and met her grandmother's eyes where she stood in front of her, now corporeal as well. A lovely woman, she stared at Seph with love in her amber eyes, her long chestnut hair flowing down her shoulders, a wind on the astral plane billowing her pale blue dress around her ankles.

"I'm going now to join your grandfather," Etta said. "He's the one who possessed Jack that first day, but when the two of you shared your first kiss, the power of your destined love mingling with mine and Anthony's allowed him to move on to the next world. Malachi let him go because he looked at his absence as having me all to himself again."

"I'm so sorry."

"No need for you to be, child. You had nothing to

do with Malachi's evilness." She cupped Seph's cheek in a cool hand. "I've been earthbound for decades, so I don't know if your mother and father are still alive or not, but I know you need answers, so perhaps you will find your parents one day."

"Where did the coven take her as a baby?" Seph asked.

"North of here," Etta said. "That's all I know."

"I'm glad I got to meet you."

"Same here, Granddaughter. Embrace the beast, but don't let it rule you." Etta turned and took Anthony's hand. He kissed her, then led her through the column of light that grew narrower by the second until it was a bright line, then that too disappeared.

Hurrying to her side, Jack hauled her to his feet and cradled her in his arms. "Is it over?"

She nodded with her face buried in his bare chest. "You're naked."

He chuckled. "My animal got the best of me when that demon attacked you."

"Your place is a disaster."

"It's just stuff, Seph. You're what's important to me."

"I love you."

"I love you too," he replied, squeezing her and rocking from side to side. "You have no idea how much, babe. No idea at all."

* * *

Bernadette gasped as Frank gripped her by an arm and dragged her outside, down the steps and onto the front lawn. The rain still fell steadily through the saturated tree limbs, but most of the thunder rumbled far to the east.

"Frank! What is wrong with you?" she protested, wounded by his treatment.

"What the fuck did I tell you when we left to help Jack?" he snarled down into her face. His eyes began glowing, the pupils shrinking. "Did I not tell you to stay behind with Luella and Puppy?"

"Have you not learned that when my powers speak to me I can't ignore them?" she shot back stiffly. As the glow of his eyes grew more intense, her inner beast responded with aggression. Heat, as though she were lying in the sunshine with her eyelids closed, seared her eyes, so she knew hers were glowing just intently as his. "Magic doesn't work like shifting does. My magic doesn't obey when I try to silence it. It's who I am, Frank, and I feel I was put here with your MC for more than just becoming your lifemate!" She wiped water out of her eyes. "I'm here to help others, regardless if they're lycanthrope or human! If you can't handle that, then we have a serious problem."

Frank blinked several times, the anger in his semblance washing away with the rain. "No, no...we don't have any problem"

Before she could react, he snatched her into his arms, his clothes warm but wet against her, and hugged her tightly, burying his face in the top of her hair. Trembles raced up and down his body.

Alarmed, she asked, "Babe? Are you okay?"

"I don't mean to be an ass," he whispered into her hair. "You scared the hell out of me, sweetheart. That thing you fought had turned into a full demon. It was pure evil and possessed enough energy to fling people through the air, but you faced it down as though it was no more than a Bible salesman who refused to pack his wares and leave."

"Seph and Jack needed me," she replied, suddenly understanding her mate's side of the situation. "And I'm sorry for frightening you, but, Frank, you have to accept who I am just as I've accepted who and what you are." She cupped his unshaven jaw. "I accepted you a long time ago, so why can't you accept me and my magic?"

"It's not that I don't accept you and your magic, sweetheart," he rumbled and drew her against his body again. "I'm scared I'll lose you. As a lykoi, you have the tools to protect yourself, and even in human form, your lycanthrope side gives you abilities over humans. But your magic puts you in the presence of dangers that I don't understand, nor can I protect you from them."

Ah, now she understood. He felt powerless to protect or help her when it came to magic and the otherworldly. As she stood pressed torso to torso with him, the rain pattering down on their heads and shoulders, an idea began to form in her mind.

"I'll make a deal with you," Bernadette said. "Since you'll be teaching me the ways of a lycanthrope, I'll teach you about magic so you'll understand what I deal with. I don't know if you can wield magic, but it's the knowledge of what's what and how to defend against something that's important. You'll have the knowledge to help me or at least know where to go for help."

He leaned back to look down at her, but as the rain had picked up again, all she could see was a watery image of him.

"You'd teach me?" he asked.

"Sure. It'll be nice to share my knowledge with someone."

"Okay, it's a deal." He grinned at her and the glow vanished from his eyes. "By the way, your eyes glow brilliant green when you're pissed at me. I'll have to watch for that from now on."

She giggled.

"Come on." Frank hooked an arm around her waist. "Let's go up on the porch out of this infernal rain."

She let him lead her across the lawn and back up the steps. From inside, the excited murmurings of the rest of the group tumbled through the door and the broken window.

Bernadette sat in a porch chair next to Mary, who had just come out to relax. The woman lit a clove cigarette and drew hard on it. The cloud of smoke she released wafted over the porch, bearing the aroma of cloves. She reached over and held her hand out, palm up, to Bernadette, who took it and squeezed.

Mary went back to smoking her coffin nail, and Bernadette sat watching the rain pound the saturated yard. So much had changed in her life. Frank gave her more love than she could possibly absorb, her powers were multiplying in strength, and she had a wonderful, caring mentor to teach her about magic, plus the MC provided a huge family for her to enjoy.

Now she was a lykoi too. It still frightened her, even disgusted her a bit with the bloodlust and chasing animals, but she also realized that the animal part of her needed it and it was natural. She'd learn just as Frank would when she began teaching him about her world of spells and things that went bump in the night. They'd grow old together and watch their children, grandchildren, great-grandchildren... She drew in a deep breath and smiled as she let it out. Yes, she was incredibly happy and well loved. She was mated to man whom she loved more than life itself and looked forward to an amazing future with him.

Chapter Twenty-Four

A week had passed, and Jack sat with Persephone, Bernadette and Frank in the front yard, their lawn chairs positioned around a portable fire pit. Evening had fallen over the landscape, and in that week, the weather had warmed substantially and the leaves had unfurled everywhere. The fire in the pit crackled high, the wolf design in the grate casting long-legged shadows across the ground. As he gazed over at Seph, he contemplated how it didn't seem as though a week had passed since she'd become his lifemate and the entity in his home had been defeated.

Seph's cell began playing Für Elise. She'd called Queen earlier, not receiving an answer, but he caught a glimpse of the display to find Queen's name on it. Good. Now Seph could put part of her past to rest and find some peace.

Seph rose, looked down at him and mouthed, "I'll take this over there." She wandered over to stand against one of the shade trees.

Frank had been telling him about the new orders for bikes, the quality of Nightshade's Wolves catching the attention of buyers outside the tristate area. Only half listening to his president, Jack wondered if Seph would ever snap out of her quiet, subservient mood since Malachi had been vanquished. Seph had learned she had blood ties to this area, only to be abandoned at a Detroit orphanage. He didn't understand it any more than she did, but as each day passed, it seemed as though Seph was pulling further and further away from him. There had to be something he could do to help her, but what? It was so frustrating that even his beast whined to him about it.

He'd broached the subject of Seph offering her services as a medium to people or inquire about working for the sheriff's department to help on cases, but she'd shaken her head, saying she wanted to put her gift to rest. However, he knew that wasn't so easily done, so maybe she'd change her mind later. If she came out of this funk.

The sound of a vehicle heralded the approach of a pickup. Soon, Phil's truck bounced into view along the gravel lane. He parked behind Frank's vehicle.

Once he'd gotten out with Daffodil, he called, "I came out to see if you would need some help installing the new windows, but it looks like you're all done."

"It's still too fucking cold most nights to put up with only plastic over the windows," Jack replied as they approached. "Beastman and Tom helped me the day after everything happened." He looked up at Daffodil, who held a big plastic bowl covered with a lid and on top of it a plate wrapped with foil. "Daffi, how have you been? It's been a couple weeks since anyone has seen you."

"Since my promotion to head clerk in the title department," she said, "I come home and crash. There's so much to remember, so many procedures, rules and laws I have to keep up with."

"Do you like it?" Bernadette asked.

"I'm not sure. I'm too tired mentally to think about it." Daffi laughed.

"I've had to work all week," Phil said, accepting a bottle of beer Frank handed him from a cooler. "Daffi made her awesome pesto dish for everyone and baked some cookies for dessert. Since we won't be working on the house, we can chill, eat and talk. What happened to Tina and the Wraithkiller boys? Since I had to go back to work the day after, I haven't gotten a chance to talk to anyone to find out."

"Deputy Williamscot tied the Wraithkiller members helping her to more weed and some meth found in the van," Frank told him, "so they'll be behind bars for a while."

"And Tina is in the psych ward in Wheeling," Bernadette added. "She thought her daddy's money made her invincible and that it could buy anyone, including Jack."

"From what I understand, Tina has done nothing but babble about werewolves," Jack said. "She's officially lost her mind and she'll be gone for a long time—if she's ever released. She paid those guys enough money to help her that they couldn't turn her down, plus she was fucking both of them to help her control them." He shook his head in disgust. "I wish I'd never gotten mixed up with her."

"Hindsight sucks," Phil said.

"Fucking A." Raising his beer to Phil, Jack nodded.

"So what did Crow say about his boys?" Phil asked.

Frank laughed. "Good riddance."

They all chuckled.

"How's Seph?" Phil pressed.

"Not the same. I don't know what to do to reach her." An ember popped in the fire, drawing Jack's attention to the steel pit. He stared into the leaping flames, then looked up at his friends, seeing spots after staring into the fire for so long. "I'm afraid I'm losing her."

"Was she...?" Daffi shot him a meaningful look.

"She says she wasn't. I believe her, but she's not right. It's as if something was taken from her."

"Let me talk to her," Daffi said. "I think I know what may be bothering her."

* * *

"I really hate to lose you," Queen said.

Seph smiled and shifted the cell phone against her ear when the signal threatened to fade. "I know, but I've found *the* one. Jack is good to me. I love him and I fell in love with the people and country down here too."

"Will you keep in touch with us?" Queen asked.

"Absolutely."

"Good. I'm going to miss you, girl."

"I'll miss you guys too. I'll visit when I come up to move my stuff and cancel my lease."

"Let me know when and we'll have a nice dinner out for everyone."

"Sounds like a plan," Seph said. "Bye, Queen."

"Take care, honey."

She slid her thumb over the End sensor. For an instant, regret hit Seph. She was giving up everything in Detroit to be with Jack. But just as quickly as the pang gripped her, she banished it. There really wasn't anything for her in Detroit. Everything here was new to her, even Jack, so it was normal to feel anxiety.

Besides, as a lycanthrope, she couldn't live in the city anyway.

She slipped her phone into her back pants pocket and walked toward her friends. It had been a few days since she'd seen Phil and she knew very little about Daffi other than she was Phil's mate. As she walked over, she couldn't help but notice what a looker the leggy blonde was dressed in simple Aeropostale jeans and a royal purple tunic, which looked an even deeper purple with the way the firelight danced over the fabric. Even the gray suede booties on the woman's feet shouted "runway model."

Upon meeting her gaze, Daffi smiled from ear to ear, then looked around the seated group. "Everyone hungry?"

A combination of comments ranging from "sounds good" to "I'm always hungry" floated over the fire.

"Seph, would you show me where things are in the kitchen?" Daffi asked and nodded toward the house. "I brought food and gooey cookies."

"Sure."

She led the way up the steps and into the house to the kitchen. Quietly, she pulled out paper plates from a cabinet as Daffi withdrew serving spoons from one drawer and forks from another.

"I realize you don't know anything about me," Daffi began, her tone light, soothing, "but I was sold to the River Rebels and abused by an incubus, so I understand how you're feeling right now."

Seph nearly dropped a glass on the floor. She gaped at Daffi, who didn't look at her. Instead, the woman focused on stirring the pesto and noodles in the big bowl.

"You're damn right I don't know you," Seph said defensively, "and you sure as hell don't know me." Where did this chick get off being so forward with her? There was no way Daffodil could know how she felt about *anything*.

"I was raped repeatedly," Daffi went on as though she'd never heard Seph. "You say you weren't raped, but you still feel violated—and that's normal."

Dumbfounded, Seph could only stand there with her mouth hanging open—and why couldn't she find the strength to shut it? Shaking assailed her. She gripped a glass in each hand, afraid she'd drop them to shatter on the floor.

"I don't beat around the bush," Daffi said, finally looking at her. Sympathy, understanding, and warmth glowed in her eyes. "You're hurting, but cutting Jack out of what's going on with you is the worst thing you can do. When Phil and I were first together, we fooled around, but we didn't make love until much later. Some of my friends from my old life made fun of me. They said with a man as handsome and virile as Phil, I should be fucking him at every opportunity. They were sweetbutts too, but none of them had gone through anything like I had. You see, an incubus will literally fuck you to death. It draws energy from people just like the dark entity in this house did, but an incubus can do it physically *and* psychically. Ezra nearly killed me—several times. And although I was attracted to Phil, responded to him sexually, I needed time to adjust to him, to adjust to how we felt about each other, and I needed time to realize that I wasn't tainted, that I could have a healthy, loving relationship, not only emotionally, but physically as well."

"I'm not cutting Jack out." The moment the words left her mouth, she knew it was a lie. Maybe she was. How many times had he asked her to talk to him this past week and she'd said she didn't want to talk? "Well, maybe I have. I guess I've been going all internal and didn't realize what I was doing to him. I didn't mean to."

"Let Jack know how you feel, what you're thinking. Trust me, it will help you heal."

"But I feel so dirty," Seph admitted. "That guy didn't rape me, but he did touch me, and now that I'm a…"

"Lykoi?" Daffi smiled and quirked a golden eyebrow.

"Yeah, now that I am, I don't feel like I'm me anymore. It's like I'm a stranger to even myself."

"*Tell* Jack that," Daffi urged, her smile growing bigger. "That's what you need to do to free yourself from the pain and uncertainty, and that's what he needs to hear so he can love and support you."

Hot, stinging tears abruptly stung Seph's eyes, then leaked down her cheeks. Her breath hitched, and she quickly bit her lower lip to keep it from wobbling. Daffi crossed the kitchen, took the glasses from her and set them on the counter, then drew Seph into her arms. Big, gut-wrenching sobs burst from Seph, both relieving and embarrassing, especially in a stranger's arms, but she sensed the sincerity in Daffi's actions and relaxed somewhat. Daffi swayed to and fro with her until Seph finally cried herself out.

"I think we're going to be the best of friends," Daffi soothed. "We understand each other. You can talk to me too—anytime."

Another sob tore free of Seph as she nodded.

"Is everything okay?" Jack asked behind them, a note of panic in his voice.

"Everything is fine." Turning, Daffi handed Seph over to him. "I think she needs a moonlight run. You two go on. I'll feed the pack out there and you guys can catch up with us later."

Leaning into Jack's warm side, Seph let him walk down the hall with her to the back door.

"Take your clothes off, baby," he said as he began removing his.

Once she was naked, he held his hand out, and she took it.

* * *

They ran and ran and ran. Seph would never have thought it possible, but shifting into her wolf counterpart freed her. She kept pace next to Jack. They chased raccoons and birds startled from the undergrowth, then they splashed through streams full of runoff and swampy areas brimming with frogs croaking to the stars. The warm night offered excitement, tantalizing odors, new noises in the forest and a strength that emanated from Mother Earth that Seph greedily drew upon.

Jack jogged into a small field where new hay grew tall, green and thick. A rabbit burst from its hiding place, and Seph gave chase with Jack only a couple feet behind her, allowing her the chance to make the kill, which she did. She caught the animal by its haunches. The rabbit cried out, but she quickly wrung its neck, unwilling to let it suffer. She shared her kill with Jack, reveling in the waning heat of animal's body, the coppery smell that permeated her nostrils.

Panting, Jack sat in the hay next to her. He rubbed her neck with his head. "Shift," he said, words guttural. "I want to make love to you."

She hated the pain of transformation, and judging by the grunts and moans coming from Jack, years of shape-shifting only made a seasoned lycanthrope tolerant of the pain.

Sweating and gasping for air, Seph lay in the tall hay and waited for the last traces of discomfort to fade. When her breathing steadied, Jack lay alongside her, his cock hard and demanding against her hip.

"Are you okay, babe?"

"Yes," she answered. "Daffodil helped me realize some things tonight. I'm sorry I shut you out, Jack. I didn't mean to."

"What do we do next?" he questioned. "I want to help."

"Well, I need to collect my things at my apartment, cancel my lease, and when you and I know what days or weekend we'll go up to Detroit, I'll call Sister Miranda and schedule a visit with her. I need answers—if she even has any—about my parents."

"I'm betting you were left at the orphanage as a way to protect you," he mused and smoothed his hand over her belly. "Lykoi can't live in urban settings without surviving on rodents and pets—or worse—whenever they shift."

She looked into his eyes.

"I almost did that," she admitted.

"But your inner beast was functioning on survival and protection modes for both of us. What you *almost* did wasn't out of fun or cruelty."

"I suppose…but this whole situation"—she tapped herself between the breasts with two fingers—"is something straight out of a storybook or a movie."

"You'll come to terms with it, Seph." Cupping her breast, Jack stared directly into her eyes. The moonlight glimmered in his hair and gilded his upturned shoulder. "Besides, you're not alone. You have an entire clan and MC full of lycanthropes who will give you help and from whom you can learn. *Lykoi* is Greek for wolf, so we use the term loosely around here because it's Frank's actual clan, but there are a few other clans mixed in with his, such as mine—which is why my mother went to live with her sister in Florida. Our clan is there. Anyway, we just need to figure out what clan you belong to, then maybe that info will lead us to your parents."

"If they're still alive. I told you my grandmother didn't know if they were or not."

"One step at a time, baby."

"Yeah, you're right."

"You're a strong woman. You'll deal with all of this just fine. Just don't shut me out."

"I'm sorry, and I promise I won't do it again."

He kissed her, flicking the tip of his tongue over her bottom lip. "I know that, baby. You've gone through a lot, and that asshole, Smokey, had no right to touch you."

"Make love to me, Jack. Erase the memories, the stain that's on me."

"You're not stained, my little she-beast. You're my lifemate, my she-wolf, the love of my life." He rolled on top of her. "And I'll never leave you. I'm your beastly lover, Persephone."

She spread her legs and he settled between her thighs, his cock pressed to her pussy. In one move, he slid into her.

"Oh!" She stiffened at the sudden intrusion. He stretched her so much, a sensation both disconcerting at first and yet so pleasurable she couldn't keep still. She hooked her feet behind his knees and pushed her hips up, seating him inside her as deeply as possible.

"Fuck, baby," he groaned.

"Yes," she said. "Fuck me now—and hard."

He began thrusting, slowly at first, pushing all the way into her until he was balls-deep, then withdrawing just as slowly until only the tip of his cock remained inside her. Again, he pushed in one inch at a time, then withdrew in the same manner. Seph dug her nails into his ass cheeks. That beautiful itch in her core was quickly rising in crescendo. Heat spread through her body, the spring within her clenching to excruciating levels, drawing tighter and tighter.

Abruptly, he changed his tactic and shoved into her—hard. She squealed and clasped him to her. Rising onto his arms, he looked into her eyes and pistoned his hips.

"Fuck…" She held on, keeping her feet hooked behind his legs.

Jack lowered himself, his cock fully seated inside her, and licked and sucked on each breast until the nipples pebbled like rocks in the cool night air. Each time he pulled a nipple into his mouth and laved his tongue over it, electrical charges bulleted straight to her core.

"Jack…damn…"

He thrusted into her over and over, his cock growing even harder. She responded by grabbing his ass and thrusting her hips up and holding him there.

"Ungh!" He tried to withdraw.

She held fast to him.

"Fuck, you're gonna make me unravel," he grunted out.

She wiggled her ass, grinding into him.

He collapsed on her and began pumping in earnest. Seph met him thrust for thrust, the coil suddenly shattering. The orgasm swept through Seph, rendering her immobile. She could only lie there as pleasure ravaged her and Jack pummeled her into the soft earth. He stiffened suddenly, a long, low groan rolling out of him as he came inside her. Seph squealed, rejoicing in the heat filling her core as he pulsed within her. He coaxed the last few drops of his essence into her, then lay between her legs while he kissed her lips, neck and the tip of her nose.

"I love you," he said.

"Oh baby. I love you too."

"Are you ready to return and join our friends?"

"Only if you promise to make love to me again after they leave," she said, grinning.

"I'll fuck you until you can't walk tomorrow," he bragged. "I'll bet I have you pregnant by fall, if not sooner."

"Well," she said, feeling him hardening inside her, "we're sure going to have fun making it happen, my beastly lover."

He chuckled and seized a nipple, forcing a delighted squeal from her.

"Our friends can wait another half hour," he said, his mouth full of her breast.

She giggled and pulled him closer.

About the Author

Ana Lee Kennedy loves writing stories steeped in lore, history, mythology, and her wicked sense of humor, although she is known to pen hot paranormal and contemporary stories too. She is currently writing the final novel in the Werewolves of Rebellion trilogy.

After many actual dreams of traveling the world, Ana Lee hopes to do so soon with her husband and young son, and their first stop will be England. When she's not writing, she can be found in her flower gardens or at one of the local lakes playing with her son and their creepily intelligent Labrador retriever. She resides in the U.S. with her family, Sir Creepy Dog, two almost-as-smart felines, and a pair of pet ducks.

Other Riverdale Avenue Books By Ana Lee Kennedy

Nightshade's Flame
Book One of The Werewolves of Rebellion

The Devil's Russian Beauty:
Book Two of the Werewolves of Rebellion

Seduced by the King
Volume One of the Valhalla Skies Saga

The Dragon God's Kiss
Volume Two of the Valhalla Skies Saga

The Sorcerer King and the Fire Queen

Invasion of Her Heart:
Book One of the Lovers of the Galaxy Series

Bounty Hunters of the Heart:
Book Two of the Lovers of the Galaxy Series

Raiders of the Lost Heart:
Book Three of the Lovers of Galaxy Series

Wrapped Around Your Handlebars

You Might Also Like

Passion of the Panther
By F. L. Bicknell

Whips, Chains and Candy Canes
by F. L. Bicknell

Collaring the Saber-Tooth:
Book One of the Masters of the Cats series
by Trinity Blacio

Embracing the Winds
by Trinity Blacio

Jeanne-Claude and Eugene's Magic Lamp
Book One: I Dream of Jinns
by Trinity Blacio